Chronicles
of
SideStreet

by

Joseph L. Thompson

CONTENTS

CONTENTS

INTRODUCTION

I n all fairness to the people of Detroit, especially folks in the inner city, times are tough. Tension is high and morale is low. If it's not one thing it's another. The war! A nonexistent job market! The Teamsters Union has just about shut America down! Make you wanna holla... (Reference to the Detroit Riot of 1967)

During slavery, Detroit's Underground Railroad was a pilgrimage to Canada that meant freedom for the slaves. One of the railroad passages that led to the river that crossed over to Canada was a hidden trail carved out by people who wanted to help the slaves in their freedom quest. By all accounts it was the quickest way to get to the river without being caught. This trail was used so many times successfully that the people gave it a name, Side Bow, because of its curvature. With its easy access to the river, during Reconstruction, folks started building structures there and decided to rename it Side Street. Then buildings began to go up all around it.

Side Street's reputation began to take shape in the '40's and by the late '50's it had become a black historical landmark. The centerpiece for peace in all of Detroit's black communities! It became a symbol of respect and honor. Ordained, no less! For years, Side Street enjoyed the prestige that comes with being Detroit's pride, a respectable community worthy of admiration. Sitting on a pedestal, if you please!

Now a new era is emerging; a change of order so to speak. Will it be better or worse? Will Side Street continue to be the cornerstone of class for the black communities of Detroit? Or will folks be forced to admit their wrongdoings and risk sullying its stellar reputation?

What would or could cause the change? Could the infidelities, lies, deceit, secrets, mistrust, illegal activities and lack of employment disrupt its fame and prestige?

Will Reverend Peters carry on the tradition and leadership in the church his father founded and built?

Will Cousin Bee's cooking continue to attract notables as the famous Eunice's Café once did?

Will Sister Johnson's sweet potato cobbler send her straight to hell?

Will Mary, Tracy, Carl and Jessie's bonding love and friendship endure revelations?

Will Housecoat Pearl's baseball bat keep peace on Side Street?

Will the dramas and tragedies change the protocol that has made Side Street famous?

Chronicles! Not of a city, nor of a town, nor of a community. It is…Chronicles of Side Street!

ACKNOWLEDGEMENTS

To my daughter Donna and sons Mark and Tony, I love you. To my deceased daughter Terri Jo, I am sorry I didn't have enough time to spend with you but thanks for loving me and for the time we shared together.

There is no greater love in the world, in my opinion, than the love of true friends. That is what Joyce Bramble and Janice Hatchett Cowan are to me! This book could not have been what it is without them. Their input and consistency in getting the most out of me paid off. I cannot describe how many times I have argued with them about their unwillingness to be any less than satisfied with my work on this book. They read, reread, and proofread it until completion. I am so blessed and thankful for these two beautiful and wonderful friends. I thank God for them… "Thank you God!"

Rebecca Annie Mae Nichols Davidson…the gateway of my dreams! One day soon I plan to write the story of Rebecca and Joseph… truly an amazing story only we can tell. Rebecca is my cousin…many think she is my sister…others think she is my mother. Others know she is my best friend. She has been and still is all of the aforementioned. It is frightening to imagine where I would have been without her in my life. She has been the nucleus of all my dreams ever since I was a child. She gave me my first start and has been there ever since with encouragement…I love you!

I am happily married to Gloria Thompson. People always ask me how is my wife doing and I tell them…she is tolerating me, so she is doing okay. My previous Mac, a Christmas gift from my wife, was destroyed when I spilled water on it. She spent her last dime and bought me another one so I could continue my writing. That is my wife whom I truly love and am thankful for! You are an inspiration to my life... Thank you!

To my brother Tim (Dickie)…A brother's love is so special! You have played many roles in my life…a supporter in all my quests! You are a person to whom I have looked up to and was proud of your achievements and accolades in high school sports. You were able to do admirably all the things I could not do… dance, swim, roller and ice skate, etc. You were a model dresser. Truly a brother's love!

Special thanks to Elaine Wright…RIP.

Also special thanks to my friends, Martha Willingham and Cleo Hill-Jackson, who have always believed and encouraged me.

Special thanks to Delena, the artist who drew the painting for the cover of this book.

Special thanks to my friend Sombat Kriangchaivet, for fine tuning and putting this manuscript into book form.

Special thanks to Carlene Lance, for final edit reading.

Special thanks to Charleston Williamson, the talented young man, who helped me in the final editing, reading and critiquing of this book/ play!

Special thanks to Ann Noell who did the final editing.

Again, everyone who has been a part of my life, in the past and present, has contributed.

God made me! I hope I will forever be that which He made me to be; forever me…Thank you all!

CAST

Jessie Barfield is a Vietnam veteran who returned home after serving three years in the Army. He is twenty-one years old and of average height and size. He loves sports and is happily married to Mary his high school sweetheart. He is emotionally sensitive, street-smart, respected and well-liked in his community. He was raised by his grandparents who moved back to Alabama when he finished high school. He lived with his Uncle Milton until he got married. Carl is his best friend.

Mary Barfield is twenty-one years old. She is somewhat naïve and gets excited very easily and sometimes is comical because of it. Her parents are deceased. She is happily married to Jessie and works as a sales clerk at Hudson's department store with her best friend Tracy.

Carl Malcolm Frank (he dropped Frank and uses Malcolm as his surname) is twenty-two years old, dark-skinned and above average height. He loves sports and is street-smart with a slightly militant attitude. Abandoned by his mother, he was raised by his father and aunt. His father was a professional boxer who now lives in Texas. Carl is a Vietnam veteran who served three years in the Army. He is respected and well-liked in his community. He is happily married to his high school sweetheart Tracy. Jessie is his best friend.

Tracy Malcolm is fair-skinned, medium height and nicely built. She is twenty-one years old with a no-nonsense attitude. She is happily married to Carl and works as a sales clerk at Hudson's department store with her best friend Mary. Her parents are deceased.

Sister Ella Johnson is brown-skinned, average height and build, and is in her late forties. She dresses very stylishly and is head of the senior choir at True Life Baptist Church. She has Southern charm and is well-respected within the community. She is considered a mother figure to Mary, Tracy, Carl and Jessie.

Nicholas (aka Rabbit) Jones is twenty-two years old, brown-skinned, six feet tall and athletically built. He was once the most famous athlete in Detroit and the pride of the community. He became a drug addict and got kicked out of college because of his drug use.

Reverend Daniel Peters is in his early fifties. He is of average height and build, with a light chocolate complexion. He is the minister of True Life Baptist Church. There is a square side to his personality that comes off when he is being humorous. He is a well-loved and respected community leader who is fond of Sister Johnson.

Page Brown is a mail carrier in his late forties. His complexion is a fair shade of brown and he is slightly overweight. He is streetwise to what is happening in the community. He likes to tease and jokes a lot… sometimes getting on everyone's nerves. He is single and slightly lazy. He is also a small-time numbers man.

Housecoat Pearl Burns is in her late forties and is married, but her husband left her. She is tanned and slender. She is an alcoholic who often wears a housecoat (i.e., the name Housecoat Pearl). She is the lookout for Side Street's illegal activities at Big Hank's poolroom. She is a no-nonsense person and has a reputation of not being afraid of too much and will use her baseball bat as a defense. She is more intelligent than she appears.

Luella and Francine are prostitutes, both twenty-two years old and sexually attractive. They were school mates and are still good friends of Carl, Jessie, Tracy and Mary.

Ernest Winslow was born and raised in Harlem, NY, and came to Detroit at eighteen. He is in his late fifties, dark-skinned and owns Cousin Bee's Café along with his wife, Bee and daughter, Ernestine. He gambles on horse racing, sports and plays the numbers (and wins quite often). He is well-respected in the community.

Bee Winslow is heavyset in her late fifties, married to Ernest Winslow, with one daughter, Ernestine. Born in Mississippi to sharecropper parents, she was the youngest and only girl of four siblings. She learned to cook at an early age, left Mississippi and followed her two older brothers to Detroit. She started working at Eunice's Café where she met Ernest, a regular customer at the café. Bee is friendly and soft spoken with a charming Mississippi accent.

Ernestine Winslow is thirty-years old, and works as a waitress and a cook in her parents' Café. She is slender, above average height, plain looking and has no boyfriend. She is very business-oriented and can sometimes fool people into thinking she is naïve by her mannerism.

Bernie is a Jewish grocery store owner in his fifties, very well-respected in the community he has served for a long time.

Big Hank Crawford is in his late forties and has a large build like a football lineman. He owns one of the largest illegal numbers and gambling operations in the city of Detroit. He is well-respected and very generous to the community which encompasses Side Street.

Adele Washington, a fair skin, middle-age creole lady, has been a resident of Side Street longer than her neighbors. She and her deceased husband were living in New Orleans with their two children when her husband's aunt, who lived on Side Street, passed away. Her husband inherited his aunt's house on Side Street. The family left New Orleans and moved to Detroit where her husband got a job in the automobile factory. While living in Detroit, one of her sons was killed in the Vietnam War and her other son moved back to New Orleans. Her grandson, Randy, was killed on the streets of Detroit. Every year during winter, Adele goes to New Orleans and stays with her son and grandchildren.

CAST OF CHARACTERS

Jessie .... Vietnam veteran returning home

Mary .... Jessie's wife and Tracy's best friend

Carl .... Jessie's best friend recently returned home
from Vietnam

Tracy .... Carl's wife and Mary's best friend

Sister Johnson .... Godmother to Mary and Tracy

Reverend Peters .... Minister, True Life Baptist Church

Rabbit .... Athlete/heroin addict

Luella & Francine .... Prostitutes

Page .... Local Postman

Bernie .... Owner, Jewish Grocery Store

Bee .... Owner, Cousin Bee's Café

Ernest .... Bee's husband/Ernestine's father

Ernestine .... Daughter of Ernest and Bee

Housecoat Pearl .... An alcoholic who lives on the second floor
of Cousin Bee's Café

Big Hank .... Owner of the neighborhood poolroom and
illegal gambling operations

Adele Washington .... Oldest and longest living resident of Side
Street

SCENES

ACT I
The Neighborhood
Jessie is home from the Army
Rabbit, the great athlete's downfall
Residents' review of Side Street's history

ACT II
Jessie's visit with Roosevelt (Army Buddy)
Carl's Chicago nightmare / Mary Alice the redeemer
Carl's conscience battle / Jessie and Carl in The Well
Roosevelt and Calloway pay Jessie a visit
Mary's reaction to Mary Alice's telephone call
Rabbit's displeasure with Jessie
Rabbit leaves Detroit
Street Party
Teamsters' Strike / Mary is pregnant

ACT III
Carl's confrontation with Jessie
Carl meets Roosevelt and Calloway
Big Hank, Carl and Jessie in The Well / Carl and Jessie's friendship
is back on
Tracy is pregnant / Carl and Jessie hit the numbers
Poolroom is raided / Rabbit returns to Detroit
Tracy has a miscarriage / Rabbit gets killed
Rabbit's funeral
Carl and Tracy's surprise gift

ACT I

SCENE ONE

The neighborhood - early morning...

It is early spring and exceptionally warm for this time of year. This unusually mild weather has the locals basking in the warmth. All over Detroit's inner city, the soulful sound of blackness can be heard from the Gospel singing to the old-time, down home Blues to the Motown Sound.

The locals welcome the warm weather after winter's long and bitter cold. Side Street is no different from the rest. Throughout the city there is an epidemic of spring cleaning; a renewing of pride in the neighborhood with its old buildings. Adorning Side Street is a barber shop, Gladys' Beauty Shop; True Life Baptist Church; Sister Johnson's house; the duplex where Carl, Tracy, Jessie and Mary live; an apartment/rooming house; Mrs. Washington's house; Big Hank's pool hall; Bernie's Grocery; Cousin Bee's Café and upstairs apartment; The Well Bar; the dry cleaners and the laundromat. These stores, houses and rows of buildings have no noticeable separation between them.

Side Street is slowly stirring, with little activity going on at this hour. The only businesses open are the laundromat, Cousin Bee's Café and Bernie's Grocery. It may be quiet now but the smell of Cousin Bee's cooking is a sure sign that it won't be quiet for long.

Adele Washington comes out of her house carrying a pail of water and a broom. Mrs. Washington is a fair-skinned, somewhat heavyset, gray-haired Creole lady. She looks to be in her late fifties and is about five feet tall. She puts the pail down and begins to sweep the porch steps and the sidewalk in front of her house. She looks down the way and sees Sister Johnson, who lives a few doors down, coming onto her porch carrying two plants.

MRS. WASHINGTON: Morning, Sister Johnson. It sure is looking' like another hot one today. How are you faring this morning?

Sister Johnson has a nice build and attractive features. It is hard to tell she is middle-aged in her late forties. She looks more like a woman in her early forties. Sister Johnson sits the plants down gently on the plant stand and looks up as Mrs. Washington speaks to her.

SISTER JOHNSON: Good morning, Mrs. Dell! Why I'm faring fine I believe. It does feel like it's going to be another hot one. I don't ever remember seeing it this warm at this time of year.

MRS. WASHINGTON: It can get as hot as it may please. Nobody is gonna complain, especially as cold as it was this past winter, no ma'am! *(Mrs. Washington finishes sweeping the porch steps and goes back into her house.)*

Sister Johnson picks up a bucket from the porch and commences to watering her plants. From the upstairs duplex next to Sister Johnson's house, the shade of the large window rises and Mary Barfield, a 21-year-old brown-skinned woman leans part of her body out of the window while grasping the collar of her robe as she bends forward. She takes a deep breath of the early morning air which is mixed in with the scent of Sister Johnson's coffee. Mary's husband, Jessie, is in the Army, stationed in Vietnam.

Not knowing that Sister Johnson is on her porch, Mary calls out to her somewhat loudly...

MARY: Good morning, Sister Johnson! I sure would like a cup of that good smelling coffee. *(Yawning and stretching)* I'm still sleepy… up late last night… but I made up my mind I wasn't going to let a beautiful morning like this escape me.

Sister Johnson puts the bucket down and walks over to the railing where Mary can see her.

SISTER JOHNSON: I'm right here, chile. I figured you all might need coffee this morning after being up so late last night. (Sister Johnson walks back into her house while Mary continues talking.)

MARY: We sure were up late; playing bid whist until almost three o'clock this morning.

Mary pulls her head in and seconds later her screen door opens and she steps outside dressed in her robe. She walks down to where her stairs are parallel to Sister Johnson's porch railing, sits down on the step, crosses her legs and starts talking without missing a beat.

MARY: I tell you, Sister Johnson that Carl and Mr. Ernest are always cheating and fussing about everything. I've never seen folks who hate to lose as bad as those two.

Sister Johnson comes back onto the porch with two cups of coffee and a rag. She goes to the railing and hands Mary a cup of coffee.

MARY: *(Continues speaking)* Carl and Mr. Ernest sure hate to lose to us women. They blame each other every time they lose instead of admitting that Tracy and I are a better team. It makes us feel good to beat them.

Sister Johnson wipes the flat surface at the end of the railing with the rag and puts her cup of coffee on the rail. She goes over to the other side of the porch and brings a chair to sit next to the railing. As she sits down she picks up her coffee cup and takes a sip.

MARY: *(Taking another sip of her coffee)* This coffee sure hits the spot this morning, Sister Johnson! *(She stretches her arms)* It's been a while since we've enjoyed this kind of time - I mean sitting out here like this.

SISTER JOHNSON: I know. This weather has sure energized the neighborhood. It seems like summer really is coming early. Folks are coming out of their houses like caterpillars coming out of a cocoon. I see folks I haven't seen since last fall. I don't blame them because this winter was cold. Lord knows we don't need any more cold weather. I don't care if it's a hundred degrees every day - I ain't complaining.

MARY: I'm with you, Sister Johnson. This winter gave our butts a real good licking. *(Sipping her coffee)* Isn't this weather strange? *(Uncrosses her legs)* It seems like only a few weeks ago it was below zero and now it's hot and humid. Strange, I say!

SISTER JOHNSON: These last few days people have been running 'round here with hardly anything on. Detroit weather will fool you. Fool around in this kind of weather and you'll sure nuff catch your death of pneumonia!

MARY: It isn't going to get cold again. Tracy says she saw old man Gene heading for the river yesterday. Now you know that's a good sign. Soon he'll be walking down this street with two buckets full of Detroit River catfish to sell. *(Pauses)* Hmmm…fresh fish and some good old homemade grits sure sounds good.

SISTER JOHNSON: That sure is some good down-home eating. *(She raises the cup to her mouth)* I knew you all were up real late. Last time I looked at the clock it was nearly one o'clock and you all were still playing cards.

MARY: We kept telling Carl to be quiet so we wouldn't disturb you. It's like talking to a brick wall when he's excited. *(Pauses, takes a sip of coffee)* If we could've taped his mouth shut we would've, but he won't keep it shut long enough.

SISTER JOHNSON: *(Smiling and defending Carl)* He doesn't need any tape on his mouth. Your noise is what makes me sleep. I like knowing you all are around. I hear you all having a good time and I sleep like a lamb. Come to think of it, I haven't heard you all having that kind of fun in - I can't remember when. It must be the weather…

MARY: …and the beer! We were having a good time. Carl won a little money at the playground and brought home some beer, Parks Bar-B-Q, skins, chips and some Faygo pop. He stopped by the bar and got Mr. Ernest so we could play bid whist. I tell you, Sister Johnson, him and Mr. Ernest drank up all but two bottles of beer! *(Mary pauses and begins to raise herself up from the steps)* I reckon I better get myself inside and straighten up. I need to put on some clothes before the street starts getting busy or Reverend Peters comes a-calling. I don't want a Sunday sermon about robe wearing on the streets of Detroit and you know he will. *(She gets up and begins to climb the stairs)* Are you working today? Maybe you, Tracy and I can get out and enjoy some of this pretty weather. Maybe go over to the river or into town.

SISTER JOHNSON: I have to work four hours today. I should be back by early evening. Maybe we can do something then, if you all like.

MARY: *(Opening her screen door)* Okay. I'll see you later then! *(Mary goes inside and closes her door)*

Sister Johnson gets up from the chair and looks up the street before entering her house.

Bernie, an older Jewish man, stands in front of his grocery store looking up and down the street. He knows business will pick up, now that the weather has changed. His old pop box is known to have the coldest pops around and makes him plenty of money when it is hot. He is also known to have the best domino games around.

END OF SCENE ONE

ACT I

SCENE TWO

Later in the morning - mail deliveries along Side Street...

Page, a somewhat overweight brown-skinned man in his forties, appears from the opposite side of the street. He's wearing a U.S. postal uniform and carrying a mailbag. He seems to be in no hurry as he grabs a handful of mail from his bag which rests on his shoulder. He peeps into the laundromat and then disappears briefly into the cleaners. Moments later he comes out, stops at the bar, looks at some letters and then drops them through the door slot. His next stop is Cousin Bee's Café. For the past twenty years Page has been this community's mailman. He also has a smalltime numbers business on the side.

From above the Café, Housecoat Pearl, a medium-brown skinned middle-aged lady, is sitting on her window ledge watching the activities on the street. She is wearing her trademark housecoat with a cigarette in one hand and a glass of vodka in the other. She notices Page as he goes into Cousin Bee's Café. Pearl, an alcoholic, plays the role of lookout for the poolroom activities.

Cousin Bee's Café is not overly busy as it is still early morning. Bee and Ernestine (Bee's and Ernest's daughter) comfortably handle the small flow of patrons with enough time to prepare the menu for the busy flow of customers that will come in later. Cousin Bee's Café has the reputation of being Detroit's most popular soul food establishment which has kept her and her family quite busy over the years. Page has always been one of her early morning regulars along with Bernie, who is usually her first customer of the day. Bernie loves her lox and eggs.

PAGE: *(Entering Cousin Bee's Café)* Morning, everybody! Bee, why don't you fix me one of your big, fat, juicy hamburgers with lettuce, tomato, fried egg, mustard and no mayonnaise! *(A few customers are seated at the long counter and Page sits on the vacant stool next to Billy Ray)*

Bee, a mature, slightly heavy-set woman with a kind face, is in the kitchen. You can only see the upper half of her body because of the counter where she places the orders. Page places the mail on the counter for Bee's daughter, Ernestine and then puts his mailbag on the floor between him and Billy Ray, a tall high school basketball player. Ernestine is of average height, a single, thirty-year-old woman; dark-skinned like her father, Ernest.

PAGE: *(Looking at Billy Ray's plate)* Billy Ray, that sure looks good. *(Teasing)* You're going to eat all that food?

BILLY RAY: *(Eating and not looking up)* Yup!

PAGE: Bee, I think I changed my mind. Let me have this here…what Billy Ray is eating.

As Page looks at Billy Ray's plate, jokingly, Billy Ray tries to cover it so Page cannot see. Page pushes Billy Ray's arm away. Customers sitting at the counter smile at their carrying on.

PAGE: Move your arm, boy - before I dust your britches! Bee let me have spam, eggs, grits and some of the sopping biscuits with apple butter jam. *(Looking at Billy Ray)* I tell you, the way this boy eats would make anybody hungry!

ERNESTINE: *(Places Page's coffee on the table; picks up the mail and says...)* Here, man. You don't need no enticement to eat.

BEE: *(From the kitchen)* Isn't this the middle of the month? You carrying folks checks in that mail bag of yours?

ERNESTINE: *(Leaning over the counter and looking into his bag)* Yeah, he got their checks. You better not let Housecoat Pearl come in here to get hers. You know she done had her nip by now.

PAGE: *(Sipping coffee)* Now why y'all worrying about them folks' checks? They all gonna get their checks as soon as I have me a bite to eat. Anyhow, you're forgetting that these checks *(Patting his mail bag)* I got here makes this, "Page Day." I'll be wined and dined by the time my route is over. I'll have cigarettes, cologne, enough liquor to last me a week and all the kissing and hugging I can handle. Y'all, this here is "Page Day!"

ERNESTINE: (Grunts under her breath very loud) Humph! This is also "Get Your Butt Whupped Day," too. Folks want their money!

Page, not paying any attention to Ernestine, looks over at Billy Ray and sizes him up.

PAGE: Boy, you sure have grown! Stand up and let me look at you!

Billy Ray stops eating briefly and stands up hovering over Page.

PAGE: How tall are you now? About 6'1... Huh?

BILLY RAY: *(Looking down at Page)* No! I'm 6'4.

PAGE: *(Standing up)* Naw! You ain't no 6'4.

BILLY RAY: I can see where you're going bald and where your roots are showing gray.

Ernestine, Bee and the rest of the patrons laugh at them, as Ernestine puts Page's plate on the counter in front of him. Page and Billy Ray both sit back down.

PAGE: *(Still messing with Billy Ray, leans over to him)* Think you can whup me, boy?

BILLY RAY: *(Glances at Page for a moment and smiles while eating)* Yep! I sure do.

PAGE: What! Do you know I was once a middle-weight boxer, the toughest in Detroit? I was the baddest dude around. Ask your daddy. He would come to the arena just to see me fight. They used to call me "Thunder" 'cause I hit so hard.

Billy Ray looks Page over, smiles, then shakes his head and continues eating.

PAGE: *(Teasing)* Boy! Boy! I could dust your britches right now. *(Pointing to his bag)* Carrying this bag every day tells me I can dust your britches. *(Shaking his fist like Muhammad Ali)* Feel these muscles!

BILLY RAY: *(Feeling Page's muscles and also imitating Muhammad Ali)* You ain't got no wind. You're too old, too slow and too fat!

Everyone laughs. Ernest gets their attention briefly as he enters the store carrying two full grocery bags under each arm.

ERNEST: Good morning, everyone! It sure feels like summer out there.

Ernest goes behind the counter and puts the bags on the kitchen counter where Bee puts the customers' orders. Bee takes the bags off the counter.

PAGE: *(With his mouth full, continues his assault on Billy Ray)* Cousin Bee, tell Billy Ray that I could dust his britches right now!

COUSIN BEE: *(Looking over at Billy Ray)* I don't know. Billy Ray looks mighty healthy to me. What do you think, Ernest?

ERNEST: I sure wouldn't want to be there to see it because that boy will beat the mess out of Page.

Everybody laughs including Page.

PAGE: Boy, don't listen to that old man!

Billy Ray finishes eating. He stands up and reaches in his pocket and pulls out some money to pay Ernestine.

PAGE: Hey! Don't you think I can't dust your britches now! *(Shaking his fist)* I'm a heavyweight, not a middleweight!

Billy Ray looks at Page, shakes his head and laughs as he walks out the door.

Housecoat Pearl is still sitting on the window ledge and watches as Billy Ray comes out of Cousin Bee's and disappears around the corner. Two gentlemen have a domino game going on at Bernie's and a few people passing by stop briefly to watch.

PAGE: *(Finishes his food and takes a few sips of coffee)* Bee, if there's a better cook than you, I'm scared of them. *(He looks at Ernestine* *teasingly)* Let me see, if I married Ernestine, I could eat here every day for free. *(He knows that Ernest wants to get Ernestine married off)* Isn't that right, Ernest?

ERNEST: *(Also teasing...not looking up)* Yep, as long as you all stay married.

ERNESTINE: Daddy! Why don't you just throw me in a cage at the zoo or put me in an insane asylum. It wouldn't make any difference to me.

ERNEST: He's got a job and I won't have to take care of you. I can remember when you used to like him.

ERNESTINE: *(Hands on hips)* Can you remember when I used to like rutabagas? Now I can't stand them! Momma, you gonna let him talk to me like that?

BEE: They are just messing with you, child!

PAGE: *(Getting up from the stool)* Don't you all let her fool you! She still wants me. *(Ernestine pays him no mind)* Ernest, I heard you had a hit on the numbers the other day!

ERNEST: I tell you. I believe every one of these buildings have eavesdropping machines hidden in the walls. Yeah! I hit for a few pennies.

ERNESTINE: *(To her father)* Look at you. You may as well give your winnings to charity. Telling him! Talk about not talking!

PAGE: *(Walking towards the cash register)* I swear! Ernest, you're the luckiest person I know. This is about the third time this year and the year ain't even halfway over yet. *(Reaching in his pocket, Ernestine standing near him)* How much I owe you, Bee?

ERNESTINE: You're so uncouth. Gimme four dollars, man!

PAGE: *(Gives Ernestine a five dollar bill)* Keep the change! If you were my wife, you could just take my whole check.

Ernestine, not paying him any mind, takes the money and walks away.

ERNEST: Now you sure can't beat that!

PAGE: *(Walking to the door)* Thanks, Bee. See y'all later... *(He winks at Ernestine as he closes the door)*

Page looks up and down the street as he exits Cousin Bee's Café. He reaches in his bag and pulls out a stack of mail with a rubber band around it. He does not notice Housecoat Pearl sitting on the window ledge looking down at him. She has a glass in her hand.

HOUSECOAT PEARL: Ain't today check day?

PAGE: *(Looking up at her leaning out the window)* One of these days Pearl you gonna fall right out of that window, vodka and all.

HOUSECOAT PEARL: You've been sayin' that for years and I ain't fell yet. But if I do I hope you won't be around to say "I told you so"!

PAGE: *(Somewhat ignoring her while sorting through the mail in his hand)* You want me to bring you your check or do you want to come down and get it?

HOUSECOAT PEARL: My husband doesn't want any mailman sneaking around his house when he ain't home.

PAGE: Housecoat, you ain't seen your husband since he told you he was going to the store for some cigarettes. That was fourteen years ago. Now bring your housecoat-wearing self down here and get this mail and bring me a shot of that old hard liquor with you.

Housecoat Pearl disappears from the window ledge. A few seconds later the door next to the Café opens wide and Pearl's standing there with her housecoat on and her hands on her hips.

PAGE: *(Walks over and gives her the mail)* Where's my drink?

HOUSECOAT PEARL: *(Taking the mail)* I forgot it and I ain't going all the way back up them stairs and then all the way back down, then all the way back up again to get you a lousy drink. The mailman ain't supposed to be drinking anyhow. *(She shuts the door in his face)*

PAGE: *(Walking away and murmuring)* I can see why your husband left you. *(He stops at the domino game in front of Bernie's, and four people are playing now)* Hey, everybody. Who's winning? *(He puts his bag on top of the pop box, takes the mail and goes into the store and lays the mail on the counter while speaking to Bernie)* I see the weather got dominoes going again. It's been hot these last few days.

Page comes back out wiping his forehead. He moves his bag and lifts the lid off the pop box and reaches into the icy cold water. After a couple of tries, he finds the pop he wants. He opens it on the side of the box and drinks it while he watches the domino game. Bernie comes out fussing with Page. This has been an ongoing ritual of his for years.

BERNIE: Why are you standing out here drinking pop and bullshitting when you got people's checks who owe me money in your bag? You ain't good for my business!

PAGE: Why don't you let the people enjoy their little money for a while? You done made enough off them. Done got rich off us enough to send two sons to college.

BERNIE: Maybe I'll be rich if you pay me for all those free pops you've been drinking. *(Everybody laughs)*

PAGE: You ain't fooling anybody! Where do you go when you leave here? I know - to some ritzy neighborhood. You've been here all these years and no one knows where you stay. Humph!

BERNIE: Never mind where I stay! Maybe that's where you live - in some ritzy neighborhood...huh! I work like you do, except harder! I don't have a government job like you. You're the one that can afford to live in a ritzy neighborhood considering the amount of money you make!

PAGE: They don't allow my kind to live there.

BERNIE: They don't allow my kind there either. Now what?

PAGE: *(Picking up his mail bag and getting ready to leave)* I see your wife riding in a new Cadillac. You think that's a good example for poor folks around here to see, huh?

BERNIE: This is Detroit, what do you expect? I see you riding around in a Cadillac newer than my wife's - huh! huh! *(Page, paying Bernie no mind, begins to walk away; but Bernie stops him)* Hey! Give me twenty-five cents for that pop you opened. *(Page pays him and as he walks away, Bernie is still talking)* Do you go to A&P and drink their pops and walk away without paying? No! *(Bernie holds up a hand full of mail that Page brought)* See these? All you bring are bills and you got the people's checks and they owe me money. I'll be in the poorhouse real soon. *(Page walks away and does not look back)*

Sister Johnson is dressed for work and sitting on her porch swing waiting for the mailman.

PAGE: *(Places mail into Mrs. Washington's mail box and hollers)* Mail! Good news today! *(As he walks away, Mrs. Washington goes to get the mail out of her box and sees her check)*

MRS. WASHINGTON: Thank you! *(She goes back into her house)*

Reverend Peters appears from around the corner and goes into the Church. He waves at Page but does not see Sister Johnson sitting on the porch.

PAGE: *(A few doors away)* Good morning, Sister Johnson!

Sister Johnson waves at Page and waits until he is closer before saying anything. Page drops the mail in the apartment building next to the house where Jessie, Mary, Carl and Tracy live. Having seen Sister Johnson, Page bypasses their mailbox to greet her.

PAGE: How are you feeling on this beautiful African-spring morning, Sister Johnson? This is the kind of morning that makes you want to just turn your music up loud and let everyone know that the butterflies are coming out of their cocoon, huh. I guess the Reverend didn't see you sitting here. If he did, he would've been here before me.

SISTER JOHNSON: *(Smiling)* I reckon so! It sure is the kind of morning that makes you want to shout. Would you like a cup of coffee?

PAGE: No ma'am, I just had two cups at Cousin Bee's Café. I wouldn't want to get caught relaxing while I'm on my route. Folks ain't friendly like they used to be. It sure wouldn't be a pretty sight.

SISTER JOHNSON: *(Smiling as Page hands the mail to her)* You're right, it sure wouldn't be...

PAGE: Here's your check, Sister Johnson. I have some mail for your children, too. There's a letter here for Mary from Uncle Sam.

SISTER JOHNSON: *(Taking the mail and looking at Page somewhat curiously)* She was down here not too long ago. *(Looking at the envelope, turns and says...)* What does it look like - good news or bad news?

PAGE: *(Taking the letter from Sister Johnson's hand and holding it up towards the sun)* I can't tell if it's good news but it sure doesn't look like any bad news either.

SISTER JOHNSON: *(Still curious and looking at the letter again)* You sure this ain't a bad news letter?

PAGE: Sister Johnson, I've been delivering mail for a long time. I don't even want to think about how long and this doesn't look like any bad news letter I've seen.

SISTER JOHNSON: *(Still nervous)* Well! Maybe you better take it up to her - you know - kind of reassure her. You know how she is about getting something unexpected like this here letter.

PAGE: *(Not wanting to climb the steps)* Sister Johnson, I just finished eating one of Cousin Bee's breakfast specials with two cups of coffee and a big Faygo at Bernie's. Now, *(moving closer to Sister Johnson and looking her in the eyes)* I heard tales about folks doing strenuous things and having heart attacks after one of Cousin Bee's breakfast specials.

SISTER JOHNSON: *(Smiling)* Man, you know you're lying on Bee. You could've been upstairs by now. You have a better chance of having a heart attack by not doing any exercise and letting all that food you eat get you too lazy to move. Walking up those steps is good for someone who has a full stomach like you. Now go on up those steps!

PAGE: Right now those steps look mighty steep. *(He starts the journey slowly, talking all the way)* I've been doing this too long and I'm getting too old for this. I would not do it for nobody but you and Mary. Sister Johnson, I think I deserve a sweet potato cobbler for doing all of this unnecessary stuff. How about that? It sure would make me feel special.

SISTER JOHNSON: *(Smiling)* I reckon I could do that for you!

PAGE: If I have a heart attack, it'll be on your conscience. *(As he nears the top of the stairs, Page stops to rest as if he's tired)*

SISTER JOHNSON: Hush your mouth!

PAGE: *(As he reaches the top of the stairs, Page opens the screen door, knocks on the door and loudly announces himself)* Mailman!

A few seconds later, Mary opens the door and Page hands her the mail.

MARY: *(Looking at Page curiously)* Why are you bringing me the mail? How come you didn't put it in the mailbox?

PAGE: Sister Johnson made me. She said to assure you that the government letter in your hand isn't bad news.

Mary is looking at the letter very cautiously.

MARY: *(Nervously holding the letter up)* How do you know this here letter isn't any bad news? Can you swear to me that it isn't?

PAGE: Mary, I ain't gonna swear but I've seen enough bad news letters to know one and I've never seen one looking like that. *(As he turns to leave, Mary stops him)*

MARY: Wait! Wait! You've got to stay here with me while I open it.

PAGE: *(Somewhat hurriedly)* Mary! I'm trying to get to the barber shop to use their bathroom.

MARY: *(Opens the screen door wider to let him in to use her bathroom)* Go on now. You better put the toilet seat back down and watch your aim.

PAGE: *(Setting his bag down, he goes inside)* Thank you, Mary!

MARY: *(Slowly she tears open the envelope)* He said it wasn't bad news. *(She takes the letter out, holds it close to her heart and says a prayer)* I ask you Lord to make him right.

Mary takes a deep breath and slowly reads the letter; as she reads, a smile appears on her face and her eyes begin to fill with water.

MARY: *(Lets out a big rejoice)* YES! Hallelujah! Hallelujah!

SISTER JOHNSON: *(Leaning over the banister)* Are you all right up there, child?

MARY: *(Crying and hurrying down the stairs, she leans over the railing and hugs Sister Johnson)* He's coming home! My man is coming home! *(Waving the letter in her hand)* It says so right here! It says he's being honorably discharged and leaving 'Nam for home.

SISTER JOHNSON: *(Expressing her joy, she looks up into the sky)* Thank you, Lord! Thank you for being the Lord that you are. Thank you! Thank you! You know Jessie is needed here with his loved ones. Thank you Lord for bringing good to this community! You know we need it.

PAGE: *(Coming out of Mary's house and picking up his mail bag)* What's all that screaming about? It scared the daylights out of me! Man can't stop what he's doing to run and see about all that whooping and hollering. *(He starts down the stairs)*

MARY: *(Hurries up the stairs and meets him. She hugs him briefly* *and kisses him on his cheek)* He's coming home. *(Hugging the letter)* Page, my man is finally coming home!

PAGE: *(Proud and bragging)* Didn't I tell you that it wasn't any bad news? I know my mail. You all got to start listening to me more often. I ain't just a mailman. I'm a "mailologist" – an expert of letters.

MARY: *(Hugs and kisses Page again)* Thank you! Thank you! Thank you! *(She lets go of Page and heads back up the stairs in a hurry)* I've got to go and tell Tracy and Carl!

PAGE: *(Going down the steps)* Carl ain't home. I saw him early this morning headed toward the playground. *(Teasing her, knowing she didn't want him to tell Carl)* I'm going back that way. I'll tell him for you.

MARY: *(Stops at the top of the stairs and turns towards Page with an ugly look)* You, listen here, man! If you go and tell Carl before I do, I'll break your neck with my teeny little bare hands. I mean it, you hear?

PAGE: Ahh, okay. I'll try. It sure is hard keeping good news locked up on the inside especially for a mailman.

MARY: *(Opening her door)* Man, you must really want to fight! *(To Sister Johnson)* Sister Johnson, if he tells anyone, don't ever bake him another pie. *(Pauses and points her finger at Page)* I'll never speak to you again as long as I live if you tell one soul!

Mary goes back into the house and Page goes down the stairs to where Sister Johnson is standing.

SISTER JOHNSON: *(Giving Page a hug)* You're sure bringing good news to the neighborhood today. Lord knows we're overdue!

PAGE: That's why they call these kinds of days "African Spring!" It only happens on the colored side of town. *(Page is thinking about what Mary said to him)* Now Sister Johnson, wouldn't you still bake me a cobbler if the secret just happens to slip out - the one you promised me earlier?

SISTER JOHNSON: *(Smiling)* That's a hard question. If I did, I don't think I could put the kind of love in it that you're used to.

PAGE: *(Leaving)* I reckon I better be on my P's and Q's today! Are you going to give Tracy and Carl their mail? I'm kinda running late on this good news day. I have a few more of these checks to deliver and then I'll go back to the station. I may not be finished until four o'clock if I don't get a move on.

SISTER JOHNSON: *(Standing up)* You go on, then. I'll put it in their box, but don't you forget silence is sweet potato cobbler at its finest.

PAGE: *(Walking away)* It's sure gonna be hard holding in good news. I ain't even been to the beauty shops or barber shops yet.

Sister Johnson watches and listens to Page complaining as he drops mail off at the church. Then he goes into the beauty parlor. Sister Johnson steps down off her porch and puts the mail in Tracy and Carl's mailbox. As she walks back up her steps, she sees Page again coming out of the beauty salon, still talking to himself.

PAGE: Now, if I can get in and out of the barber shop. *(He goes into the barber shop, we hear voices... Hey, Page! What's happening? What's the latest?)* I can't tell! *(He hurries out of the shop, looks back at Sister Johnson and disappears around the street's bend)*

SISTER JOHNSON: *(Looking up at the sky)* Thank you, Lord! We sure thank you.

Sister Johnson climbs the steps, opens her screen door and goes into her house.

END OF SCENE TWO

ACT I

SCENE THREE

Early afternoon - The neighborhood hears of Jessie's homecoming...

It is warmer and a different set of domino players are playing. The street is busier and the poolroom and bar are open. Tracy and Mary are sitting on Tracy's small two-step porch with both of their feet touching the sidewalk. Tracy is fair-skinned and sports an Afro. She is wearing cut-off jeans and Mary is wearing shorts that come to her knees. They are both joyful and happy as they acknowledge everyone they see.

MARY: Hey, Skeet! Jessie's coming home!

TRACY: Bebop! Jessie's coming home!

Mary and Tracy look at one another, smile and hug each other for the umpteenth time.

MARY: I'm so happy... I could scream it to the world. If I had a million dollars, I'd give it all up to be in my man's arms right now. That's how much I love him!

TRACY: *(Looking at Mary)* Girl, a million dollars? (Pauses) I'm not going to lie! I don't know if I would give up a million dollars for Carl even though I love that man like a preacher loves fried chicken.

MARY: Aw, come on! You know you'd give it up for him. What did you say when you knew he was coming home? *(Mary imitating Tracy..."I wouldn't trade that man of mine for anything in this world.")* Now didn't you say that?

TRACY: Okay! Okay! Maybe! If I did give up a million dollars for him, I know for sure - without a doubt *(Pauses)* they would have to put me in an insane asylum afterwards. *(Laughing, teasingly)* Mary Louise! You better start resting up. That man's got enough dynamite in those saddlebags to blow up Tobacco Road. *(Laugh-*

ing) And it isn't going to take long – maybe fifteen, twenty, thirty minutes at the most.

MARY: *(Still laughing)* It's going to be the best fifteen, twenty or thirty minutes of my life. It seems like he's been gone forever.

TRACY: It does seem that way. That's the same way I felt about Carl. Now he's been home six months and it seems like he never left. *(Getting somewhat serious momentarily)* Speaking of Carl, I'm so glad he was gone when you came downstairs because it gives us a little more time to do some strategizing.

MARY: *(Reacting to Tracy's comment)* I know one thing, when Jessie comes home Carl better not try to get to him before I do. As big as he is, I'll hurt that man and I'm not lying! **(Touching her breasts)** I've got dynamite stored in these saddlebags, too.

TRACY: That's why we've got to strategize! You and I both know how Carl and Jessie are. My husband doesn't understand anything. He's going to tell you. *(Imitating Carl, "You've got the rest of your life for that.")* Watch what I tell you!

MARY: *(With a disappointing look on her face)* We cannot let them do that. We've got to think of something. Shoot! Why would Jessie want to be with Carl anyway *(Mary traces the curves of her body)* instead of with his soft, beautiful and sexy wife?

TRACY: It isn't you, honey! It's another one of those stupid men things. *(Pauses)* When Jessie gets in the house, like I said, lock the door and wear his tail out! Immobilize him! Wear him down! You remember Carl was in the house for two days. I wore him into ah, ah… what they call it - sciatica attack!

MARY: I remember, girl. He sure wanted to get out too.

TRACY: Aw, that fool loved me pampering him! He was trying to act cool and all, but he liked it.

MARY: You're right, Tracy. I sure better wear Jessie out because once those two get together we may not see them until who knows when.

TRACY: I told you! *(She briefly changes the subject)* Has Sister Johnson left yet?

MARY: She's still in the house primping.

TRACY: I swear you'd think by the way she dresses that she was either a teacher or secretary instead of a housekeeper in one of those rich homes in Grosse Pointe.

MARY: Yeah! Sister Johnson is a sharp-dressing woman. Reverend Peters has been trying to sweeten her tea as of late. Wouldn't that be something? A preacher in the family! You know, *(Pauses)* it's been almost nine years since Big Mo, Sister Johnson's husband, passed away even though it doesn't seem like it's been that long.

TRACY: You think Sister Johnson likes Reverend Peters? He's a sharp brother.

MARY: She may, but I think he's too square for Sister Johnson. At that very moment Sister Johnson comes out of her house and onto the porch dressed very stylishly.

TRACY: Ooo-wee! You're looking mighty cute today! *(Teasing)* Are you sure you're going to work?

SISTER JOHNSON: Now, child, where else would I be going? I tell you. I'd rather be sitting right here with y'all enjoying this day than to be serving food and drinks at some rich folk's highfalutin' party. *(Walking down her steps)* With all of the good news that has sprung up on the street today, I feel like frying fish, cooking spaghetti and making coleslaw. I might even drink a beer with y'all.

MARY: *(Smiling)* I know you're just saying that about the beer, but the food part sounds good.

TRACY: Let's see, *(Looking at Sister Johnson and thinking)* the last time you had a beer was with Uncle Buck at our graduation.

SISTER JOHNSON: Well! We haven't had anything to shout about in a long time - not since Carl came home.

MARY: Sister Johnson, this day and the day Carl came home are the happiest days I've had in the last couple of years.

SISTER JOHNSON: *(Walking away)* Y'all sure deserve something good after these past few years. *(Stops, turns around and looks at Tracy and Mary smiling)* Don't use up all that joy. Save some for me when I get back this evening.

TRACY: *(Smiling)* The kind of joy we're having lasts a long time. Soon we all will be back together again. *(Hugging Mary)* One big happy family! Can I get an "amen"?

MARY and SISTER JOHNSON: A-A-Amen!

MARY: *(Loudly)* If you happen to see Carl, don't tell him about Jessie!

SISTER JOHNSON: I won't! *(As she approaches the bend of the street, looking down, and her voice fading)* Oh, Lord! I think I see the vegetable man up the street. It sure must be summer. Y'all get some sweet potatoes and I'll bake a cobbler tomorrow.

MARY: *(Being a little playful)* Now that sure sounds good, Sister Johnson, but I have to look *(Gesturing the outline of her body)* streamline for my man.

TRACY: Honey! When Jessie sees you, he isn't going to see anything but loving. When Carl came home, he didn't notice my hairdo, my new thirty-five dollar lingerie or my makeup. I mean, if I have to say so myself, I looked good but that man was so hungry that he didn't see nothing else but his honey. It lasted about fifteen minutes.

MARY: *(Sitting back down, joyfully speaking)* Fifteen minutes is a long time!

The sound of Mr. Crimple, the vegetable man, gets closer and closer; he's coming from around the bend, the same direction as Sister Johnson. It is the first time this year anyone's seen him. Mr. Crimple is an old white man who has been bringing vegetables to the neighborhood long before Mary and Tracy were born. His push-cart is full of vegetables and fruits. A scale hangs from the side and a large overhang roof shelters him and the cart from the sun and rain.

MR. CRIMPLE: *(Yells)* Vegetable man! Fresh mustards, turnips and collard greens; onions; green peppers; squash; black-eyed peas; apples; grapes and sweet potatoes. Vegetable man!

MARY: *(Waves as Mr. Crimple passes them)* Welcome back, Mr. Crimple! You have any big sweet potatoes?

Mr. Crimple waves and grabs one from the cart and raises it so they can see it as he passes. He gets near the center of the street and stops. He sets up business across the street between Bernie and Cousin Bee's Café. Before long, he is busy selling, even to Bernie and Cousin Bee. It is evident that folks are happy to see him back.

TRACY: Folks are glad to see Mr. Crimple again.

MARY: I tell you, this must be the first day of summer on Side Street. Domino games starting, fish man going to the river with his pole and bucket, the vegetable man arrives, today is check day and most of all - Jessie is coming home. This is the happiest day of my life!

TRACY: Jessie's coming home is what sparked everything else. You know, since Sister Johnson is going to make the cobbler, let's get some turnips and mustards and make a big meal for tomorrow and pig out. I'll cook the greens and cornbread if you cook the chicken and make the potato salad... and don't start talking about stream-lines either. Wait until after tomorrow.

MARY: *(Getting up and pulling Tracy with her)* What are we waiting for? Come on!

Tracy and Mary walk jubilantly toward the cart like two teenag-ers. Two girls walk between them, heading to the beauty shop. They touch elbows in a wing-like position, a friendship fad among the young crowd.

TRACY: *(As they are passing)* Hey, you sisters! (Pointing at Mary) Mary has something to tell you.

CHRISTINE and JACKIE LEE: *(Turning around)* Is it good? You all acting like it is!

MARY: *(Happy)* My man is coming home for good!

JACKIE LEE: Now that is some good news! Are we going to have a get-together?

MARY: I sure would like to so he can see everybody.

TRACY: We're going to do something. We'll let you know.

CHRISTINE: *(Walking away)* We hope you don't do a Carl on us.

TRACY: *(Loudly as she nears the vegetable cart)* I HAD NOTHING TO DO WITH CARL'S LITTLE PARTY! HE PICKED AND CHOSE WHO HE WANTED AND YOU KNOW CARL NEVER THOUGHT TOO MUCH OF YOU ALL.

Tracy and Mary get to the cart about the same time as Christine and Jackie enter the beauty shop.

From the opposite direction, male voices are heard singing a cappella and seconds later, four teenagers (Darnell, Beanpole, Fatman and Kool Breeze) appear on Side Street. Their names fit their description. Mary and Tracy leave the cart with their greens and potatoes. They see the boys, whom they know, coming toward them singing. The boys block their way, making them stop momentarily as they serenade them. Tracy and Mary try to go around them but the boys block them.

TRACY: You all sure don't impress us. Get out of the way!

Tracy and Mary push through the boys who are still following them, singing and admiring the view with comments while they are singing.

DARNELL: Ump! Ump! Ump! Y'all sho look good!

TRACY: Why don't you all go flirt with somebody your own age?

BEANPOLE: *(Being cool)* We don't want no juicy-fruit. We want exspearmint.

Everyone laughs in agreement.

MARY: Can't you all see that nobody got time for your mannishness today?

TRACY: I ought to call Carl out here on you all.

FATMAN: Go ahead. We know he ain't home. We just saw him at the playground playing basketball.

DARNELL: Yeah! He's taking money from youngsters. We want to beat his butt anyway for taking all our money at the gym last week.

MARY: Well, as soon as Jessie comes home he and Carl will out-sing you all and whip all four of your butts at the same time... easily!

TRACY: Shoot! You and I could probably beat them. I know I can beat Fatman, and Mary, you could beat Beanpole.

Tracy and Mary laugh out loud.

FATMAN: *(Speaking mannishly)* Y'all could beat up on me anytime!

BEANPOLE: *(Looking at his buddies)* That's how they get their kicks. Y'all probably are just lonely women. Jessie in 'Nam and Carl, well, he... *(Thinking)*

FATMAN: I'm potent. *(Everyone laughs)*

MARY: Oooh... you all are so mannish.

TRACY: Now you know if I tell Carl, he'll come and whip you all's behinds.

KOOL BREEZE: Tell him. We ain't shaking, are we? *(Looking over at his friends and laughing)*

Mary and Tracy are not paying the boys no mind as they approach their house and step onto Tracy's porch. The boys are still following and singing to them. They stop at Tracy's porch. Tracy opens her screen door and Mary follows her into the house without saying a word. The boys turn around and head up the street past the domino game, Cousin Bee's Café, the laundromat and out of sight around the corner as their voices fade.

A short time later...

Tracy and Mary come back onto the porch. They look both ways and then burst out laughing. Taking their same positions as before, sitting on the porch steps, they look at each other and start laughing again.

TRACY: You're thinking the same thing I am?

MARY: Yep! Carl and Jessie, Junior Boy and Rabbit!

TRACY: Sure enough, those boys act just like Carl, Jessie and their group when they were in high school.

MARY: I wonder if Carl and Jessie tried to flirt with older women like Fatman, Darnell, Beanpole, and Kool Breeze were doing just now.

TRACY: You know they did and we did, too. Remember those college boys at Edgewater Park? *(Mary and Tracy are smiling as they reminisce about their past)*

MARY: Oh, my Lord! I had forgotten about them. I can't even remember their names.

TRACY: Reginald and Cleotis! Girl, how could you forget Reginald? That boy had you hypnotized. You were *(Making a measuring gesture with her finger and thumb)* this close to losing it all and about to make me lose mine. How could you not remember them?

MARY: Now I remember. Jessie was with Carl and his father in Texas for the summer and that's why we were at the park by ourselves. Shoot, girl, we were only what... fourteen? And don't you blame everything on me. If you hadn't been blossoming like you were they probably never would have spoken to us. You know I had nothing that would attract those kinds of boys. Remember I was called, "Mary Toilet Paper." *(They laugh)*

TRACY: You may have been small in size but you were one fine black sister. You sure had Jessie going. *(Laughing)* You had Jessie beat up poor Joe Robert for calling you "Mary Toilet Paper,' *(Pauses)* yeah, old Reginald really liked you. He talked you into going to the White Castle on Eight Mile and then to Belle Isle, knowing if you did, I was going to go with you. Boy, we were dumb back then.

MARY: Thanks to Rabbit for being there and knowing those boys and what they were up to. That's one thing about him. He always looked out for us when Carl or Jessie weren't around. Even college boys didn't mess with Rabbit. *(Looking at Tracy and smiling)* You had a little crush on Rabbit, didn't you?

TRACY: Rabbit used to be one fine brother. He was an athlete, muscular and always dressed sharp. I had a little crush on him, I guess. I don't know if you would call it a crush or not. Now that I think about it, it was just infatuation. All the hip girls liked him. I never went out with him. He would just flirt and tease with me because he knew I liked him. He only dated the okay "can't say no girls." *(Reminiscing and laughing)* Remember when Mama caught me and Carl and you and Jessie necking in the basement?

MARY: Oh Lord! You're about to make my butt hurt all over again just thinking about it. Your blouse was half unbuttoned and Jessie was trying to unbutton my blouse when your mother walked in. He sure didn't care if I didn't have much there. He just wanted to explore. *(Mary and Tracy laugh)*

TRACY: I got the worst whipping I ever had in my life! How in the world Mama got down into that basement without us knowing still puzzles me to this day.

MARY: Mamas sense things, but I still say you were luckier than I was. After your mama got through whipping us she called my mama. Girl, *(Looking at Tracy)* when I got home and saw them both standing there, I was never so scared in my life and when I saw the look in my daddy's eye… that was the first and last time he ever whipped me. That time sure hurt him. Daddy was so afraid we were going to wind up pregnant like Barbara Jean and them. It sure taught me a lesson… Jessie and Carl too. My daddy scared them to death.

TRACY: Carl and Jessie were scared of your daddy. I've never seen Carl afraid of anybody but Uncle. He didn't take any mess from anyone and everybody around here knew it! Remember what he once told Carl and Jessie? *(Imitating Mary's dad...)* "If y'alls intentions are anything other than nice and respectable to these girls, you best stay away from them. I expect to be going to graduation and a wedding with the brides wearing white dresses. If it's anything other than what I just said, you boys better stay the hell away from them because if I have to come looking for you, I won't be talking. That understood?" Girl, Carl and Jessie sure were nice after that speech until we graduated and married them.

MARY: We did get married and in white dresses, too!

TRACY: Believe you me, if your daddy didn't scare the daylights out of them and us... you know we would have tried doing the do. I know we made a promise to each other that we were going to hold out 'til our wedding night, but between listening to our friends, our dreams, magazines, Carl's and Jessie's hormones running wild, and us being square, curious and dumb... I wouldn't have bet anyone before Uncle put that fear in us.

MARY: *(Laughing)* We were all scared all right! The guys were almost too scared to kiss, hug and neck with us after that. We had to make them - but tell the truth, don't you think our men felt good on our wedding night knowing that they were the first and the only? I remember Jessie was like a kid at Christmas.

TRACY: Yeah, Carl was like a kid in a candy store. He thought he had died and gone to heaven. My man hasn't been the same since. He said he grew two inches taller after our wedding night. I tell you that is still the most beautiful event in my life.

MARY: Mine, too! Our families would be proud of us. We finished high school, did a little college and got married.

TRACY: *(Overcome by sadness)* I sure miss our families!

MARY: Me, too! I know they're looking down on us and are happy and proud of our accomplishments. I just wish they were here to enjoy the moment with us. I know they are still here in spirit - still watching over us. *(Pauses)* You know, we may not have a lot but we have a home. Old as it may be, it's ours and it's paid for, thanks to our family. We have good husbands, Sister Johnson and each other. We had a lot of love back then and we have a lot of love now. Love still conquers all.

TRACY: Amen to that! Also, love is what keeps us surviving today. It sure isn't about money - although we need it.

MARY: *(Smiling and still reminiscing)* Tracy, what about daddy's brother, Uncle Buck? He was just as bad as daddy. He used to chase Carl and Jessie away every time they came to our house.

TRACY: *(Remembers and starts to laugh)* He sure did. *(Smiling)* Remember when they would be out here singing in front of the house? Your uncle would come out and chase them away. He would yell, "You all get away from here with that damn racket."

MARY: Uncle Buck thought they were rebels, especially Carl. *(Mary imitating Uncle Buck)* "Talking that Muslim talk, calling everybody sisters and brothers. Don't nobody want to be kin to that boy and his folks." Tracy, do you remember what he used to say to you about Carl? *(Imitating...)*. "You better be careful of that boy. He may snap any day." Uncle Buck said Carl was a little bit foggy *(Pointing to her head)* up there!

TRACY: Yeah! My poor baby was talked about. My daddy-in-law had been hit in the head a few times too many in the ring. Folks thought it was hereditary. My poor baby was labeled when he came into this world. I'm kind of glad daddy-in-law decided to stay in Texas with his sister, Aunt Caroline. *(They laugh)*

MARY: *(Back in the groove)* You and Carl are a perfect pair if I have ever seen one.

TRACY: Yeah! So are you and Jessie. *(Still reminiscing)* Those sure were some good old days, weren't they? Everybody was working. Not like the way things are now - brothers dying in 'Nam, jobs getting scarce, drugs soothing miseries - or so they think.

MARY: *(Sadly)* Years sure made a difference. We were on top of the world back then thinking about college and marriage and with just a blink of an eye our world collapsed around us.

TRACY: Yeah! *(Pauses)* It's hard to talk about it still, but I'm sure our parents are looking down on us with pride.

MARY: *(On a lighter note)* Also looking over us! You know I sometimes wonder if God took our fathers. *(Pauses)* You know they sure weren't church going and religious-acting folks.

TRACY: *(Smiling)* Girl, you know our mamas weren't going to let God take our fathers away from them. You know as well as I do, there wasn't anyone I know of who could pray like your mama. Shoot, Reverend Peters called on her to pray in church sometimes when the church needed a little spiritual boost.

MARY: My daddy and Uncle Buck sure kept her in practice trying to get God to forgive their blasphemous behaviors. *(Changing the subject)* Lord, my man sure is going to be disappointed when he gets home. Being right there in the battlefield, I just couldn't tell him any depressing news - like Rabbit.

TRACY: *(Trying to brighten the moment, they hug briefly)* He's going to be fine. Once he sees that fine, sweet chocolate face, his troubles will disappear.

From around the bend appears Nicholas Jones, better known as Rabbit. He is groomed nicely from head to toe. His demeanor is suspicious.

TRACY: *(Scowling)* The last person I want to see right about now!

RABBIT: Two of the finest ladies on this planet! What's happening?

TRACY and MARY: *(Not very pleasing)* Hey, Rabbit!

RABBIT: *(Oblivious)* Tracy, where's your old man? Does he know that you're out here showing all that? *(Pointing to the outfit Tracy has on)* He can't be too far.

TRACY: Yes, he knows I dress like this and you know where he's at.

MARY: *(Excited and not able to contain it)* Rabbit, guess what? Jessie's coming home and you better be straight when he gets here or else I'm going to beat you up myself.

RABBIT: *(Not paying attention, but also excited)* Naw! You mean my man Jessie is really coming home? That's my man! My main man! My man Jessie is always composed and cool. My man Jessie is all right.

MARY: You better not go to the playground and tell Carl either. If you do, I'll never speak to you again as long as I live.

RABBIT: I'm not going to say anything. *(Pauses)* Old Jess is coming home... my man! *(Looking at Tracy in an instigating manner)* Tracy, your man is still over there taking money from amateurs. He won't play me for change. He knows I will run circles around him like I used to do in school.

TRACY: You can brag. At least he's still in shape. Look at you.

RABBIT: Shoot, I could beat him in shape, out of shape, even in a decathlon and he can choose the event. *(Boasting)* I used to be the baddest. Admit it! Wasn't I?

TRACY: *(Looking somewhat disturbed)* What difference does it make now how bad you were? Yeah, you were bad all right - so bad you disappointed a whole neighborhood!

MARY: Rabbit, this isn't the time for you to be bragging on yourself.

TRACY: Let him go on and hide his miserable self in dope.

RABBIT: Aw, now, you're going to low blow me now 'cause I've been talking 'bout your man!

TRACY: You know what I mean, Nicholas Jones!

RABBIT: I'm going to get myself together again.

TRACY: No, you won't! You're just another big disappointment!

MARY: *(Sadly)* You should be ashamed of yourself. You sure are going to disappoint Jessie when he comes home. I just couldn't bring myself to tell him how much you've let him down.

TRACY: Rabbit, you have disappointed a lot of folks!

RABBIT: Aw, baby! Y'all watch. Old Rabbit will be back on his feet again soon. This is just a slight setback. That's all.

MARY: Jessie always asked about you when he wrote to me. I couldn't tell him anything while he's over there risking his life.

RABBIT: That Jess! He's my man! Never was too good in sports, but he was tough. Mary, you've got one cool man. Not like someone else I know - not mentioning any names.

TRACY: If you're talking about my husband, you're just mad because he doesn't look up to your butt anymore. That's part of what's wrong with you. You had it too good and it went to your head. Now look at you!

RABBIT: Your man has always been jealous of me, Tracy. I reckon he's okay though… a little crazy at times.

MARY: Nicholas, you have no right to talk about anyone after what you've gotten yourself into.

TRACY: Don't try and tell him anything. He doesn't care about no one but himself. He had a chance to be something for the community, but what is he? A junkie! It's just that simple. It is what it is.

RABBIT: *(Defensively speaking)* There you go again - low blowing me foul. You've never seen me take any drugs, have you?

TRACY: Don't have to. Everyone around knows that you take drugs. What did you go to jail for last month? Look how you're looking and acting now!

RABBIT: I went to jail for tickets, that's all. *(Changing the subject)* Tracy, I hear your old man lost y'alls old raggedy car playing ball with that hustler from Newark's playgrounds. I heard he was in town. If I had known I could have told Carl not to mess with the "Street Doctor." That dude is known in every playground where people play basketball. Bad dude! He's supposed to be the best there is on any playground.

TRACY: If you knew about that street and what's his name, you should have told Carl. Nobody around here can afford to be losing cars no matter how raggedy they are.

RABBIT: Carl should have come and asked me just like he and Jessie used to do when they were in over their heads. I've still got a reputation!

TRACY: *(Smartly speaking of his drug habit)* You sure have!

RABBIT: *(Saddened by the statement, yet subtly understanding)* Why you want to come down on me like that? I've always looked after y'all regardless, haven't I? Why you keep coming down on me?

TRACY: *(Without remorse)* Why do you think?

RABBIT: Aw, there you go with that again! I haven't done anything to hurt no one.

TRACY: You sure haven't done anything except make people lose their religion thinking about your behind. I know I'd lose mine every time I think about or see you. Like now, I'm about to lose it. Why don't you go get lost some place?

MARY: Nicholas Jones! You aren't going to mess up this day for me with your carrying-on. You better not come around here this kind of way when Jessie comes home either. You hear what I'm saying? Stop making Tracy mad at you.

RABBIT: *(Teasing)* Yes, ma'am! I hear what you're saying but I think the reason Tracy gets mad at me is 'cause she's still in love with me!

TRACY: Man! I'm not thinking about you. I have never loved you. I was just infatuated with you because you were *(Emphasizing)* at one time… one popular dude!

Reverend Peters, an older-looking gentleman, walks out the front door of the church. He speaks to a lady coming out of the beauty shop as she passes him. It's too late for Rabbit or anyone else to leave as Reverend Peters walks toward them.

TRACY: Oh, Lord, here comes Reverend Peters and I have on these short, tight jeans.

MARY: He sees you! I'm not wearing my Sunday sermon clothes, either!

Rabbit makes an attempt to leave but Mary grabs his arm.

MARY: You're not going anywhere. Stay right here!

Reverend Peters looks at Sister Johnson's house as he passes like he was hoping to see her on the porch or in a window.

MARY: *(As Reverend Peters approaches)* Morning, Reverend Peters! It sure is a warm one today, huh? How are you?

REVEREND PETERS: *(Smiling as he approaches Mary, Tracy and Rabbit)* Beautiful morning to you, Sister Mary, Sister Tracy and Brother Nicholas... it sure is a beautiful day. It has folks around here thinking its summer. The music is playing; folks sweeping, cleaning, dusting, painting and planting.

MARY: Page says it's called "African Spring." He says the only place it happens in America is in the inner cities.

REVEREND PETERS: Brother Page has a name for almost every-thing. Sister Tracy, Brother Nicholas, how are you?

TRACY: Morning to you, Reverend Peters, I'm doing fine!

RABBIT: I'm fine, Reverend!

REVEREND PETERS: *(Speaking to Rabbit)* Well, now, that's mighty fine! There's nothing the Lord likes better than to see his children doing fine.

RABBIT: *(Looking a bit uncomfortable, stands up straight, brushes his hair in place and prepares to leave)* Well, I gotta be going y'all!

REVEREND PETERS: Brother Nicholas, it has been quite some time since I've seen you in church.

RABBIT: Yes sir, it has! I've had some rough times lately, Reverend.

REVEREND PETERS: Maybe the Lord's house is what you need. Handling rough times is one of his specialties.

MARY: *(Getting Rabbit off the hook and desperately antsy to tell the Reverend her news)* I have some good news for you today, Reverend. *(Teasing)* Want to guess what it is?

REVEREND PETERS: Now Sister Mary, I've been praying most nights and most days for me to come out here in these streets during these troubled times just so I can hear some good news from the flock. *(Also teasing)* Now after all those prayers, you are going to make the Lord's answered prayers wait.

MARY: *(Stands and comes toward Reverend Peters)* Jessie is coming home! He's finally coming home! *(She hugs the Reverend)* Now isn't that good news?

Reverend Peters hugs her momentarily and then he grabs Rabbit and her hands for a brief prayer. Tracy, not really wanting to stand in her jeans, steps up anyway and holds Rabbit's and Mary's hands. Feeling the perspiration from Rabbit's hand, Tracy briefly wipes her hand on her jeans, then reaches out and holds his hand again.

REVEREND PETERS: There is no need to wait 'til lunch, supper, bed time or Sunday morning service. Let us give thanks to our Lord and Savior right now.

MARY: *(Holding her head down, she glances from the side of her eyes at Rabbit's nervousness)* Amen!

From the second-story window of the rooming house next door, two girls poke their heads out of the window, briefly awakened by

Mary, Tracy, Rabbit and Reverend Peters' activities. Unnoticed, they quickly pull their heads back in. From up the street Housecoat Pearl leans her head out of the window and starts looking at them, too.

REVEREND PETERS: Heavenly Father, thank you for answering our prayers. For sending Jessie, someone whom we all love dearly, back home and for blessing our humble community with your presence in our lives. We ask you to continue to give us hope and faith each day. We thank you, dear Heavenly Father. Amen.

TRACY, MARY and RABBIT: Amen!

Tracy sits back down on the porch steps.

REVEREND PETERS: I hope the rest of this day is as beautiful, with blessings like the ones we're receiving right now. Isn't our God's glory great?

TRACY and MARY: Amen!

RABBIT: *(Seeing an opportunity to leave)* Well, I guess I will be moseying on. I'll see y'all later.

REVEREND PETERS: (Speaking to Rabbit) Brother Nicholas, it sure would be nice for you to come back to church and sing in our choir. The Lord needs young men like you to praise His glory.

RABBIT: *(Walking away)* Yes sir!

REVEREND PETERS: *(Speaking to Mary and Tracy as Rabbit is leaving)* I see a troubled young man. We should pray for him that one day he may find himself and come back to the Lord where he again can have peace and hope. You all have a wonderful and blessed day. I'm on my way over to Jessie's Uncle Milton's barber shop for a haircut. Have you told him yet? I can tell him for you if you like!

As Reverend Peters begins to walk up the street, Mary remembers that she did not tell her Uncle Milton the news of Jessie's homecoming and she hollers out to the Reverend.

MARY: *(Loud voice)* REVEREND PETERS, YOU BETTER NOT TELL UNCLE MILTON! *(Grabbing Tracy's hand and pulling her up from the porch steps)*... Let's hurry and change so we can beat him over there. You know he's going to stop twenty times before he gets to the barber shop.

END OF SCENE THREE

ACT I

SCENE FOUR

Early evening...

A few scattered gray clouds have diminished the sun's heat rays. It is not as intense as it was earlier when people were wiping sweat from their brows. There is a steady flow of pedestrian traffic and a new set of domino players and spectators. Cousin Bee's Café is still doing steady business. The laundromat has slowed down and folks are going in and out of the bar and poolroom. Housecoat Pearl is sitting on an old wooden bench next to her doorway and as usual, is in her trademark housecoat with a glass of alcohol in her hand. It is too hot in her apartment.

Tracy comes out of her house and onto her porch. She has changed her clothes and put on some makeup. She goes to the edge, puts her arm around the bannister for support and leans over so she can see Mary's porch.

TRACY: *(Calling from the highest pitch of her voice)* Mary-eeee...
A few seconds later, Mary opens her screen door and comes onto her porch and starts down the steps. She also has changed her clothes and put on makeup. She seems to have forgotten something and goes back up the steps.

MARY: I forgot my purse. I'll be right back!

After a few minutes, Mary starts her journey back down the stairs. Luella and Francine come out of the next door apartment onto their porch about the same time as Mary reaches Tracy.

Luella and Francine are two girls who grew up with Tracy, Carl, Mary and Jessie. They are very attractive and sexy, which they display to their advantage. They are prostitute/call girls. All four girls see each other about the same time. Luella and Francine come over to Tracy's porch.

LUELLA and FRANCINE: Hey! Now, what's happening?

TRACY and MARY: Heyyyyy!

TRACY: What's been happening with you all?

LUELLA: Earlier we heard the little ruckus, peeped out and saw you all down here with Reverend Peters and Rabbit.

FRANCINE: That poor Rabbit - he sure looked pitiful!

TRACY: Why didn't you all bring your butts down here and get in on the prayer? You all sure could use some.

LUELLA: We sure could, but I don't think Reverend Peters wanted to see us the way we were dressed 'cause he sure would find a spot for it in his Sunday morning sermon.

TRACY: Heck, if he sees you all now he sure enough would have a sermon to preach tomorrow. Remember last summer - the time he preached about hot pants? Hello, *(pointing to herself)* that was me! He caught me wearing hot pants when I was watering the plants on my porch and to make matters worse, I think I was bending over when he passed by. This morning, he caught me in short, tight jeans. I'm not sure if I'm going to church tomorrow or not. That man can be downright embarrassing and he doesn't even call names. You all wouldn't stand a chance if he ever catches you. If he should catch you, stay at home that Sunday. *(Laughter... Pauses)*

MARY: Say what you want about Reverend Peters...he really loves us.

TRACY, LUELLA and FRANCINE: *(Speaking in unison)* Amen!

TRACY: Where you all going looking so sassy anyway this early in the evening?

LUELLA: We're heading over to the boulevard to Soft Toes for a pedicure and manicure.

FRANCINE: Where you all going? Those aren't your porch-sitting clothes.

TRACY: *(Turns and says)* Ask Mary!

FRANCINE: What's happening, Mary?

MARY: We're going to The Well for a drink.

LUELLA: Who hit the numbers?

MARY: *(Joyously hugs both Francine and Luella)* I hit the jackpot! My man is coming home! Hallelujah! Hallelujah!

LUELLA: So that's what that was all about this morning. Shoot, girl, if we had known we would've come down and joined in with you all - after we changed clothes.

FRANCINE: You all know we've got to have something for Jessie when he comes home.

MARY: We're going to give a little something...*(They Laugh)*

FRANCINE: Girl, there's no way you can give a little something for Jessie. We're talking about a real party.

TRACY: I declare, Fran. You sound just like Carl. Mary, we may as well do it because as soon as Carl finds out Jessie is coming home you know he's going to act like we're rich and spend what we don't have, just for him.

MARY: What are you talking about? Where are we going to give something big enough for the amount of people you all are talking about? You're forgetting about the money it would cost for something that big.

FRANCINE: You all can rent a hall or maybe Lu and I can get you The Hasting House. We're pretty close with Big Hank.

LUELLA: Only problem with that is he's probably booked 'til after Christmas and New Year, but we can check and get back to you.

MARY: You all are forgetting something. Sure we can get a hall or The Hasting House but a lot of the older folks and Christians aren't going to come to a place where beer will be served.

TRACY: We sure haven't thought about that.

LUELLA: We didn't.

FRANCINE: Well, whatever you all come up with we're behind you. *(A thought comes to her mind)* Hey, I know what we can give and it won't cost much - a street party!

TRACY: That's a great idea! We all could use some fun around here. Jessie's coming home street party! I think that will do it.

LUELLA: Fran, you've got a good one this time! We used to have the best street parties in the city. Everybody was there.

FRANCINE: *(Proud of her idea)* I bet Jessie will see everybody in one night.

MARY: *(Reluctant)* I'm not being negative - Jessie sure would enjoy a street party - but these people around here now aren't like they were way back when. I mean it's a new breed of folks.

TRACY: Girl, nothing's going to happen. This is our turf and you know Carl and Jessie's friends and the homesteaders aren't going to let anything happen around here. Maybe a few raids on the poolroom every now and then and that's been over a year and a half ago. This here is our world - the place we call home. It may not look like much, but most of us like it and nothing is going to happen - not on Side Street.

FRANCINE: Lu and I can vouch for that. Ever since the '50s when Detroit James and the Eastsiders gang declared this street as sacred ground there hasn't been any major problem.

FRANCINE: Remember when we were written up in Black Ivory magazine as one of the best streets in the ghetto?

MARY: *(Smiling)* All right! I'm not saying anything negative again. Let's have a street party then.

LUELLA: You all know we're going to help. Just tell us what or how much. We've got your back.

FRANCINE: Girl, as much as Jessie done bailed us out of jail, there's nothing we won't do for him.

LUELLA: You all are covered. This party is going to happen!

TRACY: We're going to get on that now. We can start by letting folks in church know what we plan to do. First time I've been excited about anything in a long time.

LUELLA: It sure seems exciting!

FRANCINE: *(As Francine and Luella are walking away)* Tell us what you want us to do.

MARY: Will do! Thanks, Sisters!

Francine and Luella throw up their hands in a gesture of understanding. Tracy and Mary watch them as they sashay up the street. Housecoat Pearl stands to her feet, her hands on her hips and right foot forward; then she sits back down as Francine and Luella pass by.

TRACY: They sure are some sexy mamas.

MARY: They're good people, too. They've been our friends forever and have always been in our corner.

TRACY: That sure is true, but I will tell you like it is. If they were not our real true friends, honey, I wouldn't let them get within ten feet of my man. They're just too fine to be testing my man's hormones and that's the truth.

MARY: They are fine, but don't forget we must be pretty fine ourselves. Look how many girls tried to get Carl and Jessie and look who wound up with them. *(Smiling)* Remember you had to whup Mary Alice's butt for telling lies about how she and Carl had a thing going on.

TRACY: Yeah, I remember her telling folks that he was trying to hit on her and she went out with him a couple of times.

MARY: *(Laughing)* You were so mad! I had to pull you off of Carl. He just let you beat on him. He didn't even know what for. Jessie and I were cracking up.

TRACY: She better be glad I didn't find her when I went looking for her because if I had, I would've whupped the black off her and put it back on. I was so mad.

MARY: Yeah, but thanks to Lu we finally caught her butt hiding in the girls' gym bathroom waiting 'til she thought we were gone. When she came out it was on, ooo-weee! I stood guard at the door.

TRACY: *(Smiling again)* I beat the mess out of that floozy. *(Thinking)* I wonder where she's at now!

MARY: You didn't see her last year at Robert Green's party when you, Chris, Jackie Lee and I went together. *(Pauses)* Naw, that's right. You were doing Chris' hair and you two came later. She came in for a few minutes just to show off it seems. Had this high-yellow, fine brother with her and told Jackie Lee that he wanted to marry her. Found out later he was already married and had three kids. *(Pauses)* I think she wanted to show off to you and Carl. She let everybody know that she was a school teacher in Chicago - smiling from ear-to-ear. She was pretty hot looking in that "can't sit down" dress.

TRACY: *(Excited)* Did she say anything about Carl? I guess she didn't know he was in the service.

MARY: She wouldn't speak to me. Jackie Lee said she asked about us and she told her that we were married to Jessie and Carl. She left about fifteen minutes later. I believe she came to show off to Carl and in front of us. She was really hot in that dress.

TRACY: I sure wish I had been there just to see her face when Jackie told her we were married. I don't care that she was hot - she's still a miserable heifer. She hasn't got what she still wants. I got him.

MARY: *(Teasing)* I think she's the kind of woman who will give it up to prove something and tell you all about it.

TRACY: All right now, don't make me go to Chicago and whup that girl's behind for what I think she might do. *(They laugh)* We've been standing here this long - we may as well go and change clothes and sit our butts down.

MARY: You know how it is when women get to talking. I almost forgot what we got dressed for. I guess I'm just happy. Did you leave a note telling Sister Johnson where we're going? She said she wanted to celebrate with us.

TRACY: *(Pulling the note out of her dress pocket)* Got it right here! Sure glad you mentioned it. I had forgotten all about it.

Tracy goes over to Sister Johnson's house and puts the note in the crack of the door. As she turns around, the same group of boys from earlier this morning, are coming around the corner from up the street singing. This time Carl is singing with them.

MARY: Uh-oh, here comes Carl!

TRACY: Let's go sing with them!

Tracy and Mary start walking up the street towards them. When they reach Carl, they put their arms around him and he puts his arms around them. Singing along with the guys, Tracy and Mary begin to do a dance routine in Motown style that Carl is showing everybody. He stops and addresses them.

CARL: Whoa… whoa… whoa… wait a minute… you all are messing up the song and the routine!

TRACY: Listen to you! We aren't messing up anything. You all didn't sound that good in the first place. We just thought we would give you a helping hand.

CARL: You all are off key. Now let me show you!

Carl commences to have them harmonize. It is natural for him because he leads the church choir. They continue singing until they reach Mrs. Washington's house. Carl, Tracy and Mary slow down at Mrs. Washington's house, but the boys continue on down the street singing until they cannot be heard.

CARL: *(Still walking arm-in-arm with Mary and Tracy)* What's there to eat? I'm starving!

TRACY: Tuna fish sandwiches!

CARL: That's it? You didn't cook anything?

TRACY: Now you know I don't cook on Saturdays. Show me one black woman who cooks on Saturdays!

CARL: Any more catfish and spaghetti from last night?

TRACY: Nope! Mary and I ate it for lunch. You win any money? I need a twenty.

CARL: *(Cool acting... takes his arms from around them and pulls out a small wad of cash)* I won a little bit. *(Giving her a twenty)* What you need twenty dollars for? Where you two going dressed up?

Tracy takes the twenty and they stop in front of their house. She and Mary turn back around and start walking up the street near Bernie's store. Carl is still standing in front of their house as Tracy yells back at him.

TRACY: Mary and I are going to The Well!

CARL: Hold on a minute! What are you going to The Well for? That isn't any place for you all without me! Who hit the numbers? Tracy and Mary reach The Well and as Tracy opens the door, she hollers back to Carl as they enter.

TRACY and MARY: To celebrate! *(As the door closes Carl barely hears them)* Jessie is coming home!

CARL: *(Briefly stunned, then heads up the street towards the bar)* Wait a minute! Did I hear them say that Jessie is coming home! Hey, wait! *(He gets to the bar and goes in)* Did you all say Jessie's coming home?

END OF SCENE FOUR

ACT I

SCENE FIVE

Six weeks have passed - Randy's funeral / Jessie comes home...

It is late Saturday morning and all the businesses on Side Street are closed except the pool hall and the bar. The church door is open, soft organ music can be heard and the folks going inside are all dressed in what you call their Sunday best.

Coming out of their establishment are Ernest, Ernestine and Bee along with Page. Bernie is also leaving his store and the five of them walk together towards the church and go inside. People are going in and out of Mrs. Washington's house paying their respects.

Mary's screen door opens and Mary walks out onto her porch. She is dressed in her black, special occasion outfit. With a hat and matching purse in hand she comes down her steps to the sidewalk, then onto Tracy's porch. She sits down in a chair on the porch and calls out.

MARY: *(Softly)* Tracy-eeee, are you all ready?

TRACY: *(Walking out of her screen door)* I am. You know how slow Carl is – besides, he doesn't want to go anyway. *(Tracy is dressed in a dark, conservative outfit)*

MARY: None of us want to go. This is just something that we have to do.

Mrs. Washington and her nephew, along with a group of people, commence to walk towards the church. Everyone is dressed in black attire. Mrs. Washington is wearing a hat with a veil that covers her face.

MARY: That poor woman! A son killed in 'Nam and now a grandson gone.

TRACY: Yeah, I feel sorry for her. Darn that Randy.

Tracy and Mary stand at the edge of their porch as Mrs. Washington approaches. She stops with her nephew.

MRS. WASHINGTON: *(Sadly)* Y'all look very pretty.

TRACY: Thank you, Mrs. Washington.

MARY: Is there anything we can help you with?

MRS. WASHINGTON: Just pray for me to have enough strength to get through this.

MARY: Yes, ma'am, we will.

Mrs. Washington, her nephew, and the group of people continue walking to the church.

MARY: It's a shame.

TRACY: So young! Live by the sword - die by the sword. *(Looking towards her front door)* Carl, you better come on here!

MARY: *(Nearly in tears)* Lord, I don't want Jessie coming home to this mess. Hasn't my man seen enough killing to last him a lifetime?

TRACY: *(Putting her arms around Mary)* It's going to be all right, Sis. You'll see.

Just then Carl comes onto the porch wearing a suit with his tie untied, eating a peanut butter sandwich.

CARL: One of you all tie my tie! Hey, what's with you all?

TRACY: *(Tying his tie)* Mary is just a little upset about Jessie coming home to all this, that's all. I told you not to eat until after the funeral.

CARL: *(To Mary)* The only thing to really break Jessie's heart right now is you. Give him a minute to adjust back to society and he's going to be all right.

MARY: I can't help it. All this killing, the dope and stuff. It hurts.

CARL: *(Putting his arm around Mary)* Baby, we all hurt because of a lot of things, but when you're told not to and you play anyway, just like Randy, you play, you pay. Jessie understands those rules. This stuff has been going on way before Jessie went into the service but it wasn't this close to home. We've just got to get past this and go on living our lives.

MARY: *(Pulling back from Carl's arm)* Why is it so hard for me to understand why we have to hurt one another the way we do?

TRACY: I guess we're doing what is expected of us to do.

CARL: Don't say that! Black folks got no excuse for what they do to one another. That's why I have no sympathy for Randy. When brothers and sisters get to the point where they are killing the foundation of our race, it's too late for them. For every child that dies, two mothers cry. Mrs. Washington is the only reason I'm going to this funeral. She shouldn't have to suffer like this at her age, but she is because of stupid stuff.

TRACY: He did cause Mrs. Washington much grief.

People emerge from both ends of Side Street going into the church. Some nod in acknowledgement at Tracy, Carl and Mary as they pass by. Two teenagers dressed in black and white stand at each side of the entrance of the church. One opens the door while the other escorts the people to their seats. The sound of soft organ music is heard each time the church door opens. Big Hank and two men from his crew stand next to Cousin Bee's Café waiting for Housecoat Pearl. Housecoat Pearl comes out of her apartment very nicely dressed and the four of them commence walking towards the church. Big Hank and his crew nod as they pass Carl, Tracy and Mary.

TRACY: Looking good, Pearl!

HOUSECOAT PEARL: Same clothes. Same occasion.

Luella and Francine come out of their front door dressed fashionably for the funeral.

LUELLA and FRANCINE: *(Looking at Mary, Tracy and Carl)* Heyyy!

CARL, TRACY and MARY: Heyyy!

FRANCINE: You all are looking nice. Are you ready?

TRACY: We've got to stop by Sister Johnson's, that's all. You all look good, too.

CARL: Come on. Let's get this over with. I don't want to spend the whole day in mourning.

LUELLA: Now that's no way to talk about one of our own.

TRACY: Don't pay him any mind. He's just mad at Randy.

CARL: I told him time and time again to stay away from those Dough Boys. I took a gun away from him six months ago. Enough of us dying in 'Nam. He didn't need a gun.

They leave the porch and stop next door at Sister Johnson's house. Carl goes up and knocks on the door while the others wait. Sister Johnson comes out and walks down the steps with Carl.

SISTER JOHNSON: You all look real nice! *(Looking up and down the empty street)* It looks like everyone is in the church except us.

All six of them walk to the church; soft organ music is playing as they approach the church doors. Moments after they enter the music stops as Reverend Peters begins to speak.

REVEREND PETERS: The spirit of the Lord is present. His love will carry us through all trials and tribulations. He is aware. Amen!

The boys standing in front of the church doors take a quick look up and down the street. Seeing no one except for the few going into the poolroom and bar, the boys close the doors behind them.

One hour has passed...

The church door opens and you hear Reverend Peters giving the eulogy.

REVEREND PETERS: There is nothing more we can do now, Lord. It's all in your hands. Randy, we take you to your final resting place here on earth and pay our last homage to you. As you make this memorable journey, the same journey we all one day will take, let us think about our lives and remember that the Lord Jesus is our only salvation.

New Orleans funeral style music plays, "Just a Closer Walk with Thee" as the funeral procession gets underway.

A gentleman dressed in funeral marching attire comes out of the church followed by two other young men dressed in black suits, then comes Reverend Peters with an open Bible in his hand. The casket, carried by Randy's friends, follows Reverend Peters. Mrs. Washington and her nephew follow with the rest of the attendees. The lead man walks in a rhythm dance, turning his head from one side to the other. Everyone follows with a rhythm movement except Mrs. Washington and family.

By the time the end of the procession gets between Luella and Francine's building and the bar, a man in an Army uniform appears from around the bend. He slowly walks towards them not saying a word until he realizes whose family's funeral it is.

Jessie throws his duffel bag on Carl's porch and begins to sing the song "Just a Closer Walk with Thee" as he follows the funeral procession. When everyone hears Jessie's voice they stop and Mary screams his name softly and runs to him.

MARY: Jessie-eeeee…

Jessie and Mary put their arms around each other and hug affectionately, as Jessie continues to sing. They move to catch up with the funeral procession, as Carl and Tracy watch them approach. Carl, Tracy and Jessie hug and Carl begins to sing along with Jessie.

The funeral procession continues, but without Bernie, Ernest, Bee and Ernestine, who leave to open their businesses. Housecoat Pearl drops off too. Jessie and Carl continue to sing as everyone disappears around the corner. Their voices fade and soft music is heard on the vacant street.

One hour later all the proprietors have opened their businesses and the street is active again. Luella, Francine, Mrs. Washington and her family, and Sister Johnson have returned from the funeral. A short time later, Jessie, Mary, Carl and Tracy come around the bend by the laundromat embraced in each other's arms. Folks wave and speak to Jessie as he passes by. Some try to hold conversations with him but Mary holds onto him tightly trying to keep him from prolonged conversations with anyone.

MO: Hey, Jessie, my man! What's happening? Welcome back!

JESSIE: *(Passing)* Mo! Mo! Mo! How you doing? What's happening?

HOUSECOAT PEARL: *(Sitting in her regular spot on the bench and somewhat intoxicated as Jessie approaches)* Now you know I don't care about that woman holding onto you. You better come here and give me a hug and a kiss before I have to get up and show off on these streets. Y'all know I will do it!

JESSIE: Now Ms. Pearl, you know I can't pass you without a big hug. *(She stands and they embrace)* Have you been good while I was gone?

Mary comes over and gets Jessie. Pearl puts her hands on her hips and looks at Mary as the two of them walk away. Tracy and Carl laugh and catch up to Jessie and Mary.

TRACY: Housecoat, now you know better than to mess with a dog in heat.

Pearl pays them no mind and goes back to her bench and sits down. Jessie with Mary, Carl and Tracy by his side, continues to shake hands and speak to friends as they walk arm-in-arm toward their house. Jessie acknowledges the greetings.

CARL: As you can see the old neighborhood is still the same - a few disappointments, but no better - no worse.

TRACY: As you can also see, the same fool rules!

JESSIE: *(Teasing)...* Now Tracy, you're not including present company are you?

TRACY: You know I am.

CARL: She'd fight an alligator for me.

TRACY: You keep on believing that, your butt will be a pair of shoes on somebody's rich feet.

Carl, Tracy, Jessie and Mary get to their house and stop out front. Carl is trying to separate Jessie and himself from the girls.

CARL: Hey, Jessie, if you were like me when I came home, you sure would wanna smell that old stinky polluted Detroit River and factory smoke, huh? *(Jessie smiles in agreement)* Why don't you change into your civvies and let's stump the neighborhood for a little while. We can be back before sundown.

JESSIE: *(Picking up his duffel bag)* Okay!

MARY: *(Pulling Jessie away from Carl)* Oh no, you don't, my brother! You all are not going to pull that one on me.

TRACY: *(Speaking to Carl)* Man, you sure are one crazy fool. They got business to take care of.

CARL: What kind of business? They aren't gonna do nothing in broad daylight. I said we'd be back before dark.

TRACY: That isn't what you said when you came home! You come here with me. *(Pulling Carl against his will)*

MARY: This is one time I'll kill you if you try and take my man from me and if my man tries to go with you. I'm not lying either!

TRACY: *(Teasing)* I'll help you and I'll dispose of the corpse for you. *(Speaking to Carl)* Come here, man! *(Opening the screen)* Help me take some food to Sister Johnson. Mary, you know dinner is ready whenever you all want to eat.

JESSIE: What you all cook? I haven't had any soul food in a long, long time.

TRACY: Well, if we had known you were coming in today we would have fixed your favorites. You know how black Saturdays are, but because of the funeral Mary and I made catfish, spaghetti, potato salad and coleslaw this morning for Sister Johnson and us after the funeral.

JESSIE: *(With a surprised look on his face)* Do you know I dreamed last night that I was eating Detroit River catfish, potato salad and coleslaw? I'm not lying. It's amazing!

CARL: It's ready now, man, and I have a couple of six packs on ice.

MARY: Uh... uh... No! No! No! Carl, you ain't fooling anyone.

CARL: Mary! Mary! I thought you trusted me. We're family!

TRACY: Girl, don't listen to Carl! You call me when you want me to fix you all a plate. Man, *(Pulling Carl towards her)* come on here!

Jessie and Carl are laughing as Tracy pulls Carl into the house. Mary and Jessie walk arm-in-arm up the stairs to their apartment.

JESSIE: *(Hugging Mary)* You can't even imagine the times I've thought of these moments. The thoughts of you are what kept me alive. Sometimes all I had going for me was the thought of seeing and being with you. Right now I'm the happiest man in the world!

MARY: I'm the happiest and luckiest girl in the world! Every moment, every danger you lived, wherever you went I was right there with you - living for this moment.

Jessie and Mary get to the top of the porch and embrace. Jessie opens the screen door and picks up Mary and carries her in. You can see them kissing through the window. Mary comes to the window, looks out smiling and pulls the shade down.
(Music) "Living and Waiting for You"...

END OF SCENE FIVE

ACT I

SCENE SIX

Early evening...

In Mary's and Jessie's living room an extension cord extends from the wall to the center of the living room and is plugged into an iron. The tables, couch and chair in the room are old but nicely maintained. Mary, wearing new lingerie, stands at the ironing board in the middle of the living room ironing Jessie's shirt. She is somewhat disappointed knowing that Jessie is going out shortly with Carl. Just as she finishes ironing the shirt, Jessie appears from another room wearing slacks and T-shirt and carrying a pair of shoes in his hands. He walks over to Mary and pats her on the butt. Standing behind her he puts his arms around her waist and kisses her on the neck then goes over and sits in the chair next to the window.

JESSIE: *(Putting on his shoes)* Almost finished, hon?

MARY: *(Turning to face him despairingly)* Jessie Barfield! Why are you going out on your first night at home? Do I have to make you aware of how long it's been? I know you don't think "bip bam thank you, ma'am" is going to make up for all the time we've been apart, do you?

JESSIE: *(Teasing)* All that work and that's all it is to you.

Mary puts down the iron and picks up the shirt in one hand while putting the other hand on her hip.

MARY: *(Teasing - shaking the shirt at Jessie)* Man, it took me longer to iron this shirt.

Mary hands him the shirt and he pulls her down onto his lap.

MARY: It just isn't fair!

JESSIE: Aw, honey, it isn't like that. I just need to unwind a bit with the fellas and get all that ugliness I've been through out of my mind and see what's going on and what's been happening.

MARY: *(Gently)* You may not be too pleased about what's been going on or what's been happening.

JESSIE: I have to get out there and see sooner or later.

MARY: I wish it was later. *(Holding him close)* I just want to hold you and give you all my love and affection. I missed you sooo much!

JESSIE: *(Assuring her with a kiss)* I missed you, too, honey. You're the best thing that ever happened to me in my life. Just knowing I have you makes this world so beautiful for me.

MARY: *(Embracing)* Jessie, can't the mixture of happiness and disappointments wait a while longer? *(Hugging him tightly)* Let me give you joy and pleasure, caress you a little while longer before you go out into those streets.

JESSIE: Honey, ever since I've known you and that's almost all my life - the torch of your love, joy and pleasure have burned inside me. Nothing is more important to my life than you. You are my eternal, my all seasons. It may be a little difficult for you to understand, but being away from home for so long is like... *(Searching his mind for clarity and trying to make sense of his thoughts)* When I wasn't on the front line, or had liberty to go into town, all I wanted to do was read the letters you wrote to me over and over again. I know every word from every one of your letters by heart like they were poems but they were letters about my life. These are our kinfolks. Before I went to war, this neighborhood and these folks were all I ever knew about. We share one another's grief and pain. This is our lifetime family, no matter where we may go or what we may do.

MARY: I know, baby. Maybe I'm being selfish or maybe I just wanted to fill you with happiness before you see the disappointments so soon after coming home. I just wish you could have come home to something more pleasant than what's been happening here. Just don't have expectations that are too high.

JESSIE: *(Lifting Mary from his lap as he stands to his feet)* I know! I got a taste of it today. *(Kissing her on the cheek as she stands in front of him)* I have someone I can come home to that can heal anything I encounter. I'll be all right, honey. I won't be out too long.

Feeling a little better, Mary watches as Jessie puts on his shirt and buttons it up.

MARY: You better not be out too late. We're going to church in the morning. I promised Reverend Peters. Tracy told Carl his butt is going to get up even if she has to pour a bucket of water on him - and we all know she will do just that.

Jessie laughs; goes to the door and Mary follows him. He opens the door and gives Mary a kiss.

JESSIE: *(Walking out the door)* See you in a little while!

MARY: *(Picking up the robe from off the chair and putting it on as she speaks to Jessie)* Be careful!

Mary comes onto the porch and watches Jessie as he walks down the stairs. She cannot see him as he enters Carl's porch. Carl walks out of his door and gives Jessie a brotherly embrace.

CARL: Sho is good to see you, my brother!

JESSIE: Oh no, it's good to see you, my brother. It's good to see Tracy and everybody.

CARL: It's gonna be all right - starting right where we left off!

JESSIE: Amen to that!

Tracy comes out onto the porch just as they step down from the porch onto the sidewalk.

TRACY: I don't care how late your butt stays out; you're going to church tomorrow.

Tracy comes off her porch and heads up the stairs to Mary's porch and stands next to her. They put their arms around each other's shoulders as they watch Carl and Jessie walk up the street.

TRACY: *(Tracy and Mary are very happy)* There they go and here we are just like old times. *(They walk back into Mary's house)*

END OF SCENE SIX

ACT I

SCENE SEVEN

Late night - Jessie and Rabbit meet up...

The only businesses open at this time of night are the pool hall, Cousin Bee's Café, the bar and the laundromat. If it were not for the streetlights, the lights from those businesses and a few residents, Side Street would be in total darkness. Soft upbeat music, barely audible, is heard on the street. Carl and Jessie are casually walking up the street with Jessie stopping from time to time greeting folks and shaking hands as they continue along the way until they disappear into The Well.

Short time later...

Francine and Luella, along with a well-dressed, older, distinguished-looking gentleman, come out of The Well. Luella has her arm lightly tucked in the bend of the gentleman's arm and their conversation is soft and indistinguishable beneath the music playing. They casually walk across the street and stand beneath the streetlight. Luella lights up a cigarette for him. She takes a few puffs before giving it to him. Francine goes past Bee's and sits on the bench where Housecoat Pearl always sits.

Rabbit comes out of the poolroom and he is obviously in another world. He slowly looks up and down the street. He sees Luella talking to a man and he sees Francine sitting on the bench. Keeping an eye on everything, he goes over to Francine.

RABBIT: *(Slow, dragging speech)* What's happening?

FRANCINE: *(Cool acting)* What you want to be happening?

RABBIT: Let me borrow twenty dollars.

FRANCINE: You mean let you have twenty dollars, don't you?

RABBIT: Now that's cold!

FRANCINE: It's a cold world.

RABBIT: I wasn't saying that when I used to bail… *(Interrupted)*

Francine, familiar with Rabbit's line and not wanting to hear it or be bothered, stands and reaches into her bosom. She pulls out some money and hands him a twenty, folds the rest and puts it back into her bosom.

FRANCINE: Here, Nicholas… now be gone!

RABBIT: *(Cheerfully taking the money and slowly walking toward The Well)* You just come out of The Well. Is Jessie in there? I heard in the poolroom that he was. Is he?

FRANCINE: *(Disappointed, as he nears The Well's entrance)* Yeah. Why you want to mess up his first night home by letting him see you like you are now?

RABBIT: *(Somewhat fooling himself)* I'm cool. Besides Jessie is my friend, my man!

FRANCINE: My brother, you ain't cool and if you were his friend you wouldn't let him see you like you are.

Rabbit, not paying her any mind, attempts to straighten himself up and turns his attention to the door, opens it and in slurred speech he yells loudly.

RABBIT: Jessieeee! I know you're in there! This is Brother Rabbit. Come on out here! I ain't seen a live soldier in a long time!

A few seconds pass by. He thinks it's taking too long for Jessie to respond so he hollers again.

RABBIT: Don't let me have to come in there and get you and leave "you know who" in there.

Rabbit turns his attention back to where Francine is, just as Luella and the gentleman pass him. He speaks to Luella as they pass.

RABBIT: What's happening, baby? *(Intimidating)* I got your back!

He walks back towards Francine not seeing Carl and Jessie come out of the bar. Jessie looks and sees Rabbit walking to Francine, unaware of his presence.

RABBIT: *(Speaking to Francine)* Y'all know ain't nobody going to do nothing to y'all as long as Rabbit's around and as long as they know you know the Rabbit. That's the truth.

Carl and Jessie are looking toward Francine and Rabbit.

FRANCINE: *(Reluctantly speaking to Rabbit)* Turn around and look behind you.

JESSIE: Hey, Rabbit!

Rabbit turns while trying to compose himself and speaks softly.

RABBIT: Jessie! Jessie, my man! What's happening? *(Rabbit and Jessie walk toward each other)* Man, am I glad to see you. *(They joyfully embrace. Feeling emotional, Rabbit pulls back)* Damn, I'm glad to see you! *(Rabbit embraces Jessie again)* Damn, Jessie, I'm so glad to see you, man. You just don't know.

JESSIE: *(Sensing something is wrong or not quite right with Rabbit)*... I'm glad to see you too, Rabbit. You know I'm glad to see you, man.

RABBIT: *(Emotional)* I know, man! You've always been my man Jessie. *(Smiling and touching in gesture as he speaks)* You are the best, Jessie. Ain't nothing I wouldn't do for you, man!

JESSIE: *(Showing concern)* I know, man, I know. What's happening with you, man? How you been?

Luella comes back onto Side Street alone. She joins Francine as they close in on Jessie and Rabbit. Jessie still shows signs of not knowing but is about to find out.

JESSIE: *(Continuing)* You still got hopes of playing pro ball don't you, Rabbit?

RABBIT: One day, Jessie. I just had a little setback. *(As Carl approach-*

es Rabbit changes the subject) Jessie, you too cool to be hanging out with the likes of that. *(Pointing at Carl)*

CARL: *(Mad)* Why don't you go jump in the river, man?

RABBIT: *(With a perky demeanor)* See how ungrateful he is, Jessie? He forgot all those times I came through for him throughout the years. Why just last month, he didn't know it but the reason the Street Doctor gave him his car back was because I won it back for him and told him not to tell. *(Proudly)* I tricked him into thinking he was that much better than me and he over handicapped me. I knew I couldn't sell that piece of junk so I told him to give it back to Carl. *(Taking a minute to think)* He didn't think I knew that he brought groceries to my house the time I was in jail. Tell him we're even, Jessie. *(To Carl, changing expressions)* I know you don't like me now, man. It's cool. How soon we forget.

Jessie slightly laughs just before realizing something was seriously wrong with Rabbit and Carl. He's thinking about Rabbit's behavior.

JESSIE: Come on, Rabbit. You know Carl likes you. Hey, man, what's going on with you? *(Being street smart, a look of disappointment comes over him as he closes in on Rabbit's features and behavior)* Aw, man, I hope you ain't gone and done something crazy! God, man, I hope not! Tell me it ain't what I think... man, I put my belief in you!

RABBIT: *(Feeling Jessie's love)* You did, didn't you, Jessie? You always thought I was one bad dude, didn't you? *(Assuring him)* I'm still a bad dude Jessie - just a slight setback, that's all. Now that you're here it's going to be alright. You watch!

CARL: *(Angry)* Setback! Look at him, Jessie. The reality is that he's a junkie - a low-life junkie! He's the kind who doesn't give a damn about no one but himself. A junkie! That's the appreciation he done showed us for supporting him, helping him all through school with his academics all those years. Now look at him. Don't feel sorry for him. Naw! I don't like you!

JESSIE: *(Upset)* Come on, Rabbit man. You ain't gonna let us down, right, man?

CARL: Forget him, man. He couldn't have made anything of himself anyway. He's too weak. He's just another sorry disappointment to the neighborhood - even to his two-year-old son living in an orphanage in Ohio.

The story is that Rabbit got a sixteen-year-old girl pregnant during his first semester in college. It was said that he did not know she was sixteen until after she was pregnant. Highly recruited, Rabbit redshirted his freshmen year and just worked out and ran track. However, in a redshirt year, a student athlete can attend classes, practice with an athletic team and dress to play but may not compete in the games. A redshirted student athlete has up to five academic years to use the four years of eligibility thus becoming a fifth-year senior. Having the extra year due to him being redshirted, the school had high hopes of playing Rabbit as long as they were allowed. Watching Rabbit work out impressed the coaches.

Rabbit met this girl at a home basketball game. She was with some college girls who came to the game from Ohio. She supposedly told Rabbit that she was eighteen, but she was only sixteen. Rabbit thought she was as old as she said, being in college and all. First few weeks she and Rabbit would take turns visiting each other. They would bring a few friends with them who wanted to go and have fun. She and her roommates had an apartment off campus. Within a month she was pregnant. She didn't want her parents to know, so she stayed at school.

Rabbit got real scared when he found out she was sixteen years old. It was considered statutory rape, so he could go to prison. She wanted to get an abortion but both were too afraid to do anything. Rabbit would come and visit her every weekend and gave her money. They had planned on him taking the baby when it was born, but then she changed her mind.

Rabbit had told her the names he wanted if it was a boy or girl. If it was a girl, he would name her Nichole Jessie, and if it was a boy, he wanted to name him Nicholas Jessie. Every weekend he was there until he started using drugs. Then he stopped going. The word soon spread about Rabbit being on dope. The school tried to help him but his grades were bad and he started failing. Eventually, he was kicked out of school. The girl gave birth to a boy, and immediately put him in an orphanage and moved to a college in Seattle, Washington.

Everyone was aware of Rabbit being on drugs, fathering a little boy and being kicked out of school. They were also aware that the baby was in an orphanage.

RABBIT: *(Trying to explain)* Why don't you be cool, man? *(Holding his head down pausing)* Jessie, man, what can I say? It happened. That's all, man. It just happened. My intentions have always been good. I intended to finish school and be good enough to go pro. *(Smile)* You know I could don't you, Jess? Just couldn't keep my grades up. I got ineligible for all sports. I was doing really well. *(Speaking to Jess)* Then I got a girl pregnant!

CARL: *(Taunting)* Cradle robbing, Jess! A sixteen-year-old girl who had to put the baby in an orphanage because of him!

RABBIT: *(Not paying attention)* I was really down on myself, Jess, and then old Satan himself introduced me to Cinderella. Soon they put me out of school. Then one day I woke up and never went back to sleep! It's been a different world ever since, man. *(He raises his head up, smiles and cheers up)* But it's going to be OK now, Jess. *(Changing the subject)* Did they tell you I've got a son, Jess? *(Pausing)* He's two. Bet you can't guess what his name is. Take a guess!

JESSIE: *(Clueless)* I can't guess right now, man. What is it?

RABBIT: *(Proudly)* Nicholas Jessie Maliki Jones! I named him after you. You my main man! I'm going to go and get him when I get back on my feet again. He's going to grow up to be as cool as you, Jess. You're one cool brother. Not like "you know who." *(Rabbit laughs as he points to Carl)*

JESSIE: *(Forcibly smiles and shows signs of sympathy)* I don't know what to say Rabbit. Thanks, man!

RABBIT: You my man, Jessie, I love you, man!

JESSIE: *(Sadly)* Yeah, I love you too, man!

CARL: *(Somewhat softening on Rabbit)* Jessie, it's been a little rough around here lately. Heavy drug scene compared to how it used to be. Folks seem more hostile. Look at Randy's funeral today. He just threw his life away. No reason that boy should have died. The ground hasn't settled well on his Uncle Ben yet. Yeah, a number is being done on us. Preying on the weak and stupid - like him. *(Referring to Rabbit)* But that's life. We can't let it get us down, my brother. We've been through this before. It isn't much different from 'Nam and we made it through that didn't we? We didn't come home in a box or screwed up in the head like some of the other brothers. As far as he's concerned, Jessie don't let something that weak destroy your homecoming, man. It ain't worth it.

Rabbit is getting a little impatient with Carl and showing signs of hurt feelings over the disappointment of Jessie seeing him in this state.

RABBIT: Hey, Jessie, my man, I'm going to mosey on. We've got to get together anyway real soon, don't we, Jessie?

JESSIE: Yeah, Rabbit… real soon, man. Real soon!

RABBIT: *(Getting ready to leave, he hugs Jessie)* I love you, man. You are for real - beautiful people. We're going to get it together, won't we, Jessie? We're going to get it together.

JESSIE: I hope so, Rabbit. We're going to try, man. I really hope so!

RABBIT: You my man! Don't forget me, Jessie. Hang in there with me, brother!

Rabbit turns and slowly walks away. He turns back and looks at them a few more times. Lights go on in some of the dwellings, including Tracy's and Mary's houses. They both come out onto their porches in their robes and looking up the street, see Carl, Jessie, Luella, Francine and Rabbit coming in their direction. Mary comes down her steps and joins Tracy in front of their house. Their eyes are glued on Rabbit as he approaches and passes them in somewhat of a gloomy trance, as though he does not see them, as he turns the corner and disappears. By this time the street is awakening. The late night music has brought some out of their homes. People are congregating in their lounging and night clothes as music plays in the background. A gathering of unity in these situations is normal.

Jessie is saddened by the events of the evening and turns to Carl, Luella and Francine...

CARL: Okay... I know this is bothering you, man. It bothered me for a minute. In fact, it bothered everyone around here but we gotta keep on living life. Keep on going. *(Pauses)* Don't let this get you down too much, my brother. Remember, we live in a bittersweet world. It ain't heaven - it ain't hell. It's just bittersweet.

LUELLA: Amen to that! In our world we have to stay strong and tough and look for the sprinkles of sweetness.

FRANCINE: Sho nuff, sugar! We take a licking and keep on ticking.

JESSIE: *(Smiling)* Thank you all! *(Speaking to Carl)* You still care for Rabbit, don't you, man?

CARL: I tell you, I really want to, man. I tried real hard to care but it just isn't happening. He hurt a lot of folks.

They all begin to walk slowly. The sound of soft music can be heard. Luella and Francine look at Carl and Jessie joyfully.

LUELLA: Look at our heroes! Together - back home where they belong!

Luella locks her arm with Carl's arm and Francine locks hers in Jessie's as they walk towards the house.

FRANCINE: We sure are glad you're both home looking out after all us sisters in the community.

JESSIE: Thanks! *(Stops for a moment, gives Francine a hug, then Luella)* Let's go on in, man. Mary and Tracy are probably up waiting on us. Besides, I've seen enough for one day. *(Looking at his watch)* It's pretty late. You know church is in the morning and the ladies are not going to let us rest until we are up in that choir singing.

Mary and Tracy sit on the porch steps with their feet resting on the sidewalk. They see Jessie, Carl, Luella and Francine before they are seen. They know now that Jessie has found out about Rabbit.

MARY: *(Sadly)* Lawd, my poor man!

TRACY: *(Putting her arms around Mary's shoulder)* He'll be okay, honey. At one time or another we all have felt like Jessie about Rabbit.

MARY: That Rabbit!

TRACY: Honey, you just take that man up those steps and keep giving him some of that brown sugar and he will temporarily forget about everything and everybody. *(Looking up the street)* Here they come now!

JESSIE: *(Thinking as they walk)* It seems as if I'm living on the street of darkness and the only shining light is our women. I've been far away risking my life to give hopes and dreams to others and my world is filled with darkness. I hear the baby in me crying for its mother's arms and breast, hoping to open its eyes to a smiling face and caring eyes. Instead, I see darkness.

Tracy and Mary stand as Carl, Jessie, Luella and Francine approach. Luella and Francine let go of Carl's and Jessie's arms as Mary gives Jessie an emotional hug.

MARY: My love will make it all right, honey. I promise you. As long as I have breath, I won't let anyone or anything keep your spirits down.

Tracy, Carl, Luella and Francine watch with sincere delight as Jessie and Mary, arm in arm, go up the stairs and into the house. Soon the lights come on and there is a shadow of them kissing through the shaded window. After a few seconds the light goes out. Carl, Tracy, Luella and Francine look at each other. They all hug each other and enter their separate homes. Lights come on momentarily, then it's back to darkness. The street becomes desolate.

Song: "Waiting, Living For You"

I prayed, how many times I've prayed
When I was away from you
To see your face
Feel your embrace--
That is what kept me going in the storms!
I was waiting, living for you, living for you.

For me, it was not easy
You being gone,
Knowing possibilities interrupting my sleep,
I prayed night and day since you've been away.
Nothing on my agenda
I was waiting, living for you, living for you.

What is life without love?
What is love without you?
Nothing! Nothing but confusion
That is why
I have been waiting, living for you, living for you.

END OF SCENE SEVEN

ACT I

SCENE EIGHT

The neighborhood church - early Sunday morning...

The activity on Side Street is slow. The poolroom and The Well are not open yet and Bernie's is closed on Sundays. Bee's Café is temporarily closed to prepare for the hefty flow of Sunday customers. A few people are standing at the church's entrance because of the overcrowdedness.

(Song)

Inside the church, Reverend Peters sits contently in a chair at the back of the pulpit. He sways, hitting his knee with his hand and tapping his feet, enjoying the lively singing from the choir. The congregation is enjoying the singing, too. Seated behind Reverend Peters are Sister Johnson and the senior choir members dressed in their choir robes. They are also enjoying the music. Jessie, Carl, Tracy, Mary and the rest of the young adult choir perform a moving, uplifting, hand-clapping, foot-stomping song. After a few moments the choir members finish singing and sit down. The effect of the song lingers as the congregation's jubilant expression of spiritual emotions resounds throughout the church. Reverend Peters waits for a moment, then stands and walks over to the pulpit.

REVEREND PETERS: What a wonderful way to start the morning with spiritual octane. Amen!

All together the congregation says... Amen!

REVEREND PETERS: *(Still emotional)* I tell you, the voices of the choir are sending spirits throughout this church - the gathering place of the Lord's flock. I'm not worried about anything because the shepherd watches over us. Amen!
All together the congregation says... Amen!

REVEREND PETERS: *(More relaxed)* I'm trying to keep the Holy Spirit from fleeing from us when we leave this safe haven of the

Lord and go back into the world of disobedience, lust and temptation. That's my job and my sermon today. I have no script so I don't know what I'm about to say. I'm going to let the Spirit guide the words from my mouth this morning. There are no clocks in the Lord's house. So don't be looking at any watches. I'm taking my time today. Amen!

All together the congregation says... Amen!

REVEREND PETERS: *(Holding up the Bible)* In here is the food of life - everything you need to cure, heal and feed your mind, body and soul. The hospital, the doctor and the medicine are all in here. *(Pauses)* There is nothing that this Bible can't heal. *(Laying the Bible back down)*

All together the congregation says... Amen!

REVEREND PETERS: As one of God's messengers and your minister, I have an obligation from birth to death to do whatever it takes to save your souls from hell's fire and to unify you with your Father, our maker. That's my obligation. We all have purpose. I feel this is my sole purpose. *(Pauses)* Have I not been here in this pulpit preaching ever since I was a young man and my father before me? *(Amen)* And have I not shared many of your joys and sorrows in birth, baptismal and in burial? *(Amen)* I've always been there for you. When you are sick and troubled, you call and I'm there. *(Amen)* In the coldest of nights, rain, sleet or snow or the hottest of days - *(Amen)* - I'm appointed by the high of the highest, God almighty, to do His will, preach His word, tell you how wonderful and beautiful His love and His kingdom is. I'll tell you, nothing could ever be as great as His kingdom - the eternal kingdom. *(Pauses)* Now I may not have gotten this through to some of you but I'm going to keep trying. I'm just as stubborn as everyone. Brothers and sisters, I'm telling you to change your course. If your life has been hampered by failures and disappointments, change your course. Let God guide you and see the rewards, the difference in your life. Put Him in your life actively and permanently. For every second, minute and hour of our lives we need Him to keep the Holy Spirit in us active always. There's no morning, noon, or night that we don't need Him in our lives. Whenever we wake up or go to sleep we have to thank Him, for there is no guarantee of either seeing the beginning or end of the day. We have to thank Him for surviving the negatives that are all around us. We continue to give thanks and praise for the blessings He generously bestows upon us throughout our daily lives. *(He pauses for a moment)*

All together the congregation says... Amen!

Music is playing in the background as Reverend Peters' voice rises. Showing his humorous side, he turns to the choir and focuses on Jessie.

REVEREND PETERS: As you can see by the upbeat of our choir today, we have Brother Jessie home from the army and giving back that voice that's been missing..."Welcome Home!" *(There is hand clapping and cheering... Reverend Peters continues, teasing)* Brother Jessie, we know how important you are to the harmony and vocals of our choir and to this community, but many of us have found out how important you are in getting some of Side Street's famous sweet potato pie or cobbler every now and then. There seems to be a shortage since you've been gone. It seems the sisters just haven't been in the mood. So from all the sweet potato cobbler and pie lovers, we welcome you back.

The piano music begins and the choir stands.

One hour later after Sunday's church service...

Tracy, along with some of the choir sisters and Reverend Peters have had a full meal and are lazily sitting on Sister Johnson's porch and steps. Likewise with Carl, Jessie and some of the choir brothers who are sitting on Mary's and Jessie's stairwell and Carl's and Tracy's porch. They all have taken off their robes. Mary comes out of Sister Johnson's house. She unties the apron she is wearing and tosses it across the bannister. She then goes and sits in the swing next to Reverend Peters.

TRACY: *(Speaking to Mary)* What is taking Sister Johnson so long? We washed and dried all the dishes, pots and pans!

MARY: She'll be out in a minute. She's talking on the phone to her sister in Louisiana.

CARL: Any more of that cobbler left?

TRACY: Man, you've eaten two bowls of cobbler. In fact, you've eaten two of everything we made and scraped the bottom of the cobbler dish. You ate up everything. *(Everyone laughs)*

REVEREND PETERS: Brother Carl, look at us the way we all are lazily moving around here. If we had a dog, I do believe he would go hungry today because we ate up everything. Scraps, too! I tell you we sure took advantage of some good eating today. I believe if a tornado comes along right now, all we can do is pray that it changes its course.

SISTER JOHNSON: *(Coming out of the house)* What's all the Amen about?

MARY: Reverend Peters was just talking about some good eating.

REVEREND PETERS: Sister Johnson, we almost forgot since Brother Jessie and Carl have been away how good your, Sister Mary's and Sister Tracy's cooking is — and those sweet potato pies and cobblers are still the talk of the town. *(Everyone says Amen)* Brother Jessie, I tell you brightness shone in the service this morning and its presence made the voices sound as beautiful as Gabriel playing his horn for the Lord.

EVERYONE: Amen!

REVEREND PETERS: I tell you, Sister Johnson, the spirits of our youth choir has helped to mend our community and their peers, especially with some of their popularities. Our community thanks each and every one of you all. *(Reminiscing)* Sister Johnson, sitting here like this, looking up and down this street reminds me of the time when the church caught on fire and we held church services all summer long right out here on Side Street while the church was being repaired and remodeled. That sure was something, wasn't it?

SISTER JOHNSON: *(Remembering)* That sure was something! This whole street was filled with folks sitting down and standing up. Folks lined up on both sides of the street from curb-to-curb. I tell you we had more guests than members. Folks came from all over. There was a revival and a concert here every Sunday.

REVEREND PETERS: Yes, sir! I tell you it attracted people from all over the city. *(Addressing the choir)* Some of your parents were cooks and helpers. I tell you, we sure had some good eating. I guess that's what made such a huge turnout and the choir singing...

SISTER JOHNSON: And your preaching too, Reverend. Don't be shy. Shoot, many folks wanted to join our church even when we went back inside. The church was always overflowing with folks sitting and standing out on the street. Reverend, it seemed like you were baptizing every week.

MARY: I remember that!

TRACY: Me, too! You, Robbie, Jeannie and I would set the tables with linen, paper napkins and plastic utensils. You all remember that!

JEANNIE and ROBBIE: Uh, huh!

SISTER JOHNSON: That's right. The boys and men would line this whole street with chairs for the service and the menfolk would set up the tables in front of The Well, Bee's, Bernie's and the pool hall after the service for dinner every Sunday.

REVEREND PETERS: That sure was some good eating! Between Bee, Sister Johnson, Tracy and Mary's mamas' cooking and Mrs. Washington's gumbo, so many folks were coming here to eat. I declare, if we had enough room, I tell you, I believe we could have filled half of Cobo Hall.

SISTER JOHNSON: Lawd, we must have fattened up the whole community and then some. I know that me, Bee and y'all's mamas made over fifty sweet potato pies, cobblers and cakes each Sunday.

MARY: You all know wherever there's some good cooking, there are some hungry black folks!

TRACY: I don't know if it was just because the street is so small but I've never seen so many people on this street at one time. You could hardly walk without bumping into someone.

REVEREND PETERS: There were so many people coming that the fire and police departments came each Sunday to keep it orderly and not over-crowded.

SISTER JOHNSON: They came out of the woodwork when they found out we were serving food. But the good thing was they had to stay 'til service was over before they could eat. Even the firemen and policemen didn't mind coming so they could get some of that good cooking. Shoot, you never saw the same ones twice. They used to even help cover the whole block with a large plastic canvas when it rained. It looked like a giant tent.

CARL: Y'all must have made a bunch of money in that collection plate!

SISTER JOHNSON: More than we ever made before! We remodeled the church and made it larger. We also bought new drapes and padded pews.

REVEREND PETERS: The Lord works in mysterious ways. Many who came to eat stayed and became members. I guess the way to the Lord for some was through their stomachs. Our service got to be the talk of the city. *(Pauses)* Remember the time the television people came and took pictures of us?

SISTER JOHNSON: Yes sir. We had this whole community going to church. Folks I ain't never seen before in church was there, even Buck.

MARY: Shucks, you know if my Uncle Buck was there, no telling who else was going to come. I never knew my Uncle Buck to be a church-going person but he sure could eat. He could eat more than Carl.

TRACY: Now that takes some plenty eating! *(Carl ignores Mary)*

SISTER JOHNSON: Well, I tell you everyone was there eating every Sunday and it didn't matter what kind of religion they were. The religion to them was food.

EVERYONE: Amen!

MARY: My honey and his folks were going to that high falutin Great Northern Baptist at the time. *(Pauses)* Remember, Tracy? They would send their big bus over to pick up us Lower East Side river folks and bring us to their Easter services. *(Teasing)* Wasn't my baby cute in his lime green suit saying his speech? Roses are red, violets are blue and Jesus is black as me and you. *(Everyone laughs)*

TRACY: *(Teasing Jessie and Carl)* He sure was and my baby, even though he didn't belong, would be right there with his friend Jessie wearing his black mothball suit. You could smell him coming a mile away. He changed after he met me. He made his daddy buy him a whole new wardrobe - trying to impress me. *(Everyone is laughing)* He didn't want to go to Texas in the summer anymore after he met me. *(Looking at Carl and smiling)* Didn't want to leave me here with all those boys chasing after me! *(Pauses)* He had Jessie and Rabbit watching after me.

CARL: *(Smiling)* You're pitiful. I remember one summer when Jessie's folks sent him to Texas with me and my dad to keep us away from you womanish, fast, city girls who'd make us get into trouble.

MARY: Now I know you're lying. We couldn't have been fast if we wanted to - and you know we were not womanish.

TRACY: Isn't that the truth! I know you all remember a man named Buck and his brother Duck *(Mary's uncle and dad)*. Sister Johnson knows the truth. *(Everyone laughs)*

SISTER JOHNSON: Now, Carl, you know these girls weren't womanish or fast except when they were around you and Jessie. You two sure had, excuse me, Reverend, the hots for Tracy and Mary since you both were in kindergarten. Jessie, remember when you were about six years old you took your grandma's wedding ring off her dresser and gave it to Mary?

JESSIE: Now since you're talking, I seem to recall a time when Tracy and Mary stole their mamas' sweet potato pies and gave them to Carl's daddy.

CARL: *(In agreement with Jessie)* Yeah, that's right. They sure did. I had forgotten about that.

TRACY: My future daddy-in-law ate both of them. Daddy laughed but Mama was so mad she went to his house and made him pay her.

CARL: He didn't care. That was some good eating for him.

JESSIE: Seemed like they were some good old days!

REVEREND PETERS: They were in many ways but we had some rough times too. There were times when it seemed like it was us against the world. As families and leaders we tried to keep the negatives away from our youths so their minds would be uplifted.

SISTER JOHNSON: Ain't that the truth, Reverend! One thing we had going for us, which may have helped, was more folks were working back then. We also had the "Brown Bomber," Joe Louis.

CARL: My daddy knew Joe Louis and Sugar Ray Robinson. He used to box down at the Brewster Street Gym and sometimes Joe and Sugar Ray would come there. I think my daddy even boxed with Sugar Ray Robinson before.

REVEREND PETERS: Brother Carl, your daddy was a good fighter in his day. There were times when he was great and there weren't many folks who would fight him in his prime. Somehow the big ones always eluded him.

TRACY: *(Proudly)* My daddy-in-law was a bad dude. Just like my man. *(Winking her eye at Carl and everyone laughs).*

SISTER JOHNSON: Did y'all know that this street has always had a reputation? Slaves used to come down this street headed to the river to go over to Canada. Some folks' music careers got started at The Well. Reverend Peters Senior started the first live radio broadcast in the church. The café was more popular in the 40's and 50's than it is now. This street sure has its history. I don't know of any other street as popular as Side Street. That's why it's so sacred to this community and every inner-city community in Detroit.

MARY: All that history! I guess we're lucky to live on Side Street. Was it still Cousin Bee's back then?

SISTER JOHNSON: It wasn't Cousin Bee's then. It was called Eunice's. Y'all's parents *(Speaking to Tracy and Mary)* moved here about the time Eunice died. At that time Bee was one of Eunice's cooks. She had been working at Eunice's for a while. Many people tried to buy the café after she died, but Bee was the only one Eunice's family would let buy it, provided she would keep up the café's tradition. To this day, most of the food at the café comes from Eunice's original recipes. That's why it's still the best and most popular soul food anywhere. Magazines have written about Eunice's. Every famous colored person that had lived or come to this city had eaten at Eunice's. It was the only place where you would have to make reservations to eat fatback, ham hocks and collard greens - every kind of soulful cooking you could think of. *(Pauses)* Since I've lived here I've sat on this porch and have seen many famous colored people coming and going up and down this street either to eat at Eunice's or go to True Life Baptist Church. Many came and received soul food from both places. Lord, on Sundays there would be a line of folks from the church *(Pointing to left and right)* to the other end of the street waiting to get into Eunice's.

Everyone is listening intensely to Sister Johnson and Reverend Peters as they reminisce about Side Street's history.

REVEREND PETERS: *(Smiling)* Sister Johnson, I'm listening to you talking and it sure is refreshing to my mind as you bring back all those good memories of yesterday. I remember times when Eunice would go out and buy a bunch of folding tables and chairs just for the Sunday crowd. She had to store them in the basement of the church. On Sunday, folks used to get their food and grab a table and chair before they were all gone; otherwise they would have to wait until others finished eating to get a table. It was a sight to see folks walking down the street with folding tables and chairs. Sunday would be so popular on Side Street that our choir sometimes gave performances right out here for them. I tell you, there isn't anything in this world that can make you feel as good as a combination of spiritual food and soul food mixed together. Amen!

EVERYONE: Amen!

SISTER JOHNSON: We had to put barriers up on both ends of the street whenever folks heard we were performing. On Sundays we had the ghettos of Detroit spiritually and soulfully enriched - from the loudspeakers outside the church, to the radio stations, to Eunice's. Lawd, the good times we had!

JESSIE: When Eunice died did she have a big funeral?

SISTER JOHNSON: Did she! The line of folks trying to get into the church to view the body was over a mile long. Listen to this. The street was so crowded that the folks who lived here had a problem trying to get out of their own homes. It was wall-to-wall people. I tell you that was some funeral. And the famous people that came - singers, dancers, athletes, politicians and many white people to pay their respects to her...! *(Speaking to Reverend Peters)* Reverend, your daddy sure preached at that funeral!

REVEREND PETERS: He sure did - and your choir sure did sing! I think Sister Eunice had a beautiful send-off. Sister Johnson, did you know that Eunice and my daddy were kin? My daddy's great granddaddy was her granddaddy's first cousin, *(Thinking)* let's see, that would make them...

MARY: *(Teasing)* Kissing cousins!

Everyone laughs.

REVEREND PETERS: Now Sister Mary, I guess that would be as close as I can sum it up without working my brain on it. She and Daddy were close. Every Tuesday night she and some folks always had prayer service at Daddy's house. *(Smiling)* Daddy used to call it dinner service 'cause they did more eating than praying. Eunice would bring whatever was left over from the café. Mama wouldn't cook on Tuesdays. Wouldn't nobody eat it if they had known Eunice was bringing food. Yes, sir, those were the days!

CARL: Too bad we didn't get to see Eunice when all those old heroes of ours used to eat there. But we still see our share coming to Cousin Bee's and True Life Baptist Church.

TRACY: Shoot, it's like we know her anyway. Her picture is the first thing you see when you walk into Cousin Bee's and there are enough pictures of her with all those famous folks on the walls. I just didn't know that she was as famous as what you all are saying right now.

SISTER JOHNSON: I tell you, I don't know a single colored soul in this city who was more popular than Eunice. Her funeral proved that.

MARY: Reverend, how did True Life's choir get such a reputation?

REVEREND PETERS: I believe Sister Johnson could answer that better than me. I might be a little prejudiced.

SISTER JOHNSON: No offense, Reverend. Your daddy was not a square. *(Everyone smiles at the comment)* Everybody knew your daddy.

REVEREND PETERS: My daddy did have a shady past before he went into the ministry.

SISTER JOHNSON: Aw, Reverend, a numbers man ain't shady. Where we live it's called a job. If he had not known so many people and as the young people would say "wasn't square," True Life Baptist Church wouldn't have been the church it was and still is today. Reverend, your daddy had some of the biggest people in vice in this city going to his church. Some of the first people to join True Life were numbers men, madams and their workers, gamblers and bootlegging folks. All those folks are what made everyone else come in. They turned True Life into the liveliest church in the city.

CARL: *(Correcting her)* You mean the "hippest" church in the city!

SISTER JOHNSON: *(Continuing)* That's it! Everybody wanted to join True Life Baptist Church and the choir. Shoot, we were the first to put speakers outside the church. True Life, its choir and Eunice's made us folks feel *(Pauses)* proud and important.

JESSIE: Wow! That's cool the way things seemed to have happened back then.

SISTER JOHNSON: Yeah! The Reverend took his life experiences and turned it into something good for the community. He helped Big Hank and the city to get that old building and field *(Pointing)* over yonder. Big Hank fixed that old building and made it into a community center for children and adults - and it's still standing today.

REVEREND PETERS: You know, Sister Johnson, you're not giving yourself enough credit on how instrumental you were in the church's success later on.

Sister Johnson is unsure what Reverend Peters is speaking about.

TRACY: What part did you play, Sister Johnson? I bet it was the sweet potato cobbler!

REVEREND PETERS: That came a bit later. With a few exceptions, our senior choir has won more trophies than any choir I know of. Sister Johnson is probably the main reason we became as successful as we are. Our choir has sung with symphonies and some of our most prestigious colored college bands.

CARL: *(Amazed)* How did you do that?

SISTER JOHNSON: *(Smiling)* Throughout those years I sang in almost every church choir in this city, so I knew plenty of good singers. Theodore and I got married and moved right here and started going to True Life. The Reverend Senior had a lively church going on at that time but his choir was pretty weak when I joined. He came to our house one day and asked me if I would take over the choir and turn it around. He didn't care about the cost. He knew he would recoup his losses if he had a good choir to go along with the kind of church he had. *(Pauses)* He needed a good choir, so I talked to the singers I knew and urged them to join our choir. Soon we were performing all over the city and that's when other choirs heard about us. We became very popular and soon had to turn folks down. I knew the choir and music directors and that's how we got Alphonso.

A CHOIR GIRL: Was the choir back then better than us now?

REVEREND PETERS: Now that's a tough question to answer. What do you think, Sister Johnson?

SISTER JOHNSON: *(Bragging)* I tell you, Reverend, these young folks are pretty good. They remind me of ourselves just before we peaked.

CARL: Whoa! Just one minute! Last part of that statement makes me think you're saying our choir was not as good as yours. I believe that was the quote, wasn't it?

SISTER JOHNSON: You all are close, but not quite as good.

CARL: *(Smiling)* Whoa! I'm beginning to feel a warm breeze blow by. You wouldn't want to go up against us, would you? I mean, I'd understand if you say no.

SISTER JOHNSON: *(Winking at the Reverend)* We've never turned down a challenge, have we, Reverend?

REVEREND PETERS: *(Smiling, says...)* I cannot ever recall one.

MARY: Hmmm, I've got a feeling they're not telling something!

CARL: The senior choir is challenging us. I think you better ask them first. *(Teasing)* They may not be up to such a task, as they seem content sitting in their chairs enjoying us - the Grambling of Choirs.

Carl, Jessie and the choir members don't know how really good the senior choir is. They were once a nationally known choir who now enjoy their present status.

SISTER JOHNSON: *(Winking at the Reverend)* I think we would be honored to sing against such a prestigious group as yours.

TRACY: I don't know why, but that man always seems to put his foot in his mouth!

CARL: Now, how long will it take to get the kinks out?

SISTER JOHNSON: How about whenever y'all are ready!

MARY: This is exciting! Our junior choir versus our senior choir.

REVEREND PETERS: I'm looking forward to this, too. It will be like the good old days of old-time religion!

Everyone says Amen.

END OF SCENE EIGHT

ACT II

SCENE ONE

A few weeks later – early Monday morning...

Jessie comes out onto the porch of his home. He is wearing slacks and a lightweight jacket over a T-shirt. Mary comes out wearing a stylish uniform. Hand-in-hand they walk down the stairs onto the side-walk, then onto Tracy and Carl's porch where Jessie sits down in a chair. Mary sits on his lap as they wait for Tracy.

MARY: *(Talking to Jessie)* What are you going to do today while we're working and Carl is out of town?

JESSIE: *(Hesitant)* I don't know. I may just ride around enjoying being home *(Pauses)* just cooling it, I guess.

MARY: *(Looking at Jessie)* Carl's been gone only one day and you're missing him, aren't you?

JESSIE: Heyyy! If Tracy was gone, wouldn't you miss her?

MARY: *(Hugs him)* Not if you're here *(Thinking)*; maybe a little, I guess!

Tracy comes out onto her porch wearing the same kind of uniform Mary is wearing.

TRACY: *(Humorous)* I thought I heard my name. You all aren't talking about me. I don't take kindly to that!

MARY: He brought your name up in comparison because I told him he's missing Carl.

TRACY: You always miss fools. He grows on you like an old stray dog.

JESSSIE: *(Smiling)* Like Carl and I grew on you all.

They walk off the porch passing Sister Johnson's house.

TRACY: Sister Johnson says that she doesn't want us eating a big lunch. She's catering a big luncheon at the Sheraton for the Bloomfield Hills Executives Housewives charity event. You all remember last year. Shoot, she brought back enough food to feed the whole block!

MARY: It was some good eating, too! We ate like rich folks for a couple of days... caviar, lamb, stuffed fish and shrimp in wine sauce. Whoever heard of wine sauce? My man better not catch me taking his muscatel and making a wine sauce out of it!

JESSIE: *(Teasing)* Good wine is for romancing, listening to nice jazz and for Sundays after supper with chicken, pot roast and Spam steaks!

They laugh.

TRACY: It's mighty fine dining. I guess it's okay every once in a while, *(Being expressive)* but I'll tell you what, it will never beat ham hocks, neck bones, pig tails and collards, mustards, turnip greens, butter beans, black eyed peas and corn bread *(A little sanctified move)*, and Lord, don't talk about fried chicken, Detroit River fried catfish and smothered liver and onions! Y'all about to make me hurt somebody!

MARY: *(Also sanctified... feet shuffle)* Add dessert... black bottom cake and some... hmmm... sweet potato cobbler and its first cousin sweet potato pie. Mercy, mercy me!

JESSIE: Y'all's cooking sure know how to make a poor man rich.

TRACY: *(Barely audible)* Yeah! We also got what it takes to make you feel like a king.

JESSIE: Yeah...Yeah...Yeah!

END OF SCENE ONE

ACT II

SCENE TWO

Same day - an hour later - Pontiac, Michigan... Roosevelt's living room...

A large archway entrance of the living room leads into a hallway. Sounds of voices and a door opening. Roosevelt comes through the front door... followed by Jessie.

ROOSEVELT: *(Speaking to Jessie)* So, you and your FRIEND like to fish, huh? Man, we got a lot of good fishing lakes around here. Jessie follows him into his dimly lit living room. Roosevelt turns on a lamp on the table.

ROOSEVELT: Hold on a second, man. Let me put a little music on!

Jessie takes off his jacket and puts it on a chair. Roosevelt goes over to his stereo system; seconds later, smooth jazz music plays.

JESSIE: *(Looking around the room)* Real nice place you have here, man!

ROOSEVELT: Yeah, my mom is letting me stay in it. She hooked up with this dude from Lansing who has a crib there. My sister was staying here until she got married and they bought a home across town. When I came back home they were glad, so I got their crib. Cool, huh? You, your family and friends ever want to come out you're welcome to stay here. We can go fishing, hunting or just hang out! See what small-city folks do!

JESSIE: I know more people that hang out here than in the city. *(Pauses)* Hey, man, I'm glad I came out today. This is really a treat for me! It's been only a few months since we were on the battlefield but sometimes it seems like it was yesterday and we were looking out for one another.

ROOSEVELT: Memories not easily forgotten.

Roosevelt goes to a closet, opens the door and fumbles around. Seconds later he closes it back. He has an eyeglass case in his hand. He reaches in his pocket and pulls out a little packet and signals to Jessie.

ROOSEVELT: Come on, man!

JESSIE: Hey, where are your two kids?

ROOSEVELT: They're over at their mom's. I get them on the weekends. They like to fish, too!

They both disappear into another room. (O.S. Sound of Miles Davis is playing.) Minutes later both re-enter the room having shot up heroin and are beginning to show signs of intoxication. Jessie sits on the couch. Roosevelt goes over to the stereo, turns the volume up louder, then turns off the light.

ROOSEVELT: *(Vocals dragging)* Let's get some ambiance in here!

He goes over to the windows and raises both shades a fraction, letting in the ambiance of sunlight, taking a hint from Jessie.

ROOSEVELT: *(Standing at the window)* How's that, my brother?

JESSIE: *(Nodding in approval)* Right on!

Roosevelt sits down on the couch with Jessie listening to the music...

ROOSEVELT: *(Speech slow)* This is mellow, man! We haven't seen each other since 'Nam...

JESSIE: *(Speech slow)* It's beautiful. No foxhole!

ROOSEVELT: No sounds of explosions and mortar fire. Just smooth sounds. It can't get any better.

JESSIE: Music of the soul.

ROOSEVELT: Right on! Like it's talking to us. Listen!

(The music continues but fades as the scene jades - O.S.)

(Fade In) Roosevelt's living room - five hours later...

The sound of jazz music slowly rises to a comfortable decibel. The shades at the window are up and the room is brighter. Jessie comes into the room looking more refreshed and alert than earlier. He picks up his jacket off the chair and puts it on. Roosevelt comes into the room, also looking refreshed.

ROOSEVELT: Are you cool, my brother? Don't want you getting any tickets! You know how Bloomfield and Birmingham police are.

JESSIE: Don't worry, I'm cool. How about you?

ROOSEVELT: Yeah, I guess so. You know how it is! You do something you shouldn't but you want to, so you do it anyway. Afterwards your conscience is kind of punishing you! Seems it punishes the hardest after the fact... but hey!

JESSIE: Yeah, I got that feeling too - premeditated sin.

ROOSEVELT: Yeah, I know!

JESSIE: Hey, the next time I come out we have to get Calloway - the three of us hanging together again!

ROOSEVELT: That will be cool. He works so much. Now and then we go out and have a drink when he's got the time!

Knock at the door...

ROOSEVELT: Hold tight!

Roosevelt disappears down the hallway. Jessie listens to the music, not hearing the conversation. Sound of the door opening and closing, it is Calloway in his police uniform...

ROOSEVELT: You must have telepathy! *(They hug)*

CALLOWAY: Saw your car - thought I'd drop in. What's happening, my brother?

ROOSEVELT: Look at you. I've got a treat for you!

CALLOWAY: Awww, yeah! Where or what is it?

ROOSEVELT: Come on!

Jessie, standing looking at wall pictures and listening to music, does not notice Roosevelt and Calloway in the entrance way. Calloway smiles when he sees Jessie.

CALLOWAY: *(Voice over the music)* Well, well, well! If it isn't fox-hole D of company C!

JESSIE: *(Smiling not yet turning around)* Let me see! I recognize that voice. An echo coming from foxhole B of company C!
Jessie turns and walks to Calloway and they embrace.

CALLOWAY: *(To Jessie)* How you doing, my brother? What's happening? This sure is a treat for me.

JESSIE: Yeah, for me too! Today is the first time seeing either of you guys since discharge.

CALLOWAY: I talk about you guys all the time.

JESSIE: I've been busy trying to fit back into the groove of things and pounding the pavement looking for a job.

ROOSEVELT: I'm tied with you on that one my brother. (Smiling) I'm just lucky enough to have a mom who's staying with her man at his crib in Lansing. Unless she gets tired of him or he puts her out, I'm cool until they call me back to GM.

ROOSEVELT: *(Teasing)* Look, Jess! He's still wearing a uniform and carrying a gun.

CALLOWAY: Different uniform and different reason for the gun.

ROOSEVELT: *(Excited)* Look at us! Standing here listening to some cool sounds, kicking it! Seems like it was only yesterday we were fighting for our lives.

JESSIE: A time when things seemed doubtful for a moment.

CALLOWAY: Yeaaah! There were scary moments.

ROOSEVELT: It was praying time and God heard our prayers, I'd say.

CALLOWAY: We sure said enough of them.

ROOSEVELT: Man, we did more praying than shooting and we sure did a lot of that.

(Laughing)

JESSIE: *(Serious)* I don't know. I've been praying a lot since I've been home. The day I came home as I turned the corner on my street, there was a funeral procession. A young brother we helped raise was killed by another brother. Seems I've been praying as much or more since I've been home.

ROOSEVELT: *(To Calloway)* Hey, man! Sit down for a minute. Ain't no uniformed police officer ever come to visit me socially. *(They laugh)*

Calloway and Jessie sit down on the couch and Roosevelt sits in a matching chair.

CALLOWAY: *(Looks at his watch)* I've only got a few minutes. I have to be at work in an hour.

JESSIE: Yeah. I've got to be heading back to the city, too, before traffic picks up. *(Changing the subject)* Hey, I thought you two promised you were coming down to hang out with me.

CALLOWAY: I haven't forgotten. I had to do basic training all over again! Remember, I had just been on the force a few months before I was drafted. I'm still looking forward to coming down there eventually.

ROOSEVELT: I've been yearning to eat in the best soul food cafe in town. What's its name?

JESSIE: *(Smiling)* Cousin Bee's!

ROOSEVELT: *(To Calloway)* Man, if you go down there and eat some of that sweet potato cobbler without me I'll flatten all your tires and put sugar in your tank! I'm ready, my brother! Just say when. I'll be ready!

CALLOWAY: *(Laughing)* I tell you, Jess! You talked about Cousin Bee's food and sweet potato cobbler so much that it has become my favorite restaurant and I've never eaten there.

JESSIE: You watch! Just like I said in 'Nam, if it's not the best food I'll put a spit shine on your shoes. You'll be able to turn the lights off and still see! Walk in the snow, mud and rain and just wipe them off and they'll still look like new.

ROOSEVELT: You talked about Cousin Bee's so much that I have no other choice than to believe you. Hey, where is that brother athlete friend of yours that was so awesome? How's he doing in college? That was one bad dude - what's his name?

CALLOWAY: You're talking about Nicholas Jones, Rabbit. Word was out that he was pretty messed up on drugs. Got kicked out of college! They say he got a sixteen-year-old girl pregnant, had a little boy that she put in an orphanage somewhere in Ohio. What a shame! The brother had everything going for him.

JESSIE: I think he'll be okay and maybe one day he will still have a chance to make it.

CALLOWAY: You have always been an optimistic dude, Jess. Drugs are pretty dangerous to fool around with. *(Looking at them closely)* I see you guys hanging out without me? I don't know if that is good or bad. Not even a call. That's not a good sign. Makes me feel slighted or suspicious. *(Jessie and Roosevelt stare at each other briefly)*

ROOSEVELT: We were talking about you just before you knocked on the door!

JESSIE: That's the truth, my brother! Roosevelt told me how your job keeps you busy. We thought you were at work.

ROOSEVELT: This is the first time I've seen this brother since we left the hospital!

JESSIE: I have my friend's car. The old ladies are at work and I decided to come out here.

CALLOWAY: *(Not too convinced)* That's cool. *(Smiling, yet serious)* You two still raise a level of suspicion. *(Staring at Jessie and Roosevelt)* I believe you guys done broke the pact! *(Jessie and Roosevelt glance at one another)*

ROOSEVELT: What do you mean?

CALLOWAY: Come on! We've been together side-by-side for nearly a year in foxholes protecting one another, telling our life stories, not being sure if we would make it! Man! We know each other like the back of our hands. Besides, I'm a cop. Remember? I'm trained for signs and behavior. *(Pauses)* Fellas! I believe the vibes of our friendship toward one another are what brought me over here today.

JESSIE: *(Confessing)* I won't lie to you, my brother. This was my first time since 'Nam.

ROOSEVELT: Mine, too!

JESSIE: We still feel bad.

CALLOWAY: What you say may be true, but we said we were going to leave all that behind in 'Nam. We swore on it! We were lucky in 'Nam… walking away. We knew we were dealing with demons then.

ROOSEVELT: *(Interrupting)* Yeah! It was like they were making us feel confident in 'Nam.

CALLOWAY: No, it wasn't confidence! That was what they wanted you to believe. Truth is they made us not give a damn - took the fear out of dying. Euphoria! Pretty soon it'll take over. It's only a matter of time before you wake up on the opposite side of the world. Jess, you of all people should know, man!

JESSIE: You're right, man... here I am trying to help a friend. You know, you're beginning to make me feel pretty low.

CALLOWAY: Sorry, my brother! We went through hell once. I hope none of us would ever have to go through it again. Even worse, like you, Jess, it will be those we know and love the most that are affected.

ROOSEVELT: You know, Jess! We had sworn on all that was dear to us -mothers, fathers, sisters and brothers, wives and children, that we would never use again. Man!

CALLOWAY: You see how wicked it is? It lures you, then it takes control. Makes you not care about anything - your morals, principles, nothing! Those few times we did it in 'Nam was because we were afraid of dying.

JESSIE: We were stupid in doing what we did but I KNOW for myself and believe that the same force that made me do it again, and you being here when you did, is kind of spiritual in a way. I've been down lately, not sleeping, having bad dreams when I do, and my friend Rabbit! No one knew it but I had gone down to the VA a few times since I've been out.

ROOSEVELT: You all right, my brother?

JESSIE: Yeah, I'm fine. I need a bit more counseling I guess - more than those thirty days in the hospital when we got back in the States. This is pretty common amongst vets in combat they say.

CALLOWAY: *(Smiling)* Yes, it is. I probably would have run into you if the police force had not sent me to their facilities.

ROOSEVELT: I must be the lucky one. It hasn't hit me yet.

JESSIE: You all are missing the point! I think all these coincidences... us being together like we are today... is the way it was supposed to happen! You know... me doing what I did today... and the feeling afterwards. It didn't feel the same as in 'Nam. In fact, it was disgusting... the whole damn ride! I'm glad it happened in a way and I'm also angry at the same time.

ROOSEVELT: I'm with you on that, my brother! I like weed better. *(Looking at Calloway)* Forgive us, Officer!

CALLOWAY: *(Smiling)* I'll stick to my Blue Nun wine...

ROOSEVELT: And I'll stick to my Night Train or Boone's Farm! *(They laugh)*

END OF SCENE TWO

ACT II

SCENE THREE

A few hours later in Jessie's home – after his visit with Roosevelt, he reminisces about the past...

Jessie's mind takes him back to Vietnam. Roosevelt, Calloway and him on the front line, side-by-side, killing others in order to live. There are folks all around them dying. The three of them are helping to retrieve and ship corpses of their comrades back home to their loved ones. The young boys, made men too soon, are not really sure what it is all about. Everyone there was trying to protect one another from harm, trying to live another day. How close all three of them came to not making it. Every second, minute, and hour meant so much.

(Flashback)

It was during one of those episodes, he remembers, when they were introduced to heroin. They were scared, not sure if they would see another day. Fear had attacked their minds like a swarm of hornets. Seemed the Devil always popped up when fear had engulfed you and always had an elusive cure. He had waited for that right moment and they all took the bait. For a moment the fear of death had taken a holiday. There was one other similar time and situation that it happened again to them. After that incident, they all made a pact and swore to never use again.

Jessie is thinking of all the people and kids in the neighborhood who look up to him because of the active role he plays in the community.

JESSIE: *(Talking to himself)* I know how Carl hates drugs and how it destroys families and communities. I hate drugs the same way. *(Praying)* Oh, Lord, please, if You just let me get through this without hurting those so near and dear to me, I promise You from this day forward I'll never do drugs again. Lord, I know I'm a hypocrite and I'll let many folks down if they find out about me. I don't want to hurt them because of something I did. Lord, I ask for Your forgiveness. I have so much to be thankful for and I'll never make this mistake again. Whatever happens, let it happen to me, Lord, but just don't let me be a reason for others to bear that which they do not deserve... Amen.

(Flashback)

Jessie is thinking about how Carl treats Rabbit and how badly Rabbit hurt Carl and everyone in their community when he got kicked out of school and got hooked on drugs. He disappointed and let down so many folks. He reminisces about their school days and Rabbit's greatness in track, football and basketball games they played. The many times when the whole community would come out to see Rabbit play. They would use the church bus to take folks to the games. Everyone was so proud of him. Jessie and Carl were so proud to play alongside Rabbit and be his friend.

Jessie believed Rabbit may have had a better chance of making it if he and Carl had not gone into the Army. In school, Jessie and Carl were the ones who kept Rabbit eligible to play sports. They stayed up all hours of the night helping him with his academics. Rabbit tried hard but he was a slow learner and without friends around him, he was lost.

Cousin Bee's, True Life, The Well, and Side Street's reputation was their community's only claim to fame until Rabbit came along. Born and raised on the Lower East Side, Rabbit was making the community proud during his high school days. He was well-known all over the state and in other states for his great athleticism. Jessie remembered how Nicholas got the nickname Rabbit. It was their sixth-grade track meet when Nicholas Jones outran everybody by a mile. The coach said he ran like a rabbit. After that they gave him the nickname "Rabbit." Having been out of school for only a few years, Jessie believes that Rabbit still has the will and the potential to become a great athlete. He wanted to help Rabbit regardless of his own hypocrisy.

Jessie and Carl finally found jobs working in a new auto parts facility near the airport. It has been some weeks and Jessie has almost forgotten about Pontiac and his Army buddies. He is almost assured that what happened will never happen again.

END OF SCENE THREE

ACT II

SCENE FOUR

Carl in Chicago with his Little League ball team - runs into Mary Alice...

For the past two weeks, the East River Panthers Little League baseball team has been in Indiana vying for the Midwest inner-city championship. Carl, being their assistant coach, is getting ready to bring them back to Detroit with a third-place finish. The season is over and all the teams and coaches that participated in the games are in Chicago to take pictures, celebrate (tradition) and receive their honors. The teams that participated were given a big dinner, a day at the amusement park and took in a Cubs game. All the coaches, assistant coaches and personnel were given a party at the hotel where they were staying.

Carl called one of his high school classmates, Leonard Templeton, now living in Chicago, to attend the affair. Leonard, in turn, called another classmate of theirs, Brewster (Red) Smith, who also now lives in Chicago. Brewster, unaware of the situation between Mary Alice and Tracy, calls Mary Alice and tells her about the party.

Telephone rings... Light comes on upstairs... Young lady in a robe appears...

MARY ALICE: *(Answering phone)* Hello!

O.S. VOICE: Alice.

MARY ALICE: Is this Brewster?

O.S. VOICE: Yeah! What's happening?

MARY ALICE: Nothing. What's happening with you?

O.S. VOICE: Hey! Leonard called me and said Carl is in town at the Lennox.

MARY ALICE: *(Excited)* What is he in town for and with whom?

O.S. VOICE: He and Alexander been here for a few days with the Little League team. They're leaving tomorrow and having a party at the hotel tonight. Wanna come?

MARY ALICE: *(Pauses)* Awww… I don't know. *(Pauses)* Are Jessie, Tracy and Mary with him?

O.S. VOICE: I don't think so. Leonard said it was the coaches' party. Why?

MARY ALICE: Oh, just asking. What time are you going?

O.S. VOICE: Oh, maybe in a couple hours. Want me to pick you up?

MARY ALICE: No! I'll meet you there. *(Pauses)* If I decide to come, I don't want to be obligated.

O.S. BREWSTER: Cool! I guess I'll see you there then.

MARY ALICE: Okay. 'Bye!

MARY ALICE: *(Hangs up the phone and is thinking to herself)* This may be my opportunity to get even with Tracy, Mary and Carl. Do I still hold a grudge? Yes! They humiliated me in high school. I threw myself, hook, line and sinker at Carl and he didn't bite. Tracy beat me up for lying about having an affair with Carl. I'll get Mary for being Tracy's friend and Carl for refusing my advances. Oh, yes, I'm going to that party!

Mary Alice is average-looking with a stunningly built body. She is someone who thinks more of herself than she really deserves and has always been a conceited and vain person. When she heard about the celebration, she went all out to glamorize herself for the occasion. Her intentions are less than honorable.

END OF SCENE FOUR

ACT II

SCENE FIVE

Lennox Hotel – Jazz music from the jukebox is softly playing in the background...

Carl, his back to the entrance, is at the bar talking with a group of men when Mary Alice walks in alone.

Mary Alice looks around to see if she sees Carl. One of the guys standing in front of Carl notices her as she walks in.

GUY #1: I wouldn't mind being the lucky guy who's going to take her home tonight! Man, look at that body!

All eyes turn to see who he is talking about. At first Carl does not recognize Mary Alice.

CARL: *(Recognizing her)* Hey, I know her! We used to be class-mates in high school. *(Pauses)* She must be looking for Coach Alexander!

GUY #2: She sure would make my daddy proud of me!

GUY #3: Mine, too!

Simultaneously, Mary and Carl see one another. She waves and walks towards Carl. Carl begins to leave when he is stopped by his group.

GUY #1: Hey, man, introduce us! She came alone. *(Joking)* I may be the lucky old son.

Mary Alice comes up to Carl and gives him a hug. He responds back with less enthusiasm and at the same time sees Red and Leonard come in. He pulls back from Mary Alice.

CARL: *(To Mary Alice)* Introduce yourself. The guys are dying to meet you. *(Walking away)*

Mary Alice, enjoying the attention, introduces herself while keeping her eyes on Carl as he embraces Red and Leonard.

Half hour later...

Mary Alice is enjoying the male attention she is getting. She knows she has the pick of the litter tonight, but is disappointed that she has not had the opportunity to be alone with Carl. At the bar, Carl and some of the people from the party are watching the baseball game on TV. There is an empty stool next to Carl. Mary Alice ends her conversation with Brewster and Leonard and goes over to Carl and sits down next to him.

MARY ALICE: *(Touches Carl's arm gently as she sits next to him)* Are you trying to ignore me? If you are, it's not going to work!

CARL: How did you know I was here? Red told you!

MARY ALICE: Does it matter?

CARL: Well, to be honest, it does. You are not my wife's favorite person and if she knows you are here I don't think she would be pleased.

MARY ALICE: *(Knowing)* I thought we were all grown up. You're not thinking about what happened seven years ago. I'm no longer a product of my teenage years. *(Sarcastically)* I'm a lady as you can see and should be appreciated.

CARL: Is it vanity I'm hearing?

MARY ALICE: No, sugar. Is that the way you see me?

CARL: Just reacting to your comment.

MARY ALICE: I'm a humble young lady trying to educate young minds so they can be nice gentlemen like you.

CARL: I heard you were a teacher. Congratulations!

MARY ALICE: Thanks. You mind if I buy you a drink?

CARL: I don't know. *(Looking at Mary Alice and telling himself that this does not feel right, he turns away and seems more interested in the game than in her)*

MARY ALICE: *(Trying to be convincing)* You want to keep on trying to ignore me, pretending I'm not here? I came here because I thought I was invited! I hadn't seen you in a long time. By the way, I thought you were with your wife. If you were, I would have offered you both a drink. I'm doing too well to let the past make my life miserable - but I still would like to buy you a drink.

CARL: *(To bartender)* I'll have a Strohs. Thanks, Alice *(Short for Mary Alice)*. I ain't going to lie, this just doesn't feel good. You see, I know and you know my wife doesn't like you. If she knew I was spending my time in your company, someone might possibly get hurt - and you know it.

MARY ALICE: It's not like we're somewhere on a date or in an intimate setting. We're just here socializing. Is she that unforgiving and insecure after seven years? Are you that afraid to have a drink with a classmate?

CARL: (Switching attention between TV and her) You know what? I would like to say she wouldn't mind us talking because she's not that insecure. It's you! I don't believe my wife would like us to be sitting in the same pew at church.

MARY ALICE: That's too bad she still feels that way. Tell you what, she'll never know from me that I was ever here. Deal?

CARL: Thanks.

MARY ALICE: Such a wonderful feeling to see home folks here! *(Lying)* It didn't have to be you! Could be anyone from home… classmates, folks I grew up with - I would still be here. I miss home a lot. Maybe I would go back but I got a job and you know how rough times are. *(Mary Alice holds up her glass and they toast)*

MARY ALICE: To you and Tracy! Congratulations. You all have children yet? How about Jessie and Mary?

CARL: None of us have children as of yet. We're hoping soon!

MARY ALICE: I heard you and Jessie just recently got out of the military. I'm glad you all are okay!

CARL: Thanks.

MARY ALICE: *(Keeping conversation)* Pretty sad about Rabbit, huh? I heard how hurt Jessie was when he found out. He sure disappointed a lot of people.

CARL: Yeah.

Leonard and Brewster (Red) come up to the bar.

RED: Who's winning?

CARL: St. Louis.

LEONARD: (To Mary Alice) Come on, Alice, let's dance!

Mary Alice gets up and leaves her drink on the counter... "Watch my drink for me."

RED: *(Looking at her)* Man, she's one sexy lady!

CARL: Yeah.

Carl and Red are watching the game. Coach Alexander comes up to the bar and sits his drink next to Carl. As soon as the dance is over, he approaches Mary Alice and they dance to the next song.

Time Change...

It is getting late. People are beginning to leave the party. Red is about to leave. He, Carl and Leonard are standing near the exit, talking.

RED: *(To Carl)* Tell Jessie he still owes me a dinner at Cousin Bee's from three years ago. I think he joined the Army to keep from paying me. *(They smile)*

LEONARD: Man, you and Jess were about the only ones who did not mind going to war.

CARL: Naww – it wasn't that way! Neither one of us wanted to go. When Tracy and Mary lost their parents, we decided to marry them earlier than it was originally planned. Then I got drafted and Jessie joined so our allotment could help on some of the costs they were enduring because of their parents' deaths. As a matter of fact, I hope one day that we may be able to renew our vows.

LEONARD: Man, you know I had forgotten all about that. What a tragedy!

RED: Yeah, I forgot! You know since the war Detroit has been called Dodge City because so many people went there to get over to Canada.

A few moments later, Mary Alice arrives holding a tray with three bottles and one mug of beer. She sets the tray on the table and gives each one a bottle of beer. She picks up the mug of beer last.

MARY ALICE: *(Toast)* Let's toast to this moment before we depart. Who knows this may be our last time meeting like this.

Everyone holds their bottles up.

MARY ALICE: *(Not wanting anyone to say anything)* My toast is thanks for letting me be here amongst friends of my youth and enjoying myself. I hope that our journeys, wherever they take us, are safe endeavors. May success and happiness always be the name of the game.

Everyone takes a drink.

RED: I second that motion. *(Everyone takes another swallow)*

LEONARD: Hear ye! Hear ye! *(Again everyone takes a swallow)*

CARL: I really don't need anymore I've been drinking beer all evening, but to my brothers… peace, love and happiness! *(Another swallow)*

MARY ALICE: *(To Carl)* I have danced with both my classmates now I would like to have my last dance with you.

Not allowing Carl to answer, Mary Alice grabs his hand and pulls him toward the dance floor.

LEONARD: Hey, I'm leaving with Red and we're heading over to Pin Ups. *(An adult club)*

They finish drinking their beers and put the empty bottles on the table.

MARY ALICE: *(Making a remark)* Pin Ups? Raunchy!

Carl beginning to feel a buzz, pauses for a moment to hug the guys.

CARL: Hey, my brothers, I'm glad to see you. Whenever you're in town, we'll hang.

LEONARD: To be sure, my brother!

RED: Hey, I'll be there next week. My old lady's father is having a birthday party!

CARL: *(Mary Alice pulling him to the dance floor)* Cool!

Leonard and Red are walking out of the room.

RED: *(Looking back at Carl and Mary Alice)* She sure seems to be after Carl!

LEONARD: *(Shaking his head)* That ain't good for him. Better not let Tracy find out...

Carl, a little light-headed, is trying to compose himself as he slow dances with Mary Alice. She is dancing as close to Carl as she can get.

MARY ALICE: I'm glad you saved the last dance for me.

CARL: You pulled me on to the floor. I had no choice.

MARY ALICE: Well, you're too classy a guy to say no or make a scene. Now here we are. Let's forget the past and enjoy this moment. *(She feels Carl's weight on her as he slightly stumbles)*

MARY ALICE: Are you all right, sugar?

CARL: *(Beginning to feel weak and uncoordinated)* Not really! I must have drunk too much… feeling light-headed. I have to get somewhere and sit down before I fall.

Mary Alice's hands are around his waist as they walk to a booth. Carl sits down and she stands.

CARL: *(To Mary Alice)* I think I'll be all right in a minute.

MARY ALICE: I was leaving after our dance but I'm not going anywhere until I make sure you're all right. You're not looking too good, sugar. Maybe you need to go lie down and rest for a minute. *(Smiling)* Looks like you had a good time and now you're paying for it.

CARL: You may be right. *(Tries clumsily to get up)* Man, I'm messed up!

MARY ALICE: *(Showing a little sympathy)* Here, let me help you. I don't think you can make it by yourself.

Carl is reluctant but knows he's in no shape at this point to deny her assistance....

CARL: I'd appreciate it if you'd just take me to my floor. I think I can make it from there.

MARY ALICE: *(Knowing his condition)* Come on, sugar, before I have to carry you.

Carl and Mary Alice are in the elevator.

CARL: This is embarrassing. I've never been this intoxicated.

MARY ALICE: You were just having a good time, sugar, that's all. The elevator door opens and she helps Carl off. Carl reaches in his pocket and pulls out his room key.

CARL: Thanks for not letting anyone see me like this. Hope none of the children see me. You can go now. I think I can make it. Thanks.

MARY ALICE: *(Concerned)* Are you sure you don't want me to help you to your room? I'll tell you what. I'll stand right here just to make sure until you get into your room and close the door.

CARL: *(Walking along the wall)* Thanks! I think I'm cool.

Mary Alice stands at the elevator watching him. He holds on to the wall as he tries to walk to his room. He stops briefly to readjust himself. Mary Alice hurries and helps him to his room.

MARY ALICE: Come on, sugar. Let me help you!

Mary Alice helps Carl to his room. She takes the key from his hand and opens the door. They go inside the room and she closes the door. She assists him to his bed.

CARL: *(Intoxicated behavior)* Think I'm all right now. *(Trying to take off his coat)*

MARY ALICE: You're okay now that you're in your room. Here, let me help you.

CARL: Where am I?

MARY ALICE: *(Assuring)* You're safe in your room. Here let me help you.

Mary Alice helps Carl up. He stands up and weakly pulls off his coat. He pulls his suspenders down over his arms. Mary Alice helps to unbutton his shirt.

CARL: *(Helplessly defensive)* Hey, what are you doing?

MARY ALICE: *(Taking off his shirt exposing his masculine upper body)* Relax, sugar. You can't go anywhere. You're too high.

Mary Alice loosens his slacks and they fall below his knees. She helps him back onto the bed, bends down, unties and takes off his shoes. She finishes taking off his slacks, folds them neatly and puts them on a hanger with his coat and shirt, then hangs them in the closet.

Carl is lying on the bed in just his boxer shorts, staring at her helplessly. Mary Alice looks at him, goes over and locks the door. With a completely different demeanor, Mary Alice stands over him and looks down at him lying there.

MARY ALICE: *(Shaking her head and smiling)* Look at you! What would your wife do if she knew you were with me in a hotel room almost naked? Don't worry sugar, she won't hear it from me. I just want you to be conscious enough to remember this moment.

Carl looks at her and struggles to rise up. She slightly pushes him back down. He realizes he is too intoxicated to argue with her. Mary Alice unbuttons the back of her dress, slowly slipping each arm out of each sleeve and letting it fall to her waist exposing her bra.

MARY ALICE: *(Vengefully)* After years of humiliation because of you, vengeance is now mine! I want you to be conscious, to remember this moment each and every day. I want you to always be aware and scared that she may find out. Am I that cruel to tell her or write her a letter describing our escapade? *(Writing in hand, while repeating...)* Am I that cruel? Remember, I'm a bitch! You shouldn't have drunk that last beer I got for you. *(Carl staring at her...)*

MARY ALICE: *(Continues speaking)* You want to know what's really amazing sugar? You no longer appeal to me. I can truly and honestly say I don't want you. As a young teenager, you were fine to look at and desirable. I wanted to be with - which you denied me! Now, I'm just paying back an embarrassment that you, your wife and friends did to me! I never forgot about it, though I pretended I did. You didn't know what it was like - until now. I swore one day

I would get even. *(Pauses)* Opportunity knocked and I jumped at it and now here we are.

Carl tries his best to comprehend.

MARY ALICE: You see, sugar, I had the pick of the litter tonight but I was seeking vengeance. *(Slowly takes off her shoes while talking)* To me, you all are losers - you and your miserable department store salesclerk wife - working the same job she had in high school. Me, I just want to humiliate you. That's all. *(Pauses)* Out of all those men who wanted me, you're the lucky one tonight, sugar!

Carl lies helpless. He is intoxicated beyond reasoning and understanding. He stares at her while she continues talking.

MARY ALICE: Remember when I wanted you and you wanted nothing to do with me? Your wife beat me up and the whole school knew about it! I was humiliated and embarrassed all because of you!

Mary Alice puts her hands on both sides of her waist and loosens the dress, letting it fall to the floor. She is wearing only her matching bra and panties. She bends down, picks up the dress, folds it and lays it on the bed. One hand reaches over and pulls her bra strap down from her shoulder to take it off while the other reaches over and turns off the lamp on the night-stand.

MARY ALICE: Your turn now, sugar. It's show time!

END OF SCENE FIVE

ACT II

SCENE SIX

Four days later - Carl and Jessie in the Well...

It is early Wednesday afternoon and most of the folks who have jobs are at work. At this time of the weekday afternoon, pedestrian traffic on Side Street is slower than in the mornings and evenings. Carl and Jessie are sitting at the bar in the Well listening to jazz on the jukebox and drinking beer. Carl has been eager to talk to his best friend Jessie ever since he returned home on Sunday evening. With Tracy and Mary off on Mondays and Tuesdays and today being their first day back at work, it allows the two of them the time to be alone.

The bar just opened up and Carl and Jessie are the only ones there besides the bartender, who, because of familiarity, ignores them as he busies himself with his opening chores.

JESSIE: *(Toasting to Carl)* Congratulations on a third-place finish. Those young brothers had to be playing some ball to come in third with all the competition they had.

CARL: *(Off-track momentarily)* I'm proud of those brothers! They played their hearts out. Shoot, we only lost to the teams that came in first and second - St. Louis Thieves and Buttermilk Bottom Bulldogs and to one team that didn't even place. We just had a bad game that time so you know my boys must be pretty good. Man, those Thieves can play some ball... and steal some bases. They deserved it. Yeah, the whole inner city's proud of our young scrappy brothers. *(Pauses, takes a sip of beer)* Big Hank and the community have purchased tickets for Coach and me to take them to the Tigers/Yankees game in two weeks. I'll see if I can get an extra ticket.

JESSIE: If you can get an extra one that would be cool. I know how hard it is for a Yankees game... I wanted to come to one of your games in Indiana... but I spent most of the time taking the girls to work and picking them up... and in between time painting y'all's apartment.

CARL: I thank you for that, my brother... that wasn't something I was looking forward to doing when I got back. *(Carl pauses for a moment, getting his composure together as he nervously plays with his drink and looks at Jessie, and says)* Jess, man, I'm in a world of trouble - big trouble and to tell the truth I'm scared. Man, I haven't the slightest idea what to do!

JESSIE: *(Seriously concerned)* What's happening? What's up, man?

CARL: *(Shamefully hesitant... takes a large swallow of beer and blurts)* Man!! I had sex with Mary Alice!

JESSIE: *(Lost for words)* Come on, man! Don't play like that!

CARL: I'm not playing, Jess. It's real!

JESSIE: *(Angry with Carl)* Come on, Carl! If it's real, man, how could you go and do that - and with Mary Alice? Man, you couldn't get any lower than that. I mean, that's lower than low, man. I don't even know what to say. I hope Tracy never finds out!

CARL: *(Sadly)* I know, man! This is all messed up for me. I started not to tell you - too shameful to talk about - but I had to tell someone and you're the only one I can tell.

JESSIE: *(Pauses)* I kind of wish you hadn't told me. We are best friends, brothers in the real sense. We grew up side-by-side. *(Looking at Carl)* Man, you've done some way out and crazy things but this one takes the cake! Tracy and Mary have been by our sides all our lives, practically. Tracy doesn't deserve this! *(Carl is sadly quiet)*

JESSIE: *(Still dubious)* How could you, Carl? Mary Alice of all people! That's like pouring salt on a wound!

CARL: I know. I can't explain it. It wasn't like you think! I'm wrong, regardless, but I was drunk.

JESSIE: *(No sympathy)* I can't accept drunk as an excuse for what you did. Careless and disrespectful - call it what it is.

CARL: *(Explaining as best as he can)* Listen; please listen for a minute, Jess! I know how you feel and right now what you think of me. I don't blame you. I feel bad too, man, but it ain't going to reverse what I did or change things. This whole thing is a nightmare and I can't do nothing about it so please listen, to my side of the story – at least what I can remember - before you sentence me to the electric chair. Maybe you might give me life without parole. *(Pauses and takes a sip of beer)* I didn't know she was going to be there. I swear, I didn't know she knew I was in town until Red told me that he accidentally told her. You see, I called Leonard Templeton and told him about me being in town and that we were having a semi-private party that night at the hotel for the coaches. Leonard called Red and told him I was in town. Red, being from the West Side, did not know 'bout the rift between Tracy and Mary Alice, or so he says. He innocently called and told Mary Alice. *(Taking another sip of beer)* I didn't invite either one. It was a shock to me, man, when I saw her there. At first I thought that Coach Alexander must have invited her. I didn't know, man. The whole night, I swear, I tried to stay away from her, but she would find me. You can ask Red and Leonard, she came over while I was sitting at the bar watching the baseball game and bought me a beer. At first I refused it. Then she asked me if I was trying to avoid her and told me that it was not going to work. I straight out told her I didn't want to betray Tracy by being in her company. That's the truth, Jess, but it didn't faze her. She was cool, Jess. Pretending how much of a lady she had become after going to college and getting her teaching credentials and how she had forgotten all about that stuff that happened between her and Tracy when they were in junior high school. She even said she had expected Tracy to be there and would have apologized and shook her hand. Again, I told her I didn't feel right being in her company and that's when Red came and got her to dance with him. After him, Coach Alexander wanted to dance with her.

JESSIE: I bet she had on something tight, didn't she? Just like at school!

CARL: Yeah. She had the men's attention - all except mine. I tried to stay far away from her.

JESSIE: Come on, Carl. You're street, man. You were hip to Mary

Alice. You knew she was a conniving, lying sneak. She's also spoiled. For you to turn her down and Tracy to beat her butt - you know she hasn't forgotten that!

CARL: You know what, Jess? I know... I know game. That's the strangest part. After I told her about how I felt about being in her company, she backed off. I mean, she acted cool with it after she bought me the beer at the bar. I mean, she was getting plenty action and stayed away most of the night until she was getting ready to leave along with Red and Leonard. *(Pauses)* I mean, she was cool. She had me convinced everything was on the up and up. She came over, brought a tray with four beers and gave each of us one and drank one herself. We all toasted. After that she insisted on having a last dance with me - promised she would never mention that we saw each other. At first I hesitated, but she said she would make a scene if I didn't dance with her, so I did. Leonard and Red said goodbye and split.

JESSIE: I'm not going to lie to you, man. I'm angry with you and at the same time I feel sorry for you.

CARL: *(Trying to understand what happened)* Jess, you know me better than anyone. You know the crazy and stupid things I do. You know I've never intentionally done anything to hurt Tracy. I'd never do anything, man... she's my world! You know how much I love my wife. I was just having a good time, celebrating with the other teams' coaches. *(Pauses)* So what if we got drunk? It was just us guys celebrating. I didn't know Mary Alice was going to be there. One thing I knew, I had too many beers but I didn't think I was that intoxicated. I guess that last beer put me over the edge. It just suddenly slipped up on me. *(Pauses)* I'm really troubled, man... I don't know what to do!

JESSIE: *(Scratching his head and looking at Carl)* I wish I could help you but I can't. No one can help you. You've got to figure this out. Good luck if you can. *(Pauses)* I just want to know how you wound up having sex with her if she was leaving after you finished dancing with her.

CARL: *(Perplexed)* That's where the confusion comes in. *(Pauses)* I remember getting a little light-headed when we started dancing. I asked her to stop for a minute. I sat down in a booth and thought I'd feel a little better but the feeling got worse and worse. It was so bad that I could hardly stand up straight. That's when I decided to go to my room. *(Pauses, shaking his head as he continues)* She got up to leave. I tell you, Jess, that high hit me so fast, when I stood up, I kinda fell back onto the seat. She helped me up. As we got near the elevator I didn't want to fall on the floor in front of my colleagues *(Pauses)* or have some of my kids see me so I asked her if she would help me to the elevator before she left. *(Takes a deep breath)* Jess, the next thing I remember I was in my room on my back in bed with my clothes off and she was standing over me.

JESSIE: *(Feeling for Carl)* Aww, man, she had you where she wanted you. She probably was watching you the whole time she was there. She watched how many drinks you were having and then she bought you two beers. She knew it was just a matter of time, especially with Red and Leonard out of the way. *(Pauses and looks at Carl)* That's why she wanted that last dance with you. She had no plans on leaving. She outsmarted you!

CARL: *(Sadly)* She's about to ruin my life. I'm lost... right now. I'd rather be back in 'Nam.

JESSIE: You don't want that but I know what you mean.

CARL: *(Remembering)* I couldn't move, man. I tried to get up and fell back on the bed. She was looking at me, talking and taking off her clothes. Then she went and locked the door and came back.

JESSIE: Remember what she said?

CARL: I remember her saying something like she didn't want me anymore; she just wanted to humiliate me, something like that, while taking off her clothes. That's all I remember until I woke up.

JESSIE: I feel for you, my brother. She's going to play with your conscience until she's ready for Tracy to know. May be months *(Pauses)* or years. She's in no hurry. She's got you where she wants you. A cruel punishment but for sure, she's going to let Tracy know. You can bet on that! Don't know when but she's going to.

CARL: *(Sadly)* I know, man. Why does crazy stuff always happen to me?

JESSIE: I hate to say it, brother, but you're a crazy dude. Not saying that in disrespect, my brother - you're as cool as they get, better than gold, smart as they come *(Pauses)* but your game sometimes can be pretty crazy... *(Remembering)*... like the time you bet a hundred dollars to this guy's one dollar. Man that was crazy!

CARL: That's because I knew I was right!

JESSIE: But, for a dollar? You aren't going to be right all the time. What about the time you lost the car playing playground ball? That was crazy. Crazy attracts crazy sometimes...

CARL: But, what did I do crazy to deserve this?

JESSIE: Mary Alice is a crazy girl and she knows you. After all, we went to the same junior and senior high school. She knew you enough to get you in bed. *(Pauses)* How do you know you had sex with her? You said you don't remember anything else.

CARL: I know I woke up naked. Her underwear *(Embarrassed)* was on my head and there was a used towel and wash cloth, a condom wrapper and one towel. Need I say more?

JESSIE: Sorry, man! *(Idea)* Hey, man. Why don't you tell Reverend Peters? He might be able to help.

CARL: I thought of that but I wanted to talk to you first.

JESSIE: I think it would help somewhat if he knew. He may be able to help calm the storm if or when Tracy finds out.

CARL: *(Nervous)* I've never been this scared in my life - not even in 'Nam. Man, I'm on pins and needles!

JESSIE: Mary Alice knew you would act in this way. This is part of her pay back and she's enjoying it. I think you should go see Reverend Peters.

CARL: *(In agreement)* Okay. Come with me. *(They both get up and walk towards the door)*

JESSIE: *(To the manager)* We'll catch you later!

BARTENDER: *(Waves)* Okay, fellas! *(Jessie and Carl leave The Well)*

END OF SCENE SIX

ACT II

SCENE SEVEN

Two Weeks Later...

Carl is at a Tigers and Yankees game at Tiger Stadium with his Little League team. At the same time, Roosevelt and Calloway are in Detroit visiting with Jessie.

Jessie, Calloway and Roosevelt are coming out of Cousin Bee's Café together.

CALLOWAY: *(To Jessie and Roosevelt)* I'm not going to lie to you, my brother! Cousin Bee's does some awesome cooking, as good or better than any I've ever had. I definitely will be coming back here!

ROOSEVELT: *(Smiling)* Wait, wait now! I only ate food as good as this one other place. Wanna take a guess?

CALLOWAY: *(Interrupting him without hesitation)* In 'Nam, when Jessie was telling us about Cousin Bee's.

ROOSEVELT: Jessie, man, you used to talk about her food so much we used to taste it in our minds and today I can truly say you weren't lying.

CALLOWAY: Amen to that!

Jessie, Roosevelt and Calloway sit down on the bench under Housecoat Pearl's apartment talking...

ROOSEVELT: Man! I had never heard of sweet potato cobbler until you talked about it in 'Nam. You sure were right when you said it was addictive. Man, I feel like going back in there and buying some to take home.

CALLOWAY: *(Smiling)* I agree! That cobbler will make you hurt somebody bad!

ROOSEVELT: *(Changing the subject)* Hey, Jess, how is your friend Rabbit doing? I saw the pictures and newspaper articles on the wall in the café. You guys sure won some championships.

CALLOWAY: Saw pictures of you with him. Makes you proud, huh?

JESSIE: Yeah, it does. He's trying to get himself together.

ROOSEVELT: *(To Jessie)* You've always been an optimistic dude. That's what I like about you.

CALLOWAY: He needs friends like you. That brother got a battle ahead of him. Tough habit to break! Speaking of which, how've you been doing, my brothers *(Jessie and Roosevelt)*, since we last saw each other? We still have a pact...

JESSIE: Straight as an arrow! I told you I would. Last time was just a moment in time I guess, like in 'Nam, but it's over, my brothers. I realized the consequences - my wife, my self-respect, friends and God - not worth it.

ROOSEVELT: I'm as cool as a cucumber. Life is beautiful, my brother.

CALLOWAY: I'm glad. It can't get any harder than where we came from and we're still here to talk about it. Let's enjoy life. We deserve it.

JESSIE: Amen to that!

ROOSEVELT: *(Standing up)* Look at us! Isn't this beautiful? All three of us home from hell, on familiar turf side-by-side. *(They stand and hug)*

CALLOWAY: Hey! We've got to head on back. Now that we know where to get sweet potato cobbler we'll see each other often, *(Joking)* if only for the cobbler. *(Slowly walking towards the bend)*

ROOSEVELT: *(Also joking)* Sho'nuff! That cobbler might get you tired of seeing us.

JESSIE: Hey! When you two have the same days off and have time, I'm inviting you and your ladies to come down and spend a day with us to meet my family. We'll barbeque and you can have all the cobbler you want. I'll get Sister Johnson and our wives to make enough, so you all can carry some home. Nobody can barbeque like me and Carl, I promise you...

ROOSEVELT: I'm in. Just say when.

CALLOWAY: Count me in. Roo and I will work it out real soon... *(They're walking toward the end of the street)*

ROOSEVELT: You know, Jess, this is amazing. This is such a cool street in the heart of the 'hood and it's for real, sacred grounds. How long did you say since there was a crime here?

JESSIE: Last I heard was *(Thinking)* about seven years ago. A brother robbed Bernie's store. He was caught and beat up pretty badly by folks in the 'hood for breaking a treaty. Only ruckus now and then is a raid on the pool hall.

CALLOWAY: *(To Jessie)* I bet you're proud to live here on this street, huh?

JESSIE: I sure am! This street is Detroit's Black community's pride and joy. *(Proudly)* Our history!

ROOSEVELT: Yeah! *(Changing the subject slightly)* You know, Jess. Way *(Short for Calloway)* and I did pretty well guessing about those folks who you always talked about in 'Nam. We kind of guessed who they were to ourselves before you introduced them to us. We got all of them right except one. We both failed on that one.

CALLOWAY: Francine! We probably would have gotten her down if she hadn't dyed her hair and I thought she was shorter. Other than that one, everything else seemed déjà vu. Seemed like we had been here before and knew everyone.

ROOSEVELT: Sho'nuff! Felt like stomping grounds. *(They all laugh as they disappear around the bend, out of sight and sound.)*

END OF SCENE SEVEN

ACT II

SCENE EIGHT

Carl gets found out by Mary...

Mary is downstairs in Tracy's house. Tracy is in the bathroom getting dressed when her phone rings. Tracy hollers out to Mary to answer it.

TRACY: Merr... get the phone!

Mary comes out of the kitchen eating a sandwich. She goes and picks up the phone.

MARY: *(Cheerfully)* Hello!

FEMALE VOICE O.S: You wouldn't be so happy if you knew what your husband and I were doing in room 626 at the Lennox Hotel in Chicago last month.

Mary shockingly listens.

FEMALE VOICE O.S: I wanted him to squirm some before I called you. I got three pleasures for the price of one. I made myself enjoy him, so I could tell you. Then I got a joy out of seeing him, in my mind, squirm, wondering if I was going to tell you. The other one is for you to be mad, angry, hurt and disappointed. Now we're even!

The phone goes dead... dial tone. Mary is still stunned when Tracy comes out of the bathroom.

TRACY: Who was that on the phone?

MARY: *(Briefly trying to give herself time to compose and think)* Uhh... Huh?

TRACY: *(Noticing her behavior)* What's wrong with you, girl? You all right? Who called?

MARY: *(Calmer, trying to think)* It was Jessie calling me! Uhh, he couldn't reach me upstairs and figured I was down here. He wants me to, uhh, uhh *(She holds her stomach - creating a lie)* all of a sudden my stomach's upset and cramping! I bet it's that two-day-old tuna I ate this morning. I better get back upstairs before I can't make it!

TRACY: Girl, I told you not to eat leftovers over two days old, especially with mayonnaise in it! Jess okay?

MARY: *(More composed)* Uhh, yeah, he just wanted to tell me he's at uhh... he and Carl are at Uncle Buck's!

TRACY: I could have told you that! Carl called me about an hour ago and told me they were over there working on his car.

MARY: *(Pretending to feel worse... pauses then walks towards the door)* I better get upstairs! I'm beginning to feel nauseous and cramping. *(Going out the door)*

TRACY: Call me! Let me know you're okay.

MARY: I'll call you but I'll probably rest awhile until Jessie gets home.

Half hour Later - Sister Johnson's House...

Mary is sitting at the kitchen table in Sister Johnson's house. She has already told Sister Johnson about the phone call. Sister Johnson, quiet in thought, brings a warm coffee pot over to the table and pours Mary and herself a cup. She sets the percolator back on the counter and sits down with Mary.

MARY: *(Looks at Sister Johnson and says...)* I knew it was Mary Alice! When she said "in Chicago" and "now we're even," I recognized the voice and knew for sure that it was her. Only a low-down, dirty, rotten person would do something like that. It was Mary Alice on the phone.

SISTER JOHNSON: I can truly say if it's true, I'm very disappointed and hurt at what Carl has done. Has Jessie said something to you? I'm sure he told Jessie even if he didn't want to. Of course, knowing those two with the pride they have in each other, they'll never tell!

MARY: *(Still thinking about the phone call)* I had to get out of there, Sister Johnson. I was too afraid I'd spill the beans. You know how I am!

SISTER JOHNSON: You did the right thing, child. You sure are a threat to let the cat out of the bag. I'm afraid if you're around Tracy too much now, you may.

MARY: Maybe I better go and stay with Uncle Buck for a few days?

SISTER JOHNSON: *(Not opposed)* That may be a good idea for you until you can settle down for a minute.

MARY: I'll tell her Uncle Buck is not feeling too well and wants me to come over there and stay with him a few days. I'll call Uncle Buck and tell him.

SISTER JOHNSON: Well, you know I'm against lying - unless it's for a worthy cause and I'd say this is a worthy cause. *(Smiles).*

Mary isn't smiling, instead she looks very sad.

MARY: *(Sadly)* Sister Johnson, I'd want my best friend to tell me if she knew my husband was cheating on me.

SISTER JOHNSON: I know you do, child. So would I! But we don't know if it's true or not! That could possibly mean that you may slip and say something you may regret later on, if all this turns out to be a lie. We all know the repercussions it would have on Carl and everyone else. Tracy is a dangerous, no-nonsense person.

MARY: I sure am afraid of what she might or would do.

Sister Johnson stands up and goes to the refrigerator and opens it.

SISTER JOHNSON: I forgot I have some leftover sweet potato cobbler.

MARY: What time is Reverend Peters coming?

Sister Johnson reaches in the refrigerator, pulls out a Pyrex dish and sets it on the stove.

SISTER JOHNSON: This is his sick, shut-in and hospital day. Said he would be here as soon as he leaves the hospital. *(Spooning cobbler into two bowls while Mary talks)* I better save him some. You know how he is about my cobbler.

Sister Johnson sets the two bowls on the table, leaving the dish on the stove and sits back down.

SISTER JOHNSON: *(Between bites)* You know, I'm supposed to be an elderly, wise person to you all, but this time I'm at a loss of that wise, elderly wisdom. I cannot come up with anything about this situation that would make sense. I just don't think telling the truth is best. We'll just have to let Reverend Peters share his spiritual wisdom.

MARY: *(Mad)* That dang Mary Alice! She and Tracy don't like each other since she told those lies about her and Carl... and Tracy beat her butt. I feel like going there and whupping her myself! I bet the Devil in her sure was tempting Carl. She sure got the body Satan loves to exploit.

SISTER JOHNSON: Well, Satan works on the mind, sugar, not the body! Satan can only think short term. That's what fools you.

MARY: Sister Johnson, if Jessie doesn't know, should I tell him?

SISTER JOHNSON: Why don't we just wait and ask Reverend Peters? Somehow I believe he already knows.

Telephone rings...

SISTER JOHNSON: *(Answering the phone)* Hello, *(Pauses)* she's right here. *(Pauses)* She's better. I gave her some hot tea. *(Pauses)* Okay. *(Hangs up the phone)* That was Tracy checking on you. Said since you were better she's going to run over to the Boulevard and get Carl some socks and underwear.

MARY: Whew! I'm going to go and call Uncle Buck and Jessie now and pack me a few clothes and catch a bus over there since Jessie is already there. I don't know what to tell him. He's going to want to know why I'm staying over at Uncle Buck's for a couple days - not that he cares, but he sure is going to want to know. Then I have to tell him a lie. I already have four people I'm lying to. Why do we have to lie, Sister Johnson?

SISTER JOHNSON: Because it will protect us and others from unnecessary pain and suffering.

The doorbell rings...

SISTER JOHNSON: *(Getting up)* Probably Reverend Peters.

MARY: *(Getting up and following her to the door)* I better get on up there. I wouldn't want Tracy to see us all together.

Sister Johnson opens the door and Reverend Peters comes into the house. She leaves the door open as Mary is on her way out.

REVEREND PETERS: Hello, everyone! Sorry I couldn't get here any sooner. *(To Mary)* Sister Mary, you about to leave? I thought it was you who wanted to talk to me.

MARY: I did. But you took so long getting here! No fault of your own. Now I have to leave. Sister Johnson will tell you everything. *(Looking at Reverend Peters and Sister Johnson and their being alone)* I can trust you, can't I?

SISTER JOHNSON: *(Intervening and joking)* Don't worry, sugar, he's still in hibernation.

REVEREND PETERS: *(Smiling)* This is what I left the sick and shut-in for?

MARY: *(Walking out the door)* Reverend, I hope you have some good advice for us after Sister Johnson talks to you.

SISTER JOHNSON: I'll call you later, honey.

Fifteen minutes elapse...

Sister Johnson and Reverend Peters are sitting at the same table where she and Mary had been sitting. He is eating a bowl of sweet potato cobbler. Sister Johnson has informed him about Carl.

REVEREND PETERS: *(Joking)* Sister Johnson! In the ministry, chicken is classified as our favorite food...I don't know where it came from, but they would say "this tastes like chicken."

SISTER JOHNSON: *(Pretends to enjoy his un-humorous jokes)* Well, Reverend, next time I'll offer you chicken.

REVEREND PETERS: *(Serious)* No... No... No! I didn't mean it like that at all. Chicken cannot compare to your sweet potato cobbler. You know that, Sister Johnson!

SISTER JOHNSON: *(Loves to make him squirm)* For a minute, I thought maybe one of those good sisters whose house you be going to for Sunday dinners may have put a potion in their food - better than what I put in my sweet potato cobbler! About to make me jealous!

REVEREND PETERS: *(Smiling)* Now, now, Sister Johnson! I make it my business not to have dinner alone at the single and widowed ladies' houses. Rumors float around this community like hot air balloons. But if it is true, your potion got the whole community talking about sweet potato cobbler. Guess I'm just one of the lucky ones - getting some cobbler when it's not a holiday or special occasion. Preachers do have some advantages!

SISTER JOHNSON: You sure know what to say to keep that cobbler coming out of the oven. *(Serious)* You know, Reverend, Carl's being drunk is still no excuse for what he did.

REVEREND PETERS: Very true! He did something he could have prevented. Just by not doing one thing could have prevented the other, but I'm a messenger asking God to forgive. Brother Carl came to me with Brother Jessie as soon as he got back from Chicago. He told me the whole story. That kind of told me he was sorry. You know, Sister Johnson, I doubt if I could fill the front pew of the church or have what you call a congregation if not for the sinners. I probably wouldn't or couldn't have been a preacher but God is more forgiving than man.

SISTER JOHNSON: Mary being at Tracy's at the time she was, was surely a God intervention!

REVEREND PETERS: I believe Brother Carl truly loves his wife.

SISTER JOHNSON: I believe that. I don't know what happened, but I do know temptation is an addiction and you know as well as I do, whether you want to admit it or not, men's hormones are like rich people - the more they get, the more they want!

REVEREND PETERS: Weakness of the flesh – that's the Devil's fuel. Cancer of the mind and soul! *(Pauses)* Brother Carl grew up more unconventional than most young kids. He was raised by his aunt, and a father who stayed in training camps more than at home. He was exposed to a lot of things early in life.

SISTER JOHNSON: When that boy's mama had him, she brought him to his father's house and dropped him off. He hasn't seen or heard from her since! His dad raised him the best he could. He was not too bright upstairs after being hit in the head a few times. *(Pauses-upset)* You know, Reverend; I can just imagine how hurt Tracy is going to be if she finds out. I don't want to see them break up and we both know that would be a good possibility. Not only will they hurt, but we all will be hurting. She and Mary have had enough hurt to last them the rest of their lives. Their husbands are their worlds. *(Getting angrier)* No matter how sorry Carl is, I'm angry at him! Why would he have to mess with the girl everyone knew Tracy truly dislikes? He knew that when he laid down with that home wrecker. That was just downright evil. Tracy doesn't deserve that. I'd like to have said a cuss word then!

REVEREND PETERS: Now Sister Johnson, you better calm down.

SISTER JOHNSON: I'm respectful of you; otherwise some choice words would have slipped right off my tongue.

REVEREND PETERS: I know how you must feel being so close to them like you are. You're almost like a mother to those children. I agree that his action was sinful. Brother Carl is pretty heartbroken over it. He's afraid. Afraid of losing his wife and all of you, who are so close to him. He came to me because he believes Tracy will leave him if she finds out.

SISTER JOHNSON: That's not a belief, that's the truth and I wouldn't blame her! I'm hoping she doesn't find out, though I believe it's wrong to hide something like that. Personally, I know I'd want to know if my husband was fooling around. I just don't know what to do or say. You and I being their mentors, what are we going to do about this situation? God did His part by having Mary there to answer that call.

REVEREND PETERS: That's why I tend to believe that it's going to be all right.

SISTER JOHNSON: Well, what did you tell Carl to do, Reverend... besides pray?

REVEREND PETERS: That was and still is a difficult answer. Knowing Sister Tracy as I do, it doesn't leave me with a lot of leeway. I just don't see a common ground to this situation. I pray for answers and God's intervention to this matter.

SISTER JOHNSON: So you're just like the rest of us. I thought you, being the preacher, would have come up with some divine answer.

REVEREND PETERS: Sometimes we aren't always deep enough to receive an assessment of the outcome. That's why I'm exploring the idea of talking to sister Tracy and brother Carl together, or talking to sister Tracy alone regarding this matter. I'm not quite ready to tackle that forthright. I'm sort of afraid to do something as much as do nothing. Even though I have known for a few weeks, this day made me realize the urgency of the matter at hand and I'm still in a dilemma on how to select the right course. They all seem unsafe and equally dangerous right now in my eyes.

SISTER JOHNSON: In other words, I guess you're saying we're gonna have to burn the midnight oil on this one, so to speak.

REVEREND PETERS: Yes, *(Pauses)* Sister Johnson, I feel that as a minister I should have enough wisdom to be able to find some solace to this situation. However, I don't.

SISTER JOHNSON: I think we both are too close to the situation. We saw these kids grow up every day of their lives. You're human, Reverend, with weaknesses and faults just like all of us, even though at times we all depend on your spiritual wisdom and knowledge to salvage our situations.

REVEREND PETERS: I surely have been searching and praying for it! I kind of feel bad I haven't found it yet. That doesn't mean you need to give up on me. Maybe this is God's answer - Job's patience. I must be going, Sister Johnson.

They both rise from the table. Sister Johnson takes his bowl and puts it in the sink.

REVEREND PETERS: *(Looking around in the house)* You know, Sister Johnson, I haven't been in this house for quite some time, since your late husband Theodore went to be with the Lord. *(Looking around)* I just didn't remember how lovely your home was.

SISTER JOHNSON: *(Teasing)* Why, thank you, Reverend! You haven't seen it all. *(Playing)* You want to see the bedrooms?

REVEREND PETERS: *(Smiling)* In some sort of way you're going to tongue-tie me, aren't you, Sister Johnson?

SISTER JOHNSON: More like hog-tie you! *(Both smiling)*

They are both near the front door.

REVEREND PETERS: I definitely enjoy talking to you. I think you're wise, intelligent, talented and the best cook I know. Sometimes your rawness and bold behavior can be intimidating. I'm still somewhat old-fashioned.

SISTER JOHNSON: *(Teasing)* So am I, Reverend! I believe that skirts are too high, bras are too few and pants are too tight. Yet, the well-dressed men and supposedly upstanding citizens I see are still rooting for more short skirts and tight pants. *(Teasing like always)* What must I do? Stay a sweet-old fashioned girl with love, and joy *(Making him nervous)* keeping my imagination in chastity... until I get lucky? You sure aren't like your daddy... though I can see a little of him in you.

REVEREND PETERS: *(Smiling)* I tell you, Sister Johnson, you're something else but a treat to know!

SISTER JOHNSON: Am I too much of a treat?

They are both standing in front of the screen door.

REVEREND PETERS: *(Smiling)* Don't you and Sister Mary worry! I think the end results will turn out fine. Sometimes the worth of the lesson learned can heal the scars.

SISTER JOHNSON: Very well spoken, Reverend.

Reverend Peters opens the screen door and walks onto the porch.

SISTER JOHNSON: *(Looking from inside her screened door - still playing)* Reverend, I have a question to ask you.

REVEREND PETERS: *(Stops on the porch and turns around toward her)* Sure!

SISTER JOHNSON: *(Beginning to tongue-tie him again)* How much do you like my sweet potato cobbler?

REVEREND PETERS: Why? You're going to make me a whole one?

SISTER JOHNSON: I might!

REVEREND PETERS: *(Clearing his throat)* Sister Johnson, if your cobbler is on the menu that's what I'd choose. Why?

SISTER JOHNSON: I'm just trying to make a comparison.

REVEREND PETERS: To what?

SISTER JOHNSON: Well, *(Playing and looking him straight in the eye)* if I'm as good as my cobbler, will I be at the top of the menu?

Reverend Peters looks at Sister Johnson, smiles, turns around and walks off the porch.

REVEREND PETERS: Good day, Sister Johnson!

Three days later... Mary and Jessie's living room...

Jessie and Mary are in their living room on the couch dressed in pajamas and listening to jazz music before going to bed. Jessie is lying down with his eyes occasionally closed and his head on Mary's lap. Time after time he looks up into her face and her eyes would also occasionally be closed. At times, they catch one another and reward the other with a smile and a gentle kiss. Mary does not catch Jessie one time as he stares briefly and curiously wondering about her solemn-looking behavior all evening. Suspecting something is bothering her, it causes his own conscious to rattle like it has been lately at the slightest thing. He thinks to himself that it may be about his trip to Pontiac. He silently prays not to let that be her reason.

Mary, eyes closed, is listening to the music, still trying to sort out in her head the events of a few days ago. She is still stunned and confused, and finds it hard to believe the phone call... how it all took place with her being there and Tracy being in the bathroom at the time of the call. How strange the timing was of her intercepting the phone call intended for Tracy. Her spiritual belief was that God placed her there at that time to receive the call instead of Tracy. God did not want to break Tracy's heart.

Mary is now sure that it was Mary Alice's voice she heard after she had time to think about it and put two and two together. She believes she should not tell Tracy about Carl cheating on her, whether it is true or not. Yet, it is her best friend and she believes Tracy would tell her if she knew Jessie had cheated on her. But knowing Tracy like she does, it could be very dangerous for Carl and Mary Alice, for sure.

How could Carl do that to them after all they have been through in the last few years? she thinks to herself. She is angry and disappointed in him. It flashes through her mind briefly and has her wondering if Jessie had ever cheated on her. At that moment, she feels a hurt in her heart. She looks down into his face tenderly and wonders if he knows about Carl and Mary Alice. She knows how they hide very little between them, just like she and Tracy.

Mary opens her eyes and catches Jessie staring at her.

JESSIE: *(Nervously concerned)* Everything okay, honey? It's as if you haven't been here today.

MARY: *(Hesitating...looking straight into his face, and then blurting it out)* JESSIE BARFIELD!!! Did you know Carl and Mary Alice had sex?

JESSIE: *(Stunned and relieved at the same time)* How do you know?

MARY: Ohhh... so you did know! How could he do that to Tracy? *(More upset)* If you knew, have you been cheating, too?

JESSIE: *(Rises from her lap, grasping his hands)* Come on! Is that what you think? That's how little faith you have in me?

MARY: *(Puts her hand over his hand and apologizes)* I'm sorry. I'm truly crazy and angry right now.

JESSIE: *(Lifts Mary up from the couch and hugs her)* It's okay, honey, let's go to bed.

END OF SCENE EIGHT

ACT II

SCENE NINE

Rabbit finds out about Jessie's use of heroin and confronts him...

It is late on Wednesday evening. Side Street is deserted. All the residences have called it a day. The businesses are closed, except for the neon light over the bar and poolroom entrance which is open. From the opposite end of the street, Rabbit appears from around the bend onto Side Street. He's intoxicated. As he slowly walks past the barber and beauty shops and the church, he comes to a halt at the end of Sister Johnson's porch, near Jessie and Mary's stairwell. Without respect to anyone, in a slow drag Rabbit is speaking annoyingly loud.

RABBIT: Jessie! Hey, Jessie! I want to talk to you right now! Come on out here!

The lights from Carl and Tracy's home come on.

RABBIT: *(Again)* Jessie, I want to talk to you.

The lights in Jessie and Mary's house come on. As Tracy comes out the front door, Carl follows close behind.

TRACY: Man, you done lost your mind - out here screaming like a nut at this time of night!

RABBIT: *(Paying no attention to Tracy)* Jessieeee, you in there?

CARL: *(Irritated)* Hey, man, why don't you cool it? Take it somewhere else!

RABBIT: Why don't you and your old lady go back in the house?

CARL: *(More irritated)* Why don't you take that crap somewhere else like I said?

RABBIT: Why don't you come off that porch and make me?

Carl starts walking and Tracy gets in front of him blocking him from coming off the porch. At that same moment Jessie and Mary come onto their porch. Jessie is dressed in his night wear of boxer shorts.

TRACY: Rabbit, you aren't doing anything but stirring up trouble!

RABBIT: I'm calling for Jessie. You're the one coming out on your porch being nosy.

TRACY: Why don't you go before a ruckus starts?

RABBIT: Who wants to start a ruckus with me? Your old man? Tell him to come on. Let me see if his old man taught him anything. *(Looking up at Jessie)* Jessie, I've got to talk to you right now!

By this time, Sister Johnson has come out onto her porch. Luella and Francine and some of the other tenants in the building are leaning out their windows. A few stragglers have come out of the bar and poolroom. Housecoat Pearl, looking out the window and straining to see and hear what is going on, pulls her head back in. Seconds later she appears out of her front door in her signature robe with a baseball bat in her hand as she walks toward the "carrying on." Jessie hurries down the stairs as Carl furiously pulls away from Tracy and comes off the porch to confront Rabbit, only to be met by Housecoat Pearl with her bat over her shoulder, ready to use it.

HOUSECOAT PEARL: Somebody better act like they got some sense if they don't want a knot upside their head. You know I ain't lying!

Tracy pulls Carl back onto their porch. Mary continues to stand at the top of the stairwell.

JESSIE: *(Approaches Rabbit angrily)* What are you doing, man? Why are you out here disturbing the neighborhood at this time of night?

RABBIT: *(Showing signs of anger)* We've got to talk right now. I ain't leaving this street 'til we do.

HOUSECOAT PEARL: *(Holding the bat back on her shoulder)* This bat says you're going someplace!

JESSIE: What's so important for you to say to me?

RABBIT: *(Walking away)* Meet me in the poolroom in ten minutes. If you don't, I'll be back here doing the same thing and I ain't scared of Miss Pearl's bat. *(Housecoat Pearl walking behind Rabbit)*

HOUSECOAT PEARL: That's what they all said before they went to the hospital.

As Rabbit walks toward the poolroom, he turns around once to see where Miss Pearl is, knowing Pearl's reputation with the bat, before he goes into the poolroom. Pearl turns around and goes into her building.

JESSIE: I better go and get some clothes on and see what he wants before he comes back again.

CARL: *(Speaking to Jessie)* We'll see you in the morning. If you need me, I'm here for you, my brother.

JESSIE: Thanks, man!

Jessie heads up the stairs wondering what Rabbit wants to talk to him about that is so important. He and Mary go into the house. The street is deserted once again. The poolroom is empty except for Big Hank, his two partners, the poolroom manager and Rabbit.

Rabbit is at a pool table shooting balls alone. Big Hank is sitting with the manager counting receipts. His other two partners are sitting on stools near the front door. A few moments later the front door beeps and Jessie walks in. He goes to the table where Rabbit is and grabs a pool stick. Big Hank senses something in the air and stops what he is doing as he watches Jessie and Rabbit. (The room is so quiet you can hear a pin drop).

JESSIE: *(Speaking to everyone)* What's happening!

Showing signs of anger Rabbit tosses his pool stick on the table. He looks disgustedly at Jessie, catching him and everyone else off-guard.

RABBIT: You ain't no better than me, man!

JESSIE: *(His gut is churning on the inside)* What are you talking about, man?

Big Hank catches Jessie looking at him, shrugs his shoulders in question as if this is also his first time hearing this.

RABBIT: You know what I'm talking about. You can't hide it any more. I know man. I know. *(Sounding depressed)* I know, man. I know!

JESSIE: *(Knotting up on the inside and trying to keep a straight face)* What is it you know? Tell me!

Everyone's attention is now on Rabbit and Jessie.

RABBIT: *(Exploding)* You're using, man!

There is a brief moment of silence as the shock wave saturates the room.

JESSIE: *(Somewhat in a panic shock)* Where you come off with that, man?

RABBIT: *(Not looking at Jessie, walking around the pool table very upset)* You're using! You're using! Jessie, I know you're using!

JESSIE: *(Defending the salvation of his world)* Is somebody lying to you?

RABBIT: *(Sadly)* Naw, man! You're the one lying. Ain't nobody lying but you!

Jessie is thinking to himself and wondering how Rabbit could have known for sure. He has never used around any of his friends or associates. Jessie sticks to his lie. Big Hank and his staff continue to watch and listen in somewhat of a confused state as Jessie walks towards the side of the pool table where Rabbit is standing.

JESSIE: Why are you listening to hearsay? What have I done to you to make you believe what someone else says?

Rabbit avoids Jessie's approach while looking upset. He gets to the opposite end of the table, stops, reaches in his shirt pocket, pulls a 4x5 picture out of his pocket and throws it on the pool table toward Jessie.

RABBIT: *(Angrily)* Do you know what this is, man?

JESSIE: *(Somewhat confused, picks up the picture, looks at it questionably)* It's a picture of our senior high school basketball team.

RABBIT: It just so happens that an associate of mine stopped by my house a few days ago. While he was there, he noticed a bigger picture of that same picture you're holding which was hanging on the wall. *(Looking at Jessie straight in the eyes)* He just so happened to pick you out of the lineup as a person who he had seen recently with another guy.

JESSIE: And that's your case for accusing me - a basketball picture of us and what some guy said to you?

RABBIT: *(Emotionally sad)* I wanted to hit him, Jessie, for accusing you. I swear I was about to hurt him. I gave you all kind of ways not to be the one, but he picked you out of our graduation picture and yearbook too. Man, he blew me away! You may as well admit it, man. It was you.

JESSIE: There are people in prison, especially black people, because of mistaken identity.

A look of disbelief begins to reflect on the other faces in the room. Rabbit, somewhat teary, still starring at Jessie, pulls from his shirt pocket another 4x5 picture and throws it on the pool table toward Jessie.

RABBIT: I still could have been easily convinced that it wasn't you but that picture, *(Pointing at the one he just threw on the pool table)* confirmed you.

JESSIE: *(Looking at the picture)* This is the picture I sent you of me a year or so ago while I was in service.

RABBIT: Who are the other two guys in the picture with you?

JESSIE: Roosevelt and Calloway - my Army buddies! We were on the front line together.

RABBIT: You know I have pictures all over the house of us in sports. That picture you're holding is a picture of my best friend (you), Roosevelt and Calloway in 'Nam. *(Sadly)* My associate just happened to see it and pointed out your friend Roosevelt as the person you were with at the time you all were up there in Pontiac at the dope house.

You could hear pins dropping on cotton. There is a sadness of expressions in the room from everyone as Rabbit (teary-eyed) continues...

RABBIT: *(Standing face to face in front of Jessie, with the tears running down his face)* All this time I've been trying real hard to quit because of you Jess. I couldn't wait 'til you came home. I knew deep down in my heart if anyone could help me, it was you, Jess. I'd listen to you, man. I looked up to you, man - more than anyone. I named my son after you. You're my idol, Jess. I believed I was going to make it and I was doing good, man - all because of you. This really killed me!

Silence fills the room.

JESSIE: *(Breaks down emotionally)* I'm sorry I hurt you and anyone else Rabbit. I'm truly, truly sorry. I had hoped no one would've found out - especially you, my family *(Looking around)* and my friends. I'm so sorry. I'm sorry most for betraying the faith, trust and love everyone had in me. *(Pauses - A tear falls as he continues to talk to Rabbit)* I have no excuse and nothing I say can change this moment or change the way you're feeling. I wish there was something I could do. Oh God, how I wish there was something I could do! I have prayed every night since that time in Pontiac that this moment would never happen. I know it won't be the same between us but you're still my friend and I believe you can and will make it one day, my man. *(As Jessie walks toward the door, he continues speaking)* I can't stop anyone from talking. I just hope you give me a chance first.

Jessie leaves the poolroom. There is silence. Rabbit is still at the pool table stunned and staring at the door as it closes behind Jessie.

Big Hank, standing at the bar, speaks up...

BIG HANK: I sure wouldn't want to have been through what that boy has been through in the last few years. He's lost both his wife's mother and father and his wife's best friend's mother and father at the same time. He went to a war where he had to kill human beings to save his own soul in support of his country. Jessie never has been one for violence. Then he comes home to all this mess. He thought you were in college, Nicholas. No one ever told him about you and drugs because they knew how much it would have hurt him. Yet he comes home and still tries to help. He was doing a good job, too, I might add. That's what I call a friend - overlooking himself for a friend. It's getting late. I'll see y'all later.

END OF SCENE NINE

ACT II

SCENE TEN

Weeks later - Mary and Tracy prepare for Jessie's homecoming party...

Friday afternoon sitting on Tracy's porch, Mary and Tracy are blowing up the last of the twenty-five balloons as they rub their jaws. Up and down Side Street other decorations are already up. We can see all the proprietors; Bernie's, Cousin Bee's, the salon, the bar, the beauty and barber shops, and the laundromat putting up preparations for tomorrow's street party.

TRACY: Whew! I don't think I could blow up one more balloon.

MARY: *(Full of glee)* Isn't it wonderful - us all together again?

Dressed nicely, Sister Johnson comes around the bend onto Side Street. She carries a shopping bag in one hand and a purse in the other. She waves as she sees Tracy and Mary sitting on the porch. She walks past her house and stops at Tracy's porch and sits the bag down between them.

SISTER JOHNSON: These are some things I got from work - I thought we could use them. There are paper plates, napkins, plastic cups, utensils and paper and ribbons for hanging. No need to spend money. Lord, let me rest these feet before they decide to act ugly on me.

Sister Johnson sits on one of the steps that leads up to Mary's place and takes off her shoes, stretches her legs out and sighs.

TRACY: Talking about no need to spend money, Carl and Jessie will be getting their first full paychecks. Now we all know they're going to celebrate. I just hope they bring some money home if they don't want to see some ugly sisters.

MARY: *(Pulling stuff out of the bag)* Isn't that the truth? That little money they're getting, since they haven't had any in a long time is going to make them think they're rich tonight! Shoot, I'll bet you that they think they own the whole world with that paycheck they're getting today. *(Seriously joking)* Carl might come home with a brand new car if he can convince them to finance him. You know I'm not lying! Right, Tracy?

TRACY: *(Smiling)* Who you telling? If you say something to him about it he'll tell you in a minute - proudly.

MARY and TRACY: *(Speaking in unison)* A fool and his money will soon part!

TRACY: Girl, Jessie is just as bad. He'll spend money on just about anything you don't need. I bet you have more new unused stuff that he has bought... more than anyone in the neighborhood. You all are the only ones that I know *(Laughing)* with an electric can opener and an electric shoe shine kit. Now, you know that's lazy white folks' gadgets.

MARY: *(Laughing)* He's just trying to make living a little bit easier for me. That's why he bought me a secondhand vacuum cleaner - to vacuum wood and linoleum floors. Our men want us to be ghetto rich!

TRACY: You mean ghetto fabulous. Look at that so-called mink coat Carl paid some shyster fifty dollars for believing it was real mink. I sure was fine in it *(Laughing)* until that time it rained and the coat got wet. When it dried, it was shedding mink all over the floor.

SISTER JOHNSON: *(Laughing)* Don't get too upset at them for wanting you all to have the good things in life. They're showing their appreciation any way they can while keeping their dreams alive.

MARY: All Carl and Jessie have been through - I don't think anything can stop them from dreaming.

SISTER JOHNSON: You all can because you're the foundation of their dreams. Your smiles each day are their building blocks. You make them feel rich. Your deep love is their flowers and sunshine. Remember, you two are your men's lifelines.

TRACY: Right on, Sister Johnson! Our men know they can depend on us. We've been our men's backbone ever since I don't know when. I guess since when we *(Smiling)* first stole our mamas' pies and shared our lunches in elementary, junior, and senior high school when they had none.

As Tracy speaks very highly of Carl and Jessie, the thought of Carl's alleged infidelity causes Mary and Sister Johnson to pause and make brief eye contact with each other.

MARY: Right on, sister! We are and will always be the best thing that ever happened to them. *(Sassy)* When they go to bed we make them feel like kings and millionaires when they wake up.

TRACY: *(Tracy and Mary hug each other)* Right on, sister!

SISTER JOHNSON: And don't you girls forget to keep making them feel that way!

TRACY: Sister Johnson, we love our men better than hogs love slop and preachers love fried chicken, fatback and collard greens!

SISTER JOHNSON: *(Thinking)* I tell you, having this party may be something that we all need around here. It's something to keep lifting our spirits.

TRACY: If this good energy keeps flowing, and it keeps our men working, that will keep my spirits lifted.

MARY: I'll say "Amen" to that and if you throw a baby, in I couldn't ask for more.

TRACY: I'll second that! This party is beginning to be exciting. I remember when we were young. Folks around here used to have these kinds of street parties all the time.

MARY: *(Thinking)* The last party we had on this street we must have been dancing with our mamas and Brother Theodore was dancing with you, Sister Johnson.

TRACY: Folks were barbequing and fish frying in those big old tin tubs. It's a wonder we're not fat today with all that food we ate at those street parties. You know, I don't ever remember anybody acting too big a fool either!

MARY: With Mr. Ernest, our daddies, Brother Theodore and Uncle Buck, who would be fool enough to act up? *(Thinking)* Lord, I hope no one tries to act up.

TRACY: Girl, don't you start that worrying. With Carl, Jessie, their buddies, Big Hank and his folks and Uncle Buck, we're still tough. It will be just like back in the day.

MARY: I sure wish Rabbit and Carl would make up from that episode last month. You know Rabbit is coming to the party even though he doesn't come around like he used to.

SISTER JOHNSON: For the sake of me, I still don't know why that boy acted the way he did that night. Do y'all?

MARY: Jessie never said what happened in the poolroom that night. He says it was all a misunderstanding. I asked Jessie the other day why Carl and Rabbit still don't speak. He just says to give it time. Still no telling what may happen when Rabbit comes. Those were pretty rough exchanges going on between him and Carl.

TRACY: Quit worrying. Nothing's going to happen, but I do hope Rabbit comes to the party with some sense. Now, as far as them making up I hope they do so soon. They've been friends almost all their lives. You all know how stubborn Carl is. Rabbit really disappointed him and I can assure you that Carl is not thinking about making up with Rabbit.

SISTER JOHNSON: Y'all still young. If Carl did not care he wouldn't be so angry at Nicholas. We all have had people whom we appreciated so much that at one time or another they *(Thinking)* disappointed us. *(Pauses)* When I was y'all's age and younger, I had a real good friend… she was my best friend - close like you two.

MARY: What was her name?

SISTER JOHNSON: Rose Lee Bauroppi. I thought so much of that girl. She and I grew up together, lived in the same neighborhood and went to the same schools. She used to eat at our house all the time and practiced church songs with my older brother, Louis, who was our church pianist. We both sang in the church choir. Lord that girl's voice was so beautiful, it could make you cry. Everyone knew that Rose's voice would one day make her famous and I couldn't wait 'til she became famous so I could proudly say she was my friend.

TRACY: Are you making this up, Sister Johnson? It sure sounds similar to Carl, Jessie and Rabbit.

SISTER JOHNSON: It's the truth. I remember I was graduating from high school that summer. Rose was a year older and had finished high school a semester before me. A few weeks after my graduation, Rose was hired by this gospel promoter *(Pauses)* to go on a three-month gospel crusade as a soloist with some of the biggest gospel performers in the country at that time. She was getting a nice salary and all her expenses were paid, including paying for her to have two background singers travel with her. I just knew I was going to be one of them. *(Pauses)* Do you know she didn't pick me?

MARY: Why didn't she pick you if you were her best friend?

SISTER JOHNSON: I didn't know until years later. I tell you I was so hurt and mad at that girl! I knew I couldn't sing as well as she could but I was pretty good and she knew I could sing better than the ones she had chosen. I just didn't understand. I cried and cried over that. I was so mad at that girl that I never wanted to see or talk to her ever again. To make matters worse, she would write me letters while she was out there like nothing had ever happened. I would hear how she was packing churches and halls. I was so fed up with hearing about her that I asked my mama and daddy if I could come to Detroit and stay with Daddy's sister, Aunt Caroline, for the summer. They said "yes" and I came out here, got a job and stayed.

TRACY: Whatever happened to Rose?

SISTER JOHNSON: The last two weeks of her tour my brother Louis called and told me that she had gotten sick and came home. Wasn't anything wrong with that girl except she was pregnant! At first I was selfishly glad because she didn't take me with her, but then I began to feel sorry for her because it might ruin her career. She had a lot on her shoulders then with all those people believing in her.

TRACY: What happened after that?

SISTER JOHNSON: It turned out the man who got her pregnant was a young preacher from Tennessee. Anyway, a few weeks later they got married and she moved to Tennessee where he lived. I reckon getting married and having a baby changed her mind about becoming a star. She seemed happy being a preacher's wife. Sure disappointed a lot of people but she still traveled from time-to-time doing gospel crusades and with her husband in his ministry. It ended her career as a famous star and they wound up having twelve children.

MARY: Wow! That sure was a lot of babies. Did you ever forgive her?

SISTER JOHNSON: I did and still do whenever we talk. I eventually realized that my dislike of her was based on anger, hurt and disappointment because of my own selfishness. There was nothing in this world I have ever wanted more than seeing my friend thrilling all those people and becoming a star, with me singing background.

TRACY: Did you all ever become friends again?

SISTER JOHNSON: Yes, we got back to our friendship. It took me years trying to make up with her. As a matter of fact, I spoke with her on the phone the other evening.

MARY: You still haven't told us her reason for not choosing you to be a background singer.

SISTER JOHNSON: I'm still ashamed to this day to say. The only reason I'm telling you this now is because of friendship, hurt and misunderstanding. We made up right here in Detroit about three years later. There was a big summer gospel revival going on here and Rose was one of the main attractions at the revival. Our back-home gospel choir was also performing and was going to do background for Rose. During the same time my Mama and Daddy had come here to visit with me and Aunt Caroline. My brother Louis was here with the church choir. *(Pauses)* By that time Rose knew I was living in Detroit. Like I said, I had forgotten all about being upset with her and I had this chance to see her perform for the first time since the times we sang in our church choir. Even though the revival had been going on for a few days, Louis and the choir and Rose were not going to perform until the last two days. Louis stayed with us the whole time in Detroit. It was a few days before their performance. *(Pauses)* Louis, Mama, Daddy and Aunt Caroline were sitting down in the living room chatting. I had just finished washing dishes and came in to sit down. There was a moment of silence and then Louis spoke. He wanted to tell me something before Rose and I met and I found out the truth. I liked to have died when he told me that Rose did want me to sing with her and had told Louis to ask Mama and Daddy. Because of what Louis told them from his experiences regarding all the things that go on out there on those revivals and crusades, it made Mama and Daddy not want me to go - which made a perfect case for them when Rose became pregnant. Child, I cried 'til my eyes had swollen as big as plums. I was so mad at them. I reckon if I could have said what I wanted to, I probably wouldn't be here today to tell about it. You didn't talk back to your parents like young folks do today, no matter how wrong they were. I just went into my room and stayed 'til Aunt Caroline came and got me.

MARY: Hummph! All this time you were mad at Rose for something she didn't do.

TRACY: You made up with her at the revival!

SISTER JOHNSON: That was one of our happiest moments. While I was in my room, Louis went and got Rose and brought her over. When I came out of the room and saw that girl we burst into tears, ran into each other's arms, hugged and cried like babies. I just kept apologizing to her. She told me how much she wanted to tell me but dared not, even though it meant losing our friendship. Every time we speak to each other we keep apologizing.

TRACY: Well, that is a story with a happy ending! I truly hope ours turns out okay, too.

SISTER JOHNSON: Wait! Let me tell you the good part. I sang background for her in my old back-home church choir. Then she and I sang a duet together and got a standing ovation but her singing alone had people crying and jumping for joy at the same time. They said that was the best performance she had ever given.

Page, the mail carrier, comes around the bend. He is not wearing his work uniform. He briefly opens the door of the beauty shop and yells...

PAGE: Y'all better look good when you come out. *(Seeing Sister Johnson, Tracy and Mary, he walks up and sits on Sister Johnson's porch steps.)* You must have lockjaw blowing up all those balloons.

MARY: We haven't seen you coming around to help.

PAGE: Now you know if I had known you needed help I would've come.

TRACY: Let's see how many times we've heard that lie. He's never around for work but always around when we fish frying or barbecuing. *(Mocking Page...)* "I just happened to be in the neighborhood." Your nose must be good for something other than knowing everybody's business.

MARY: You do have a reputation of always being around folks' place when food is done and never around when there is work to be done. *(Teasing)* One of these days someone is going to take offense at that and feed you the wrong thing. You know how you like to eat from anybody.

Being from Louisiana, Page believes in witchcraft.

PAGE: Hush your mouth! Don't you be giving people the wrong ideas! You know some folks around here believe in witchcraft and voodoo.

TRACY: Yeah! You're one of them! *(Everybody laughs)*

PAGE: Uh… uh! I just want to stay away from that kind of thing. I'm scared of it. I know what it can do!

SISTER JOHNSON: No more than what you let it. I come from Louisiana too.

Page reaches in his pocket and pulls out some money. He takes a twenty dollar bill from the money and hands it to Sister Johnson.

PAGE: Here is my portion, Sister Johnson. You all sure know how to change a man's appetite. I was going to Cousin Bee's for a sandwich - ain't hungry now. Tracy, got a Faygo in your refrigerator? Sure would like to have a nice cold one.

TRACY: *(Rising up from her chair)* You know you are truly worrisome sometimes. If it isn't food, it's a pop. *(She goes into the house for the pop)*

PAGE: I was hungry until Mary opened her big mouth talking about what folks can do to your food. You all haven't been putting mojo on me, have ya? You all have been feeding me for a long time.

MARY: If we had, you wouldn't be loafing right now. Your butt would be working. You better be worrying about those folks whose checks are always late and those you've been flirting and lying to. You think we don't know anything about that stuff.

PAGE: *(Teasing)* I don't know. Sister Johnson must have put something on some of these men around here. She got them eating out of her hand, including the Reverend.

Tracy pushes the screen door open with her body to get out. In her hands she has the soda pops, which she gives to each person.

MARY: *(Looking at Sister Johnson)* Page is right about you having some of these men folks wooing you, Sister Johnson, but I think it's because you're just one fine lady.

SISTER JOHNSON: Always remember - men howl at the moon!

TRACY: If I could conjure up something for Page, I would conjure him up a girlfriend, which he can't seem to get these days! *(They all laugh)*

PAGE: *(Defending himself)* No girlfriend? All the girls around here like me. I'm a player.

MARY: *(Teasing)* You too cheap to be a player! You are the cheapest man in town. All the women that you dated say they quit you because you're so cheap. They say you took them to the White Castle for dinner. You took so many women to the White Castle on dates they know you by your first name.

PAGE: I just happened to have dated women who loved the White Castle ambiance. *(Speaking to Tracy)* You and Carl got engaged there.

TRACY: *(Laughing)* You're lying, man. It was Big Boy!

PAGE: Same thing!

MARY: Every woman around here that you ever dated talks about you and your pocketbook.

PAGE: They still want me!

TRACY: They want your money. That's all. You're so cheap they think you got it stashed in old tin cans somewhere.

PAGE: I ain't cheap! It just so happens that the girls I date like hamburgers and fries instead of steak and baked potatoes.

SISTER JOHNSON: *(Getting in on the fun)* Now Page, I remember five or six years ago when you took my sister, Colleen, out on a date. You took her all the way to some club in Pontiac because it was ladies' night and drinks were half price for ladies and the place you all were at got raided while you all were eating. Y'all almost went to jail.

PAGE: That's the truth and we still had a good time!

SISTER JOHNSON: With all that went on that night, I don't know how in the world she could have had a good time but she said she did.

PAGE: *(Boastfully speaking)* That's because she was with me. I took her where the stars hung out. *(Smiling)* Said she had more fun with me than she ever had.

TRACY: Sister Johnson, is that your sister who has been and still is living with your Aunt and Uncle Bogads down in Tilda Swamps, Louisiana, population forty-nine?

SISTER JOHNSON: *(Shaking her head)* That's the one!

TRACY: Man, you could have taken her to Jack-In-The Box and let her see the clown jump out of that little box and she would have thought she had been to Disneyland. *(They all laugh)*

MARY: Tell us what stars she met if you took her to where they hung out.

PAGE: *(Seriously funny)* Let's see, she met-ahhh-Mr. Cool, Wino Willie, Big Shot, Razor Lee and his wife, Hammer Annie. She also met 44 Shirley, Double E Irene and John Horsey. *(Everybody is laughing at Page)*

MARY: Anyone ever heard of them?

TRACY: That's because he's lying!

PAGE: What are you talking about, Tracy? Those people are legends. She was so excited meeting them she took pictures with them. Tracy, Mary and Sister Johnson are smiling while shaking their heads.

SISTER JOHNSON: *(Laughing)* Stop fibbing on my sister like that!

PAGE: I'm not lying. The next time I come around I'll bring you a picture of her, John Horsey, 44 Shirley and Double E Irene all together. It was so rare I got one for myself. She took her picture back home. Said she wanted to let the folks down in Tilda Swamps see how big-city folks live. *(Everyone laughs)*

TRACY: Page, you're crazy!

MARY: We talk about how cheap he is but he has a brand new hog *(car)* every three or four years.

PAGE: *(Changing the subject)* Y'all heard yet?

EVERYONE: Heard what?

PAGE: Now, I promised I wouldn't tell anyone - especially y'all.

TRACY: Anyone who told you a secret must really want it to be broadcasted!

MARY: So what's the secret?

PAGE: Rabbit is in Chicago.

MARY and TRACY: In Chicago!

SISTER JOHNSON: What in the world is he doing in Chicago? He's in some kind of trouble?

PAGE: No ma'am. It's the opposite. His Muslim cousins from Chicago picked him up a few weeks ago. I heard Rabbit himself called them.

TRACY: I don't believe you.

MARY: I know he would have told Jessie if that was so. Who told you that gossip anyway? Probably some drunk from the bar!

PAGE: His mama told me. *(Pauses)* She was so happy even though Rabbit didn't want her to tell a soul - especially y'all. If there is anyone he wants to surprise, y'all know it's Jessie. His mama said she just had to tell someone.

TRACY: That all seems well. I just cannot understand why you?

MARY: I'm not telling a soul, but I'm going to see Mrs. Jones to find out if you're telling the truth.

TRACY: I'm with you!

PAGE: Now don't do that! She'll know I told you! She was just so happy for him she had to tell someone and that someone happened to be me. We all know how much of a disappointment it would be for Rabbit to know that his own mother broke her promise to him. If you can't trust your own mother, then who can you trust?

SISTER JOHNSON: Page, you aren't fibbing or gossiping are you? We know how carried away you get sometimes.

TRACY: What I can't see is why Mrs. Jones would tell a mailman a secret - especially this one?

PAGE: I've been holding this in for two days without telling anyone. I've been so excited about this. I just had to tell y'all. Mrs. Jones said Rabbit didn't want anyone to know because his cousins are going to set him up with this semi-pro football team after he gets himself together and he doesn't want anyone to know if he didn't make it. If he does, he wants to surprise everyone, especially Jessie for sticking by him. That's all!

SISTER JOHNSON: I guess we'll have to believe you.

MARY: I guess we will. I sure wouldn't want to tell Jessie that anyway. He would be so happy if Rabbit did surprise him. Outside of me having a baby, I think that would be the next happy thing for him and Carl, too.

TRACY: I'm glad you told us your story, Sister Johnson. Carl isn't mad at Rabbit for himself but for what he thinks he has done to the neighborhood. He'll be as happy as anybody.

Page finishes drinking his pop, stands, stretches and sits the empty pop bottle on the table next to the bannister.

PAGE: Well, I think I'll go up here to the poolroom and see which young buck thinks he can whup an old man for a few dollars today. What time Jessie and Carl getting home?

TRACY: Today is payday and your guess is as good as mine. They are supposed to be meeting with Ernest to pick up the fish, ribs and chicken for tomorrow. What time are you starting to barbeque?

MARY: They are supposed to take all three of us out for dinner this evening.

PAGE: *(Leaning on the bannister)* Hmmm, let's see... Ahhh, tomorrow afternoon, it's going to be mostly the church folks, non-drinkers and the kids. Ahhh... what time should I start? How about eleven-thirty? *(Strategizing)* Let's see, I'm only doing half my route so I should be finished and back here by ten o'clock. It's going to take me an hour and a half to make up the sauce and prepare everything. I think I'll prepare everything tonight.

MARY: We'll have the pits hot and ready for you when you get here and you better not be drinking in front of those church folks and children either. You can wait until after they leave.

SISTER JOHNSON: *(A sly smile)* Page, you're going to be in for a big treat tomorrow. Our senior choir is going to go up against the choir that Carl, Jessie and the girls are in. It's going to be exciting, don't you think?

PAGE: Y'all better be careful. Y'all don't know the senior choir like I do.

TRACY: We aren't saying anything. That's Carl and Jessie boasting.

PAGE: *(Walking away...)* You see how calm Sister Johnson is? I'll see you all tomorrow.

SISTER JOHNSON: Ain't that some good news about Rabbit?

MARY: Lord, I sure hope it's true. That will brighten this whole community up.

TRACY: Maybe he'll be our hero after all. I sure hope so!

MARY: So do all of us! *(The telephone is ringing in Tracy's house)*

TRACY: *(Getting up)* Now who can that be? I'll be right back. *(Tracy grabs the empty bottles and takes them with her into the house)*

MARY: Hope it's not more cross-town folks wanting to come tomorrow!

SISTER JOHNSON: Child, you could whisper and folks seem to be able to hear you when it comes to food. I believe they can smell the food before it starts cooking.

MARY: *(Laughing)* Don't you know it? *(Pausing)* Sister Johnson, this is going to be the most fun we've had in a long time. A street party-I almost feel like a kid on Christmas Eve.

SISTER JOHNSON: It sure is good for this community. We need a good uplifting around here. Look at the street decorations. The whole community is getting excited.

Tracy comes back on the porch.

TRACY: That was Carl on the phone. He says they are with Mr. Ernest at the meat packing plant. They'll be home in half an hour and want us all to be ready so they can take their baths and be ready to leave in an hour.

SISTER JOHNSON: *(Walking to her porch steps)* Well, I think I had better get going now if I'm going to be ready in an hour. You know it's going to take me a while.

TRACY: You don't need to fancy up. They're going to take us to some place where there's beer.

MARY: Where do you think that is?

TRACY: Your guess is as good as mine!

MARY: *(Rising)* I know I'm not going to put on my make-up and nice clothes to be taken to some bar with a pool table.

SISTER JOHNSON: *(Climbing the steps to her porch)* I don't think they would take an old lady to any old place.

TRACY: Oh, Sister Johnson! I almost forgot to tell you something. *(Smiling)* The fellas wanted to know if you would like for them to invite Reverend Peters along to keep the wolves from you.

SISTER JOHNSON: *(Opening her screen door)* What difference do the clothes make? A wolf is still a wolf. *(Everybody laughs)*

MARY: I say "Amen" to that. *(Grabbing the bag and some balloons)* Tracy, let's set this in your house and finish up in the morning.

TRACY: *(Opening her screen door)* Bring in what you've got in your hand. Jessie and Carl can do the rest when they get home and finish up with the decorations tomorrow. They never like the way we do it anyway. I guess that's another man thing.

Tracy goes into the house and Mary follows.

Next evening - The Street Party aftermath...

It is a warm early night and Side Street is nicely decorated from end to end in celebration of Jessie's recent return from Vietnam. A banner hangs across Jessie and Mary's porch which reads "WEL-COME HOME JESSIE". The street party has been going since early afternoon. All the businesses are closed except for The Well, which has a sign that reads "Invitation Only". Folks in festive behavior fashionably parade the street in colorful attire. The beat of music plays softly beneath human sound. Jessie and Mary are sitting with Carl and Tracy on their porch steps. Sister Johnson sits comfortably in a chair behind them on the porch. Carl and Jessie are drinking beer. Mary and Tracy are drinking pop.

SISTER JOHNSON: Lord, this has been a wonderful day. The weather was nice and we had plenty of food. The children had more fun than they have had in a long time and the rest of us folks today felt like children.

EVERYONE: Amen!

SISTER JOHNSON: I'm feeling good. You boys mind if I drink a beer with y'all?

CARL: *(Being sarcastic)* Sister Johnson, sometimes the way you say things to us makes me kind of believe there is a slight tail-wind behind it.

JESSIE: It does seem that way. *(Repeating Sister Johnson's question...)* "You boys mind." Now why would we mind giving you a beer?

MARY: Because she and her choir gave us a good shellacking!

TRACY: Ooh-whee! They're pretending to be cool but your choir slapped us - that's all! We got embarrassed because Carl, with his big mouth, kept bragging about taking advantage of senior citizens. I tell you, Sister Johnson, you all are bad... bad... bad.

SISTER JOHNSON: We did sound pretty good if I do say so myself. *(Teasing)* But I didn't know my children would forsake me over this.

MARY: We aren't forsaking you, Sister Johnson. That's our men who don't like to be outdone by women - that's all.

JESSIE: We didn't know you all was that good! I mean we've never seen you all perform like that in church. You all just blew us away with your soulful expressions - especially you, Sister Johnson.

CARL: *(Having fun)* Let's be honest about it. We underestimated you. Your coolness threw us off. We've known you almost all our lives and we've never seen you get down like you did today. I mean, in such a soulful expression. You all really should have been disqualified.

TRACY: *(Knowing how to shut Carl up)* Sister Johnson, don't make them any more sweet potato cobblers.

CARL: Okay, we'll accept defeat this time, but the fat lady has not finished singing yet. Next time we'll be ready.

Sister Johnson is grinning from ear-to-ear.

CARL: *(Somewhat speechless)* Did you all see her? How she... I mean... I couldn't believe it.

JESSIE: *(Looking at Sister Johnson)* For a minute, I'm not going to tell a lie, when you jumped up and started doing that shaking and strutting back and forth screaming I was about to come and get you before you hurt yourself.

TRACY: Folks would have jumped on you if you had interfered with that woman's performance.

Page comes out of The Well and walks in the direction where Jessie and everyone are sitting. He is dressed somewhat loudly.

PAGE: *(As he approaches)* Y'all, this sure is a nice affair. I haven't seen anyone this whole day not having a good time.

JESSIE: Hey, thanks for everything, man! You really helped to make it nice. What are they doing in The Well?

Carl is going into the house to get Sister Johnson a beer.

CARL: *(Looking at Page)* Man, you ought to open your own barbeque joint. I've never tasted ribs like yours. Now I do *(Pauses)* barbeque ribs myself but you're a better rib man than me. I'm getting a beer for Sister Johnson. Do you want one?

PAGE: Yeah! Give me a Stroh's if you have one. *(Speaking to Sister Johnson)* You sure deserve a drink behind that performance you put on today. *(Speaking to Jessie)* Awww, they aren't doing anything at The Well. Just listening to the jukebox and telling lies.

JESSIE: Who's all there?

PAGE: *(Replies)* Housecoat, Luella and Francine, Ernest, Samson, Pert and Ernestine.

SISTER JOHNSON: Bee must still be in the restaurant cleaning up after all the food I saw folks bringing from in there to set out on the tables.

PAGE: Many of the church members helped her clean up. They were finished before it got dark. If y'all want any more food, Ernest took the rest to the bar. There's plenty left. I'm telling you, you sure can tell when it's free. I've seen folks gain ten pounds.

MARY: Man, you haven't seen anybody gain ten pounds in that short period of time.

Sister Johnson is smiling and enjoying the moment.

PAGE: Sister Johnson, you've probably seen folks today that you haven't seen in years, huh? I've seen a few I haven't seen myself in years and I'm the mailman.

SISTER JOHNSON: I sure have. I tell you, I have enjoyed this day.

Carl comes onto the porch with four bottles of beer. He gives Sister Johnson her beer, Page, Jessie and keeps one for himself.

CARL: *(Joshing as he hands Sister Johnson a beer)* Are you sure you didn't have a few little nips earlier today?

TRACY: Women don't need no stimulants to whup men. I'm always beating you, 'til you start cheating.

CARL: Now just what can you beat me in that I don't let you beat me in?

MARY: *(Agreeing with Tracy)*... Ha!

TRACY: *(Looking at Carl)* Anything except for basketball, pool and maybe softball but everything else including roller skating, whist, tonk and checkers. You won't play me poker or dominoes anymore. Don't even comment because we know what you're going to say - you and Jessie.

TRACY and MARY: *(Mocking Carl and Jessie)* Let the truth be told, we let you win!

MARY: Jessie, Carl and Mr. Ernest cheat all the time in bid whist - giving each other signals or signs. *(Mary and Tracy mocking and demonstrating Carl's and Jessie's antics)*

MARY: You all are going to the club tonight!

TRACY: I don't have any money but my heart wants to go. *(Everybody laughs)*

PAGE: Speaking of Ernest, he may have hit the number this evening. He said he thinks he did.

CARL: That's one lucky man!

JESSIE: Mary, didn't you write and tell me a couple of years ago that he had hit really big?

MARY: Yeah, he did! I still don't know for how much but I know he bought a new car and paid cash. He paid off their house mortgage and fixed the café up.

TRACY: *(Sweet talking Page)* How much did he hit for, Page?

PAGE: He didn't play with me. Y'all know I won't take those kinds of bets. I'm a nickel and dime man. He played with Big Hank. *(Pauses)* There was a time I'd take those big bets years ago but no more.

CARL: Why? What happened?

PAGE: See, it's like this! Ninety-five percent of the folks around here are nickels and dimes players and when they get a hit, they can win for a hundred or two hundred dollars. I can handle that but those big bucks bettors - five, ten, fifty dollars - that's Big Hank's neighborhood.

TRACY: Those nickel and dimes add up to thousands of dollars when you finish counting.

PAGE: That's correct and all it takes is one or two hits like Ernest was doing the last few years and you're in a deep, deep hole. Someone like Big Hank, it won't bother his pockets none because he's got other activities to compensate, such as poker, blackjack, craps and roulette over at his Hasting Street house. Plus he's got the bookie joint and the poolroom up the street. I, on the other hand, don't have those kinds of resources. It happened to me only one time for me to know that I'm not in that league. You want to know something? Too much luck will kill a numbers man's business. Isn't that right, Sister Johnson?

SISTER JOHNSON: *(Smiling)* If you say so, Page. I don't know squat about numbers.

PAGE: *(Remembering)* Yeah! But your husband Theodore sure knew how to play.

MARY: *(Excited)* What happened?

SISTER JOHNSON: I believe Theodore hit the numbers once for a bit of money from Page.

PAGE: A bit! Now Sister Johnson, I had to take out a loan to pay that man off. I swore then that I'd always be a nickel and dime numbers man.

SISTER JOHNSON: I used to get so mad at that man for spending money playing those numbers. He always said that one day I'd be glad he played and when that day came he would quit. He was right on both accounts. Lord rest his soul, he never played numbers again.

TRACY: We remember you all bought us new bikes.

MARY: Yup, sure did and you fixed up your house - right?

CARL: How much did he hit for?

SISTER JOHNSON: *(Trying to remember)* Let me think! I can't say exactly how much but it was a nice piece of money. Page, you remember the number he played?

PAGE: 661! I won't ever forget that. That was one number that was more than my pockets and my bank account could handle.

JESSIE: *(Curious)* Wow! How does somebody come up with a number that they would put a big wager on?

PAGE: Hunches! It's called hunches and sometimes they pay off real good. Right, Sister Johnson?

SISTER JOHNSON: I guess you may be right. I guess that was what he had - a hunch. Theodore would ask me every day what my dream was and I'd tell him nothing because I never dream. Anyway, one morning I did have a dream. I remember it was something about us driving to Louisiana to visit my sister in the swamps and a crocodile chased me. I told him how scary and real the dream was. Now how he figured out what number to play is beyond me. *(Smiling at the memory)* I just know he came home that evening happy as a jay bird singing. At first I thought he had a nip or two but I didn't smell any liquor on him. He even brought home ribs from Bar-B-Q City. I tell you that sure was some good eating. When I asked him why he was so happy, he said I would know in time. Well, not quite a week later he came home one night and woke me up. He had a shopping bag in his hand. I remember him turning and shaking that bag all over the bed and Lord have mercy that was the most money I had ever seen in my life. He was the happiest man on this here earth. All he could say to me was "I told you one day."

PAGE: I tell you he taught me a lesson. From then on I never took more than I could afford to pay. You just can't beat luck.

JESSIE: You know who else is lucky? Carl. He used to win nearly every raffle and contest in school and church. He's won a TV, hi-fi stereo system, washer and dryer, camera, lawn mower. He also won tickets to football, baseball and basketball games. He's one lucky soul. Just last week at the new grocery store opening he won a year's supply of baby diapers.

MARY: *(Hugging Jessie and speaking to Tracy)* You better hurry up and get them or we may need them!

TRACY: How can you get babies with headaches and backaches? Everybody is laughing at the antics.

CARL: Jessie, you know that stuff they gave us in the Army? I slipped it in her coffee and pop. That's the only way I can control her.

TRACY: One of these days lightning is going to strike you for lying so much. As far as Carl being so lucky - he's just as unlucky. Like when he lost the camera, lawn mower, car and the washer. What good is a dryer when you're washing on a scrub board?

PAGE: Say what you want, *(Getting up)* I still say no one can beat luck. I'm a witness. *(Walking away)* I think I'm going back to The Well. Thanks for the beer. *(He walks on up the street and into The Well)*

Sister Johnson is drinking her beer.

CARL: You know I've won way more than I've lost. Shoot, look at all the money and stuff I've won while I was out of work. *(Speaking to Jessie)* Man, they've been living like queens while you were in 'Nam - her and Mary *(Everybody laughs)*

TRACY: You're one crazy man - that's all I can say.

CARL: She wouldn't know what to do without me. *(Everybody laughs)*

MARY: I wonder what we'd do if we had that much money.

JESSIE: I know what I'd do. First I'd pay off all our debts, help out my brother and sister and Mama. *(Meaning Carl, Tracy and Sister Johnson)* Then I'd buy us a car and you *(Mary)* some fine clothes and me some too. I'd take all of us on a trip, maybe to the Bahamas or Hawaii. The rest I'd put away for the baby and our future.

CARL: Now if I had that kind of money I'd do the bill thing for all of us like Jess says. Then I'd buy us a brand spanking new hog *(car)* - black on black in black.

TRACY: We're going to be broke!

CARL: *(Continuing)* Wait now, I'm not finished. Then I'm going down on the Avenue and buy me the clothes I want without looking at the price, then...

TRACY: *(Chiming in on Carl's conversation)* We're going to be broke!

CARL: *(Continuing)* Maybe me, Jessie and Page will open us up a rib joint and call it "Nothing but the Truth Bar-B-Q".

TRACY: Again, we're going to be broke! What about me?

CARL: It's all for you, baby. I was saving the best for last. I'm going to let you go and buy whatever you want. You can get a mink coat - whatever your heart desires. Then I'm going to send you, Mary and Sister Johnson on a month's vacation, maybe to Texas, to visit with my dad and aunt, then to Louisiana and Alabama to visit y'all's kin folks. Y'all can drive my hog.

TRACY: We'll definitely be broke by then.

CARL: No, we'll have plenty left!

MARY: Oh no! Nobody wants to visit relatives with that kind of money. They're just going to beg you for some and your daddy - he likes to hug and talk too much.

TRACY: Don't anybody want to go stay with your dad and aunt! Why don't you go? Furthermore, if we had any kind of money do you think I'd leave and leave you here with money? You must be crazy. I'm scared to send you to the bank with my checks.

MARY: Nobody said anything about a house. What about a house?

CARL: What about a house? We've got a house.

TRACY: Man, I don't know why I'm going to ask you this but I am. Don't you want to buy a nice house and move someplace else? Since you always acting like money grows on trees anyway. What about that?

MARY: Is that the way you feel, Jessie?

Jessie is looking up and down the street noticing his friends.

JESSIE: I never thought much about it. This neighborhood is where our friends live, parents lived and where I met you. Then there is our guardian angel, Sister Johnson.

SISTER JOHNSON: Don't worry about me. I'll be fine. If I get too lonely, I'll sell my house and move closer to y'all.

CARL: Why does everybody want to move when they get a little money anyway? If I had the kind of money you all talking about and thought I was rich, I'd be richer here than I'd be someplace else. That kind of money someplace else is just ordinary and I would just be ordinary. But here with that kind of money, I'd be looked up to. Folks would call me cool breeze. Little snotty-nosed kids would run up to me and I'd buy them ice cream - take them for rides in my hog *(car)*. I'll make sure they have a good Thanksgiving and Christmas. With that kind of money in this neighborhood, I'd be rich!

JESSIE: Right on, my brother, right on!

CARL: *(Getting pumped up)* In other neighborhoods the kids' parents would tell their children... *(Imitating)* "You all stay away from those strange acting folks always trying to act nice." *(Looking around he stands, pulls out a wad of money from his pocket)* This is where I'm appreciated. With or without money I'm the same.

Luella, Francine, Ernest, Pearl, Ernestine and Page come out of The Well headed towards Sister Johnson, Carl and Jessie's house. Carl goes into the house. A few seconds later music is heard from within as he comes back onto the porch. He pulls Tracy onto the sidewalk and they begin dancing in the street. They are the main attraction momentarily then Jessie and Mary join them. Sister Johnson surprises everyone by getting up and dancing and Page joins her and soon everyone is dancing.

END OF SCENE TEN

ACT II

SCENE ELEVEN

Teamsters' strike / Mary is pregnant / Labor meeting ...

It is late September and the leaves have begun to serenade the trees with their many earth tones of colors. A crisp of chill highlights the mornings and evenings this time of year. Soon the evening daylight will concede defeat to the night.

The nationwide strike by the Teamsters Union has crippled the nation. Every business that depended on trucks and other Teamsters' operations has shut down, including automobile manufacturers. Many people are laid off from their jobs. The inner-city communities across America were the hardest hit. Blacks were the first to be laid off in many of the job markets and there have been substantiated reports of an underground network secretly letting whites know where jobs were available. Today the community leaders will be coming together to speak of the present job crisis, its effect on the community, and offer help, encouragement and support to many of the laid-off workers and their families. Carl and Jessie are also laid off because of the Teamsters' strike and are among those who will be attending the rally.

It is Friday morning and the coolness of the weather is a sign that winter is nearing. Tracy is at work at Hudson's department store and Mary is off today because of a doctor's appointment. Today is Sister Johnson's day off. Carl and Jessie are once again out looking for work. They were only working a few months and their job future looked very promising before the strike. It was looking so good that Carl had bought a late model used car and Jessie bought a new stereo system and television. They are now behind in their payments.

Mary comes from around the bend wearing a blazer and dressed fashionably, Detroit style. Carrying her purse over her shoulder, she waves and speaks to the familiar faces as she walks towards her house. She stops at Sister Johnson's, goes up the steps and sits in the swing on the porch.

MARY: *(Sighs)* Sister Johnson, I'm back!

Christine and Annie Mae come out of the beauty shop. Seeing Mary sitting on Sister Johnson's porch, they wave and approach her.

CHRISTINE and ANNIE MAE: Heyyy!

MARY: Hey. Y'all's hair sure is looking good. Y'all must have a little money today. I sure could have used some of that as hard as times are.

CHRISTINE: Girl, if we had known you'd be home, we would've come to you and saved ourselves some of those dollars. We both thought you and Tracy were at work and we couldn't wait 'til you all got off. We had to get cute for the gathering here this afternoon. Going to be some cute men there!

MARY: What gathering are you talking about?

ANNIE MAE: You haven't heard. They're having a big community meeting right here on Side Street later on today.

MARY: What meeting and about what?

Sister Johnson comes out of the house and gives Mary a cup of hot tea on a saucer.

SISTER JOHNSON: It's getting a little nippy today. Thought you might like some hot tea. Good morning, girls! I'm sorry to interrupt you, Christine, go ahead, hon.

CHRISTINE and ANNIE MAE: Morning, Mrs. Johnson!

CHRISTINE: *(Continuing)* We're telling Mary about the gathering here today and talking about how bad things are right now job wise. Girl, do you know that the whole community is out of work because of the Teamsters' strike?

ANNIE MAE: You mean the whole country. You know it's getting bad when elevator operators and gardeners are white people.

MARY: Now that's something! What time is the meeting? I sure hope Carl and Jessie will be back by then.

Page is seen coming out of Big Hank's poolroom and coming towards Mary.

CHRISTINE: I don't know. Do you know, Annie?

SISTER JOHNSON: If y'all talking about the meeting, here is Page, I'm sure he knows.

MARY: I know Jessie and Carl wouldn't want to miss this.

ANNIE MAE: Someone in the beauty shop said three o'clock this afternoon.

PAGE: Hey, everybody! What's going on? Y'all heard about the meeting this afternoon?

MARY: I was just asking about it. What time does it start?

PAGE: It's supposed to start at three o'clock but you can hope for three thirty and be thankful for four.

As Christine and Annie Mae begin to walk away...

CHRISTINE: Be seeing ya!

ANNIE MAE: Be seeing ya!

MARY: I knew it was pretty bad but it must be worse than I imagined.

SISTER JOHNSON: *(Sitting in the swing next to Mary)* I guess so, child - I reckon so.

PAGE: Nawww. The meeting is about trying to help some of these folks out around here during this strike. You know there are more of us out of work than is working.

MARY: *(Pulling her blazer closed as if she is cold)* It's getting a little cool. Won't be too much longer before winter is here. I can feel it.

PAGE: I almost forgot to tell y'all, so much is going on. Y'all should be the first to know.

MARY: Know what?

PAGE: I spoke with Rabbit's mother this morning.

MARY: *(Interrupting before he can finish)* He isn't hurt, is he? Is he okay?

PAGE: Let me finish. You're always jumping the gun.

MARY: I'm sorry. Go on.

PAGE: As I was saying, I spoke with Mrs. Jones this morning. She told me that Rabbit is doing really fine. But the good news is that he's coming home sometime soon for a week and he's got a surprise for everyone - especially for Jessie.

MARY: Ohhh, thank the Lord! Hallelujah! I cannot wait to tell Jessie and Carl and Tracy.

PAGE: Now there you go again. She's always jumping the gun.

MARY: Look who's talking! I bet Mrs. Jones told you not to tell anybody and look what just happened.

PAGE: I'm telling y'all only because of Jessie but I wouldn't tell Jessie. Don't you know that Rabbit wants to surprise Jessie, himself? Why you going to go and open your big mouth and spoil everything? Remember, Jessie is his biggest fan. Sister Johnson, can you explain to this leaking bucket why she should keep her mouth shut? I swear - and y'all talk about me.

SISTER JOHNSON: Now you wouldn't want to go and tell Jessie, right, child?

MARY: *(Understanding)* No ma'am! I wouldn't think of letting that cat out of the bag.

PAGE: *(Walking away mumbling)* I tell you. Can't tell people anything!

MARY: I'm so happy for Rabbit. This sure will brighten Jessie's life - nearly as much as the other news I'm going to tell him.

SISTER JOHNSON: *(Responding to Mary)* Lord, all we need is some more good news and maybe we will forget about all the other news. Now tell me, child, is it what I'm thinking? What did the doctor say?

MARY: *(Hesitantly)* Well, it's going to take a few days before the tests come back but the doctor feels *(Jubilantly hugs Sister Johnson)* confident that I'm going to have me a baby!

Mary is momentarily silent, as she thinks about the present condition.

MARY: Why is it when something good happens the Devil always tries to destroy the joy you're having? He sure gets a kick out of making you miserable. I mean Jessie and I want a baby so badly but he wanted to be working and have a little money saved. You know what I mean, Sister Johnson? I don't feel good telling him while he's out of work. It's only going to make him worry more - not like he doesn't have enough to worry about already.

SISTER JOHNSON: *(Putting her arms around Mary's shoulders)* The Devil is nothing but a miserable soul trying to make everyone like him. Don't let him do that to you. Don't let the conditions spoil such a joyous occasion. Let Jessie enjoy the fruits of his labor - the making of his image. If he sees you happy, he's in heaven. I've been around much longer than you. Now that I think back,Theodore and I, Lord rest his soul, have had some pretty rough times, but it didn't seem rough at the time. You know why? I never made that man feel like we didn't have enough. Though the furniture was tattered and worn I kept it neat and tidy. I always had him a good meal... sometimes Detroit catfish and dandelion greens from across the street from the field. I'd pick up potatoes, corn and fatback from Bernie's store and I took Spam and made it taste like chicken. That man never felt like we didn't have and he paid me back for it a million times over. Put your faith in the Lord, child. This could be the start to much better things. The Lord is giving you something precious - a life.

MARY: *(Hugging Sister Johnson)* Oh, Sister Johnson, we wouldn't know what to do without your wisdom. Why am I acting like this when I'm really happy? I won't tell Jessie until I get the results back, just in case there's a slip-up.

SISTER JOHNSON: That's the girl I know!

MARY: You know, Sister Johnson, from now on nothing like this is going to worry me anymore - I promise you.

Tracy comes from around the corner past the laundromat carrying her purse and a bag. She sees Mary and Sister Johnson before they see her. She is dressed professionally and seems tired.

SISTER JOHNSON: *(As Tracy approaches)* You're off early, ain't ya?

Tracy does not say anything as she sits on Sister Johnson's porch step. She pulls off her shoes and takes a deep sigh of relief.

TRACY: *(Exhausted)* Do you know this whole city is on strike! I had to walk all the way from the square to the house. *(Rubbing her feet)* Have you ever heard the expression, "You don't have to say nothing to say something?" Well, I tell you the truth, right now my feet are calling me some dirty names. *(Pauses)* How did the tests go, Merr? Will you and Jessie be using the diapers before us?

MARY: *(Smiling and standing up)* The results are not in yet but the doctor thinks…

TRACY: *(Interrupting Mary)* I knew you were pregnant. I told you two weeks ago that you were. I guess you all will be using the diapers before us. You sure are lucky. Girl, if that doctor would have told you that you weren't pregnant, I was getting ready to give you and Jessie a run for your money.

Tracy pulls some sexy lingerie out of her bag and holds it up so everyone can see.

MARY: Wow! That will make him hurt himself!

TRACY: Girls, I got oils, lotions, new colognes and other stuff. I was going to fry up a skillet of oysters, too. I was going to get pregnant or that man would have been so worn out they would have had to hospitalize him.

SISTER JOHNSON: *(Smiling)* I tell you, with what you got in that bag, it will only be a matter of time before you'll be coming with the same good news. You just watch.

TRACY: *(Reaches into her purse and pulls out a piece of paper and hands it to Mary)* Oh, I forgot to tell you. We're laid off!

Three o'clock - The Labor meeting...

It is the middle of the afternoon and all the businesses are temporarily closed. A few people, including Reverend Peters, stand on top of a small platform in the middle of the street in front of Bernie's and the poolroom. A crowd of people including Tracy, Mary, Luella, Francine and Sister Johnson are standing in front of the platform listening to a speaker. We also see Bernie, Bee, Ernest, Mrs. Washington and Page; but Housecoat Pearl listens from her apartment window. The present speaker is finishing up his speech.

SPEAKER: There are also American auto parts companies in Windsor that will be hiring twenty-five people next week if the strike is still on. The jobs will consist of clerical, shipping, packing, maintenance and inventory; the pay will be less. Every day we're getting more job listings. Some may be as far as 25 to 100 miles away and pay less than the factories normally pay but at least we can keep a roof over our heads and milk and bread on our tables until we can go back to work. *(Applause)*

There are two more things I want to say. If any one of you are interested in little daily odd jobs, Bernie, Ernest and The Well's management need a few people with cars and trucks to pick up fruits, vegetables, bread, milk, beverages, etc., from some of the farming communities and warehouses. I'm advising union people not to cross picket lines. For those of you who may be interested in some labor trade classes, most of the high schools in the metropolitan area have staff willing to teach crafts and trades free of charge while the strike is on - but you better hurry because the classes are rapidly filling up. Our next speaker you all know. He's an activist and a fighter for the betterment of our community, Brother Man X. *(Applause)*

MAN X: As-Salaam-Alaikum! *(Peace be unto you)*

AUDIENCE: Wa-Alaikum-Salaam! *(And unto you peace)*

MAN X: I don't have much to say but we should look at this situation as an eye- opener for the future. We're too dependent. Look around you. Most of the ones that are not here, that we know, are working. They are working in places like the barber shop and beauty salon, Jake's car wash, Bloomfield/Birmingham Gardening Service, all the restaurants, cafés and stores. Yes, even the poolrooms and bars. If I were you, I'd be the first one down at those schools trying to learn some sort of trade. You don't see any painters, carpenters or plumbers standing here, do you? If you called Benson up and told him your toilet was stopped up, I'm willing to bet you he'd tell you he's too busy to come right away and he'd be telling the truth.

PAGE: *(Screaming from the crowd)* Yeah. He took so long I had to go to the gas station. *(Everyone laughs)*

Carl and Jessie come around the bend onto Side Street.

CARL: *(Speaking to Man X)* As-Salaam-Alaikum, my brother!

Everyone turns as Carl and Jessie come up and stand with the rest of the crowd.

MAN X: Wa-Alaikum-Salaam, my brothers! As I was saying, Black Willie, in case some may not know him, is Mr. General Electrician of the ghetto. He sent two of his children to college. How many of us have worked for all these people at one time or another? *(Many raise their hands including Carl and Jessie)* I know I have. They've been at some point in our lives a needed blessing. Point of fact is, without more black business explosions we'd always be vulnerable to these times and its crisis. My brothers and sisters, it's time for us to come together and make better opportunities for you and me. *(Applause)* Learn trades, be productive entrepreneurs, make a way so your brothers and sisters can have jobs or job options. Take advantage of what the schools are offering you. I bet when these times come again and they will come - your chances of survival will be terrific. Look who's offering you help right now - small businesses in this community. Let's have more of them.

As Brother Man X walks away with applause and cheers, Reverend Peters comes to the front to speak.

REVEREND PETERS: Let's give Brother Man X another round of applause. *(Applause continues)* The concern and care of our community is felt by everyone. No one can live in this community without feeling the others' needs. Every need of this community is all of our needs, so we all must play our part. This community is our home and you know in our community we must all play our part to make our house a home. *(Applause)* The churches in this community have formed an alliance to better serve and help those in need the most. Right now we're making sure that no one is going to be without food, gas, electricity and a roof over their heads. We've already contacted the water and power companies. They're in our corner, so to speak. You can go to any of the churches, give them your utility bills and they'll handle the rest. This goes for anyone in the community. You don't have to be a member or belong to any church in order to receive assistance. All you have to be is a member of this community. I also want to elaborate a little more on what Brother Man X was speaking about. I've spoken with Birmingham/Bloomfield Gardening, Benson Plumbing and Black Willie Electrical Service. They have volunteered to teach as many as possible their trades, so let's get out there and prepare for the future of this community. *(Loudly)* LET US ALL COME TOGETHER RIGHT NOW!

There is a lot of cheering and applause as music begins to play.

END OF SCENE ELEVEN

ACT III

SCENE ONE

Carl hears Jessie is on heroin and confronts him in the poolroom. Still angry, he goes to his house and walks in. Tracy is talking on the phone to Mary.

TRACY: Girl, if she puts a white girl in my position, all hell is going to break loose! Come tomorrow morning as soon as they open up, I'll be staring my supervisor in the face with my union representative.

MARY: That sure is cold if she did that. I'd do the same thing if it were me.

TRACY: You know she never liked me but this time she may have gone too far! If it's true, I'm going to tell her a thing or two.

MARY: In all honesty, you should be the supervisor anyway! You know way more than that biddy... just because she's kin to the manager.

TRACY: She has hired someone from outside when this whole city is laid off. Plus, she's white, too. Just because she doesn't want to have to labor herself... trifling woman! Oooh, girl!

MARY: Just remember, girl... we need our jobs!

TRACY: That woman has gone too far. *(Tracy looks up as Carl walks in looking disgusted)*

TRACY: *(To Carl)* Who done ruffled your feathers?

MARY: Who you talking to?

TRACY: *(To Mary)* Carl. He comes in here with a face full of ugliness.

CARL: *(To Tracy)* Who you talking to?

TRACY: *(To Carl)* To Mary. Why are you in my business?

CARL: Hang up the phone! I've got to talk to you.

TRACY: *(To Carl)* Man, can't it wait? You see I'm in the middle of something.

CARL: *(Agitated – pacing back and forth)* Come on! It's important! *(He goes back into another room)*

TRACY: *(To Mary)* Merr, I'll call you back. *(She hangs up the phone as Carl comes back out sipping a beer and sits at the dining table)* What are you all excited about?

CARL: *(Hesitantly)* Give me a minute.

TRACY: *(Concerned, goes over and sits at the table with him)* You okay, sugar? You seem really upset. Ain't nobody hurt or something worse is it?

CARL: Naw, but just as bad, though.

TRACY: *(Reaches and puts her arms around his shoulder)* Tell me, sugar, what's wrong?

CARL: Let me get a grip. I don't really know if I should tell you or not. I'm worried you may tell...

TRACY: *(Pulls back)* Now you tell me to get off the phone, then you tell me you don't know if you should tell me or not. I'm married to a fool!

CARL: You've got to promise me that you will not tell anyone – I mean no one!

TRACY: Who have I told when you told me not to tell?

CARL: *(Hesitant)* I heard Jessie is using.

TRACY: What do you mean "using"?

CARL: Heroin! *(Pauses)*

TRACY: *(Covering her mouth with her hands)* No! Don't say that! How can you let someone tell you a lie like that? I don't believe it.

CARL: *(Hurt)* What if it's true? What if he's using? I mean... what?

TRACY: *(Somewhat in denial)* Stop saying that! What proof is there? You know as well as I that he couldn't keep something like that from us.

CARL: *(Near tears)* What if it's true? He's my best friend and I love him. You know that. I wouldn't let anyone talk about Jess. *(Pause)* I just don't know. Jessie knows how I feel about drugs.

TRACY: Lord, I sure hope not. Poor Mary! I just hope it's not true.

CARL: So do I – but it's hard for me to rationalize after everything. I mean, it's beginning to look like "maybe."

TRACY: Who told you anyway?

CARL: I was in the poolroom when I overheard Page telling Big Hank what Rabbit's mother told him.

TRACY: Now I know it isn't true! Why would you believe what Page says? That man spreads more Sugar, Honey, and Ice Tea *(SHIT)* than a crop duster.

CARL: I know. But you know Page wouldn't say anything bad about Jessie un-less it was credible. It came from a reliable source – Rabbit's mother!

TRACY: I'm not being disrespectful but how in the world would Mrs. Jones know something like that about Jessie – the only one trying to help her son. *(Pauses)* Why would Page tell you, knowing how much you hate people doing drugs?

CARL: He didn't tell me. I overheard him and Big Hank. They were both surprised when they realized that I overheard their conversation. As I approached them, they stopped talking. *(Pauses)* I was about to make a scene if they hadn't told me.

TRACY: *(Sits on his lap)* This is too hard for me to believe. I just can't see how Mrs. Jones would know anything about Jessie.

CARL: You remember that night Rabbit came over raising all that hell – wanting to talk to Jessie?

TRACY: Yeah.

CARL: Well, Rabbit found out about Jessie. Page said Mrs. Jones had to stop Rabbit from beating up some boy because the boy saw one of Rabbit's football pictures and recognized Jessie in it. *(Pauses)* The boy told Rabbit that he saw Jessie and another man enter a dope house at the same time he was coming out. *(Pauses, teary-eyed)* I don't know, Tracy! To hear my best friend is using… my best friend!

TRACY: Lord have mercy if he's using. Honey, he probably didn't tell you because he knows how you feel about drugs. He may be afraid to tell you! *(Pauses)* I just want to know how he could be using and helping Rabbit at the same time. It doesn't make sense. *(Sadly)* If he is, poor baby, and if he's afraid to talk to you, he has no one to talk or turn to.

CARL: Yeah! Yeah! But he knows how I feel. I'm pretty upset right now!

TRACY: *(Soaking it in)* I know you are but you've got to talk to him. You're his best friend. You've got to talk to him. Poor Mary!

CARL: *(Holding her closer to him)* You cannot say anything to her. *(The front door opens. Mary walks in and sees Tracy sitting on Carl's lap.)*

MARY: *(Insinuating)* What are you two up to this early in the day?

TRACY: *(Gets off Carl's lap)* Getting ready to prepare dinner.

MARY: *(Laughing - not noticing)* You can't fool me. Ain't no dinner being discussed sitting on his lap. Y'all talking baby talk, huh?

CARL: *(Gets up from the chair and tries to compose himself)* Yeah, and you done broke the mood now. I'm out of here.

MARY: *(Laughing)* Uhh huh! *(To Tracy)* I just come to finish our conversation about our jobs. *(Carl goes out the door)*

Next day... Carl's confrontation with Jessie

It is an early weekday evening. Traffic is light. Carl is sitting on his porch and seems irritated and tense as if he is waiting for someone. Mary and Tracy have been out all day. Sister Johnson is at work. After a few minutes, Jessie comes around the bend onto Side Street and sees Carl siting on the porch. He bypasses the bar, café and poolroom and joins Carl on the porch.

JESSIE: *(Approaches without indicating that anything is going on)* Hey, what's happening, my brother?

Carl does not reply to Jessie - just gives him negative vibes.

JESSIE: *(Shows concern for Carl's behavior)* Hey, brother! Everything alright? Has something happened? *(Pauses)* Our ladies, Sister Johnson, is everyone all right?

CARL: *(Harshly)* They're cool.

JESSIE: Well, who done took a bite out of your apple?

CARL: *(Long pause)* You, man! You! That's who.

JESSIE: *(Not understanding)* Whoa, my brother! Explain yourself! If you've got something to say, say it.

CARL: *(Rises up from the chair and looks up and down the street at Sister Johnson's house and the rooming house next door)* You running around here in the neighborhood pretending to be "holier than thou" and shootin' up drugs just like the other low-lives in this city! Man, you're a big hypocrite!

JESSIE: *(Perplexed because he had forgotten what happened to him in Pontiac and with Rabbit. He and Rabbit are friends again and he is still helping him.)* So you found out, huh?

CARL: *(Angry)* That's all you have to say, "So you found out?" You're supposed to be my best friend and here I'm the dummy running around with you telling kids and others to stay away from drugs and you're using and I didn't even know it. Man, you're a joke – a pitiful joke. I bet everybody who knew felt sorry for me, knowing my best friend is using and I didn't know. That's what you think of me!

JESSIE: Hey, let's get this straight! First of all, I'm not using now! Yeah, I used before but think what you want if you want. I didn't tell you because of this right here. I just knew that this would be the way you would've reacted and I was right. That's why I didn't want you to know.

CARL: You know what, Jess? You ain't shit! I thought you and I were gonna help the children of the neighborhood. Now I don't know if you are the problem or the helper.

JESSIE: *(Standing up for himself)* Man, behind those words you just said to me, if I didn't have leftover love and respect in my heart for you, my wife, your wife, and Sister Johnson, we would've been to blows by now! I don't appreciate your comments!!

CARL: You're right, man. That's the only reason we aren't at it. Man, you broke my heart! You know how I am about heroin. I lost an uncle and my mother abandoned me. Man, I ain't no forgiving dude! *(Carl leaves and goes into the house and slams the door behind him)*

Jessie stands there for a moment with a hurt expression on his face trying to figure out what just happened. Then he goes up the steps into his house.

END OF SCENE ONE

ACT III

SCENE TWO

It has been almost two weeks since Carl's and Jessie's confrontation and they have not spoken to each other in all that time. Although Page and Tracy are the only ones who know the reason for the tension in the atmosphere, Mary, Sister Johnson and Reverend Peters sense that something is wrong. Carl stays at home or at the playground most of the time.

Jessie is at the V.A. hospital for his monthly private therapy sessions. Tracy and Mary are at the movies and Sister Johnson is at work. Carl is alone sitting on Sister Johnson's porch swing, reflecting on his life and trying to understand why he has more disgust for Jessie than he has for Rabbit. It hurts not being able to speak to Jessie, and deep in his heart he misses his best friend, but he will not back down from his principles. It has been very hard to keep this knowledge from the rest of the family circle, especially when he is in the company of Sister Johnson, Mary, Reverend Peters, Ernest, Luella, Francine and other close associates. He knows the rift between him and Jessie is having an effect on everyone.

Carl thinks about his mother whom he would not recognize if she were standing right in front of him. For all he knows she may have passed him on the street a hundred times. He had been told while he was growing up, by older people in his life, that his mother dumped him in the hands of his daddy, aunt and uncle before he was a year old, to do drugs with a drug dealer. Then his favorite uncle, his father's only brother, succumbed to heroin and eventually overdosed and died when Carl was eleven years old. Then it's Rabbit and now Jessie. Carl swore he would never do drugs or ever want to be around it or anyone associated with it.

Two guys (Roosevelt and Calloway) pass Carl sitting on Sister Johnson's porch without recognizing him. They stop at Mary and Jessie's stairwell and begin to go up the stairs when Carl stops them.

CARL: *(Nonchalantly)* No one's there.

CALLOWAY: *(Recognizing Carl from Jessie's description)* Hey, man, are you Carl?

CARL: Yeah!

CALLOWAY: Jessie used to always talk about you. That's why we recognized you. *(Both turn and come to Sister Johnson's porch steps)* My name is Calloway and this is Roosevelt. We were best friends in the war on the front lines with Jess. Hey, brother, I just want to tell you, you've got a cool brother as a friend! We love the dude ourselves.

CARL: *(In an awkward position)* Uhhh, Jessie and I ain't friends no more. *(Both stunned)*

ROOSEVELT: Wow! That's a blow!

CALLOWAY: That's a shock to me, too! I mean, we came down here because Jess invited us down to meet you and the wives. You were at a baseball game last time we came.

CARL: Yeah, he told me. Nice meeting you guys!

ROOSEVELT: We're sorry, man. We didn't know. I ain't trying to be disrespectful, my brother, but all he ever talked about in 'Nam (beside his wife and his close-knit friends in the neighborhood) was you and this dude named Rabbit.

CARL: Yeah. Shit happens. *(Changing the subject to Callaway)* You the cop, ain't you?

CALLOWAY: *(Smiles)* Yep, that's me.

ROOSEVELT: *(Getting in on it)* He's still the only one that wants to wear a uniform.

CARL: Yeah. I heard about you guys.

CALLOWAY: Hey, we don't want to pry or anything. We came down to kind of surprise Jess and we also wanted to eat some more of

Cousin Bee's food and hang out with you guys. Guess we came down at a bad time. That's life!

CARL: *(Nonchalantly)* Hey, The Well is right next to Cousin Bee's. By the time you finish eating, he'll probably be back before you guys leave. He usually stops in The Well or the poolroom.

ROOSEVELT: I know one thing, I'm not leaving here until I have some cobbler!

CARL: Yeah, that's good food.

CALLOWAY: *(Thinking and looking at his watch)* Today is Thursday. I'll bet he's at the V.A. The last Thursday in the month is our therapy sessions. I bet that's where he is. We can eat and have a couple drinks in the bar and we'll probably see him before we leave. *(To Carl)* Hey, my brother, it's still cool to meet you. Peace...

ROOSEVELT: Same here, my brother! Wish it was on better circumstances, but that's life's curves. *(As they turn and begin to walk away, Carl stops them)*

CARL: What do you mean, "V.A." and "sessions"?

CALLOWAY: Jessie and I have been going to counseling two Thursdays each month since being released. The only difference is he goes to the V.A. and I go to where police officers go. Same kind of facility.

ROOSEVELT: See, when we left 'Nam, man, our heads were really messed up because of the war. I think we were on the front lines longer than anyone we knew. Didn't Jess tell you? All three of us were in the hospital thirty days after we got back to the States before they sent us home. Some like Way *(Calloway)* and Jessie needed more than others. I guess I was the lucky one.

CARL: *(Surprised)* What kind of therapy did you guys have? I was in 'Nam and on the front lines and all they did for us was made sure we were not carrying any diseases so we could get medical clearances.

CALLOWAY: *(Reserved)* We were just trying to get our heads back on straight, that's all! Just trying to get our heads back on straight! *(They head back toward Cousin Bee's)*

A few days later at Carl and Tracy's house... Carl's mood seems lighter as Tracy comes through the door and sees him on the couch in the living room listening to jazz for the first time in a while.

TRACY: *(Seeing Carl's demeanor)* We've hit the numbers?

CARL: *(Smiles)* Yeah. Yeah, we did.

TRACY: Where's the money? I want it before it's in your hands too long …

CARL: It's in a safety deposit box.

TRACY: *(Sensing Carl's composure, puts her purse on the table.)* I'll bet you done made up with Jessie, huh?

CARL: *(Smiling)* Not quite, but I'm not mad at him anymore.

TRACY: *(Happy, she runs and hugs him)* Whew! Ohhh, baby, I'm so glad I could scream!

CARL: *(Bewildered)* But Jessie doesn't know yet.

TRACY: Well, tell him! What are you waiting on?

CARL: It's not that easy! I said some pretty rough things to him. I don't know how he's going to react.

TRACY: *(Thinking)* Yeah, I know. Mary says he's pretty bitter. What made you change?

CARL: I went to the V.A. hospital yesterday. *(Pauses)* Did you know that Jessie's been going to the V.A. twice a month?

TRACY: Naww! I don't think Mary knows either. How did you find out?

CARL: It was Jessie's friends *(uhhh)* Roosevelt and *(uhhh)* Calloway. They came looking for him the other day. We got to talking and they told me about Jessie being in therapy. So, I went to the V.A. to see.

TRACY: Ain't that kind of low?

CARL: Yeah, it is, but I had to find something to keep me from carrying this burden around.

TRACY: You're always jumping the gun. Jessie is, and has always been, your best friend. He deserves a rebuttal, at least. I bet he would have allowed you that opportunity before passing judgment.

CARL: Now wait a minute! I'm not going to defend no one for using drugs. That isn't me. If that be the case, then I would have to forgive my mother for abandoning me because of drugs and the person who turned on my uncle who overdosed. I would also have to forgive Rabbit for being a disappointment to the neighborhood – especially the children who looked up to him. That definitely isn't me! The brother has been in therapy all this time without telling anyone, which means that he's facing some tough challenges – whatever they are.

TRACY: I don't believe Mary knows or she would've told me. I sure hope you two brothers get it together again. It has been rough on Mary and me and Sister Johnson. I bet it's been hard on Jessie, too. First Rabbit, then you! *(Pauses)* Look, Carl, you can't continue to allow your life to be affected by the actions of your mama, uncle, Rabbit and Jessie. None of us would have friends if we want everyone to think like we think. No one experienced what you've experienced but you. Why should they have to pay because of your experiences? I mean, I'm with you all the way. I hate drugs and what it does to our folks, but I ain't going to let my feelings destroy something so precious to me, like my husband or my best friends without giving my all to help. Look how many people came home from the war messed up.

CARL: *(Pauses)* Yeah, yeah, yeah. Maybe I need to be in therapy.

TRACY: *(Getting up to humor Carl)* I've been telling you that for a long time!

CARL: *(Gets up to leave)* Ain't promising anything. I'm going to The Well. Let's see what happens. *(He walks out the door to the Well)*

AT THE WELL... Big Hank and Jessie are sitting at the bar talking when Carl enters. One of Big Hank's men is sitting at the end of the bar facing the front door. Carl freezes for a moment, then walks up to them, smiling...

CARL: Y'all probably talking about me, huh? *(Jessie doesn't answer)*

BIG HANK: *(Knowing the situation, says to Carl)* I ain't one for holding back or biting my tongue! I ain't too happy about what happened between you and Jessie. As street-smart as you are, you made a dumb decision to lose friendship with Jessie because of bullshit you heard from Page and me without knowing the circumstances. Look, you two are the coolest guys around, bar none! Why you think I trust you guys to do work for me? That ain't changed. Now you guys have gone far enough. I mean I can't tell you what to do, but you have been through a lot together and life ain't over yet. A lot more disputes are going to come y'all's way before it's over. This shouldn't be one of them! *(Not biting his tongue)* Carl, son, you've been through a lot and have seen a lot! You lucked out – got a beautiful wife, good friends and people around you that look out for your ass – including me. You're too quick to jump the gun, son! Sometimes you've got to look at the whole picture and not just a situation. We don't know half of what Jessie went through. Whatever it is, he still seems the same to all of us. I ain't seen no change in him except he seems to care for our young brothers and sisters even more than before he went in the Army. *(Pauses)* He ain't hurt you or nobody else. He's still helping Rabbit when you and no one else wanted to. I ain't never seen a junkie trying to make another junkie quit. *(Still talking to Carl)* I knew your mama and your uncle and neither one was bad people. *(Pauses)* We all make mistakes, son. Try not to let it come back to haunt you.

CARL: *(Nervously sits down on the stool on the opposite side of Big Hank and talks indirectly to him)* You're right! Everything you said is right. *(He leans across the front of Big Hank to speak directly to Jessie)* I'm sorry, man. I said some pretty ugly things to you and for that I'm truly sorry. That's all I know to say. I can't change something overnight that's been with me all my life, but I'm beginning to see how it's messing with me. *(Carl is handed a beer by the bartender)*

Big Hank looks at Jessie who is sitting quietly, listening to what is being said, then looks at Carl. "Bitches Brew" by Miles Davis is playing on the jukebox and all appear to be listening to it. As the song is ending, Jessie reaches past Big Hank with a bottle of beer to toast with Carl.

CARL: *(Leans over and extends his bottle to Jessie.)* I'm sorry, my brother!

JESSIE: *(Clinks his bottle with Carl's)* Apology accepted!

BIG HANK: *(Rising from his seat at the bar)* Hey, it was just a big misunderstanding. Now, I've got to get on up the street. Glad this mess is over! You boys had everybody on pins and needles. *(He exits through the door.)*

END OF SCENE TWO

ACT III

SCENE THREE

Better Times in the Neighborhood: Saturday morning - 2:30 am...

All the businesses are closed except Big Hank's poolroom. The street is deserted until Carl and Jessie come out of the poolroom with Hank Crawford (Big Hank), two employees (Big Hank's bodyguards) and two other patrons of the poolroom. The two men playing pool against Carl and Jessie walk up the street toward the laundromat.

JESSIE: *(Speaking to the two players)* Thanks for the game!

CARL: Thanks, man, see you guys!

They throw their hands up in acknowledgement as they disappear around the corner. Jessie and Carl wait until Big Hank's bodyguards lock the doors.

JESSIE: *(Speaking to Big Hank)* Thanks for the overtime. It was a good night for us. *(Jessie hands a twenty to Big Hank)*

BIG HANK: Naw, you keep it. I'm glad to see you guys win a few dollars. Both of you played pretty good tonight. I know those boys and they aren't slouches.

CARL: Yeah! I've been beaten by them before. Tonight it was heart!

BIG HANK: Yeah! A few times they had you guys but you played smart pool. *(Walking away)* Don't forget if you guys get uptight you can make some change by doing some running for me. Everyone knows you guys. *(Hank shakes Jessie's and Carl's hands)*

JESSIE: Thanks for looking out for us. Really appreciate it!

CARL: *(Responding to Jessie's comment)* Right on!

Carl and Jessie watch as Big Hank and his bodyguards walk toward the laundromat and disappear around the bend. They turn and slowly walk toward their home. Only the streetlights and Carl and Jessie are seen on Side Street. The rest of the street is shut down.

CARL: *(Counting his money)* I made a few bucks tonight - exactly seventy-nine dollars. I would have made another twenty, if I hadn't missed that 15-ball. You made more than I did!

JESSIE: Yeah! *(Counting his money)* I made a hundred and twenty-two dollars! We can take the ladies to a movie and dinner. You pay for the movies and I'll pay for the dinner.

CARL: Right on!

JESSIE: It sure is a beautiful night. In 'Nam, I used to always think of these kind of nights here on Side Street where my family and friends live, when we'd walk down to the river and see the Canadian lights just a stone's throw away.

CARL: Yeah, me too. But I thought just the opposite. In 'Nam I thought about the factory smoke and Detroit River smell on those hot, sweaty, humid summer nights; drinking nice cold Stroh's with you, Mary, Tra, Sister Johnson and other friends and family; not worrying about a thing! Then I'd smell Cousin Bee's cooking; hear jazz and blues coming from The Well and some spiritual food. I knew I was home. Man, I wouldn't trade what I have for anything!

JESSIE: I hear you. How beautiful our life has been in spite of all that we've been through. We're home, my brother!

CARL: *(Approaching his home)* Hey, the girls are probably over at Sister Johnson's. You want to sit out for a while and drink a few beers?

JESSIE: *(Sitting on Carl's porch)* It sounds good to me.

Carl goes into the house. Jessie sits on the porch with his feet touching the sidewalk. Carl comes out with four beers. He gives Jessie two and sits down next to him. Soft jazz is playing inside his house.

JESSIE: *(Toast)* Brother to brother!

CARL: *(Toast)* Brother to brother! To our wives and to our future babies!

JESSIE: *(Still toasting)* To our wives and babies and our dreams becoming reality!

CARL: Amen! Amen! *(Changing the subject)* Man, was I glad you came at the right time. I knew I wasn't going to beat both of them at nine-ball. I saw right through that. They wouldn't play each other but each of them was taking a crack at me. When the three of us were playing, I noticed they left better openings for themselves than they left for me. I caught on pretty quickly but they had the advantage until you got there. You came just in time!

JESSIE: We played them before at the West End pool hall. They were trying to sucker us into nine-ball games with them back then.

CARL: I remember. We stuck to eight balls because they knew those tables too well.

Silence...

CARL: *(Nervous)* Has Mary said anything else to you about Mary Alice?

JESSIE: No! We don't talk about it. Hey, what about Tracy, has she said anything about me?

CARL: No, she hasn't mentioned anything. *(Pauses)* She won't speak of it, not unless I do and you know I don't want to talk about it.

JESSIE: I guess we both have some people upset with us.

CARL: I know Mary's still upset with me. You know you can feel those things. It's undetectable, but I can feel it.

JESSIE: Yeah, I know.

CARL: Believe it or not, my brother, I'm cool with it *(Pauses)* now that I know. *(Pauses)* I ain't going to lie, man... I was really hurt!

JESSIE: I just couldn't tell you, knowing you like I do. *(Pauses)* Even though, I really wanted to. I needed you, man; but I couldn't tell you.

CARL: Jess, you don't have to talk about it if you don't want to, but I'd just like to know what happened to you and your two friends *(Roosevelt and Calloway)* in 'Nam? If those two dudes didn't come looking for you and ran into me at the time, *(Pauses)* I don't want to think about it... but I do know that God came through for me again.

JESSIE: *(Takes a sip of beer)* Yeah, I guess. It started in 'Nam. Me, Calloway and Roosevelt were together the whole time in 'Nam. It seemed like we were in combat every day for the entire time that we were there. Each day, it got pretty scary at times, when all we would see around or next to us nothing except death. We three had come to realize that it may be just a matter of time before it's one of us. *(Pauses)* Do you know how it feels to be next to someone every day and night trying to protect one another and at the same time hoping it would be them instead of you – as if we have more to live for. It was crazy. We all felt that way and yet no three people could have been as close at that time as we were. Thinking that we may never see our family again, it was on a night when the enemy didn't let up. We had already lost five soldiers in our company. *(Pauses)* One of the sergeants, a rich white dude from Connecticut, turned us on. Neither of us was dumb, but this dude, in all that was going on around us, was cool as a cucumber. We tried it then and again at another time under the same circumstances. We thought it was helping us to be brave, but in reality it was making us not give a damn about anything. We swore and made a pact with each other that when we got out we'd never do it again. Roosevelt and I broke our oath. I have never felt so low in my life. I prayed no one would find out.

CARL: *(Stops Jessie from saying anymore)* Don't need to say no more... I was just wondering, man.

JESSIE: I didn't want anyone to know about me and the therapy sessions either. I would have to explain. Besides you know how we *(Blacks)* think when they hear of us and a psychiatrist.

CARL: *(Smiling)* Yeah, I do, but I'm just the opposite though. They *(Blacks)* think me and my old man really need one. *(Pauses)* I'm glad you told me, now let's move on, man. Anyway, I kind of blame myself too. My mother and my uncle sure made me a doozy. *(Pauses)* Jess, you are the only real, true, best friend I have and ever had. You don't know how glad I am for us to be back together. I missed you, my brother.

JESSIE: *(Smiling)* Same here. I ain't going to lie. I was pretty lonesome those days without having my friend. *(Toast)* Here's to you, my brother. May you and I, and our wives stay together forever! That God has for us better tomorrows.

CARL: Amen to that! *(Back to his fear)* I guess I'll still be on edge with my situation. Man, I truly believe that God put Mary there just as the Devil brought Mary Alice. I'm hoping that since Mary Alice thought she was talking to Tracy when she called, she might not call back again.

JESSIE: My senses tell me that if Mary Alice has any common sense she wouldn't call back. She knows Tracy. I don't believe she wants to put salt on her wound. I would bet all the tea in China she won't show her face around here knowing Tracy like everyone does. Why do you think Reverend Peters and Sister Johnson had no solution to the situation? *(Pauses)* If no one else knows, you may be free – except for your conscience.

CARL: I hope you're right, man! My conscience is whipping me every day and night. I love my wife, my family and my home. I love my world. I just want this scar to heal and disappear like it never was there. I'm on pins and needles every time I look into my wife's face. It's funny how some mistakes never go away.

JESSIE: Yeah! I know where you're coming from, my brother. That's why I was upset with you like you were upset with me because of how beautiful our wives and our world have been to us. Even when we have no jobs and are struggling to make ends meet, *(Smiling)* our wives make us feel like some rich dudes. *(Expressing feelings)* We drive Cadillacs, Lincolns, live in mansion and eat chicken and Spam prime rib. We have a beautiful home, loving wives and friends. What more can we ask for... I pray for both our situations.

We have a beautiful world. Friends and a community where we are loved, honored and respected. We're truly lucky.

CARL: *(Both feeling better... in thought)* You know, Jess, we're a couple of pretty cool dudes. I mean, besides what we are enduring now, we are spiritual, don't mind working, ambitious and people look up to us and respect us. I think that regardless of what happened, we're also pretty good husbands. We make mistakes and sometimes do stupid things, but we're cool people.

JESSIE: Yeah, we are. *(Brighter note, smiling)* Sitting here like this makes me think back of the years growing up and walking on this street, passing this house and not knowing that one day I'd be living here.

CARL: This street used to be our shortcut to school, to the river to fish and the youth center. We bought tamales off the cart in front of The Well.

JESSIE: Man, we're truly blessed brothers!

CARL: I always think about those times - ice skating on this street, hiding under Sister Johnson's porch throwing snowballs at folks.

JESSIE: You hit Sister Johnson and Reverend Peters!

CARL: *(Laughing)* Oh, no! If you're talking about that time me, you and Rabbit played dare, it was you that hit Reverend Peters and I hit Page and Mary told on us. Hey, remember when you and I went to Texas with my dad and his car broke down on the way back and we had to catch a train? Man, we had so much fun.

JESSIE: Aw... yeah... yeah! Remember at school when we put garden snakes in the girls' gym lockers while they were in gym class? The teachers and the principal thought it was Johnny "Snake" Griffin because he was always doing crazy stuff like that.

CARL: Well, to tell the truth, he did inspire us to do some of those things. He used to do so much stuff and never get caught, even though everybody knew it was him.

JESSIE: Yeah! If anything crazy happened, more than likely it was Snake. Like the time he put the snake in Miss Pecklin's desk drawer. What about the time when he took our lunches that Mary and Tracy had made for us - meatloaf sandwiches and sweet potato pie? He exchanged yours for old mean Mr. Smith's sardine sandwich lunch and he gave mine to Rabbit for his old stale bologna and liverwurst sandwiches. Man, you screamed so loud in the cafeteria when you bit down into those sardines, and did they smell. Whew!

CARL: That old man Smith didn't say a word. He was enjoying that sweet potato pie and meatloaf and so was Rabbit.

JESSIE: That Rabbit used to do a lot of stuff to us, too! What about the time when we were in the shower after gym. He took our clothes, including our underwear and gym clothes, and hid them in the girls' locker room. We had to wear other kids' gym shorts in every class until your daddy came with some clothes for us to wear. Boy, the whole school was laughing at us.

CARL: Shoot, it was below zero. What about when he took the whole basketball team's clothes and put them up in that big old tree behind the school's auditorium? Man, our drawers were frozen.

JESSIE: Yeah, we got him back for all the things he had ever done to us when we slipped Ex-Lax in his chocolate cake after the football game in Lansing. Man, we had to stop every fifteen minutes for him to go to the bathroom.

CARL: Yeah, but that one time he didn't make it. Man, did that bus stink! And the time we put that rat in his hall locker.

JESSIE: *(Laughing)* I was getting scared. I thought he was going to have a heart attack at first. We knew he was afraid of rats. Hey, we got even with Snake, too, didn't we? We put skunk perfume in his underwear in gym class.

CARL: Everyone thought Snake shitted on himself. Man, all the things we did. Yeah, but nothing compared to when you lit those firecrackers and threw them into the school men's bathroom and turned out the light on Principal Klinger. Boy, I'm glad he never found out who it was. We would still be expelled if he had caught us. I didn't believe you had the nerve to do it.

JESSIE: I didn't until Rabbit told me about Jo Roberts being sent to Principal Klinger's office for calling Mary – "Mary Toilet Paper" and how Principal Klinger burst into laughter. That really got to me. Nobody talks about or makes fun of my girl, my future wife and the mother of my child and gets away with it. I was glad I did it. *(Smiling)* We've loved Mary and Tracy a long time, huh?

CARL: *(Smile)* Yeah, longer than we've loved ourselves and more than a hog loves slop.

JESSIE: Remember how they used to always make enough lunch for us?

CARL: Shoot, we never had to bring lunch to school and man, we ate good sweet potato pie and cobbler. I tell you, they sure brought joy to our lives, huh?

CARL: Yeah! They made the times growing up beautiful for us. *(Thinking)* All except for Daddy Cooper and Uncle Buck. They definitely didn't bring us any joy until after our graduation.

JESSIE: I guess they finally realized after all those years that we were serious and loved each other.

CARL: Naw, that wasn't it! They had accomplished their mission. They wanted to keep the girls as virgins by putting fear into us and our hormones.

JESSIE: I guess you're right. They definitely did put fear in us. Remember the time we won state championship and their mothers convinced their fathers to let them go on the school bus to our championship game in Marquette? And afterwards because of the blizzard, all highways and roads were closed down and we couldn't leave Marquette until the next day.

CARL: Aw, man, we were scared. Even though they stayed with the cheerleaders, we were still scared. We didn't sleep all night thinking Daddy Cooper and Uncle Buck would somehow get through the blizzard and roadblocks and kill us.

JESSIE: *(Now laughing)* Shoot, the whole basketball team was afraid. All those things Rabbit used to tell about them - especially that time Uncle Buck caught him and Virgil stealing pop out of Bernie's pop box.

CARL: *(Laughing)* Yeah, like always, Virgil thought he was so tough and confronted Uncle Buck like he would do something. That was a mistake! Uncle Buck wrapped his arm around Virgil's waist, lifted his 200 pounds off the ground 'til he nearly passed out. Good thing Housecoat came down and made him stop.

JESSIE: Uncle Buck took the wind out of his game real quick. After that, Virgil mellowed way down. Nobody fooled with Uncle Buck.

CARL: *(Still reminiscing)* Yeah! Remember the first time the girls called and told Tracy's mother that they were snowed in? Then they called a few hours later to assure them they were fine. No one answered the phone at either place. Everyone sure got scared. We just knew Daddy Cooper and Uncle Buck were on their way. Then later we heard that the phone lines were not working down there.

JESSIE: You and I always believed that Daddy Cooper and Uncle Buck were sitting by that phone.

CARL: I just believed that old man and his brother knew they were scaring the daylights out of us. Boy, when we got back home the girls had to face the music all by themselves. That was one time I was glad I didn't have to face it with them.

JESSIE: That's for sure - and I was glad Sister Johnson told us to stay away for a while. Both mothers tore into both fathers. Mary brought a tear to her father's eyes because he didn't trust her.

CARL: It didn't faze Uncle Buck though. He still raised hell.

JESSIE: He thought we had too much black power in us.

CARL: He thought I was militant, calling folks brothers and sisters. Told Tracy I was crazy like my old man. My old man wasn't crazy.

JESSIE: Your old man was cool and still is. Ain't nobody around here had as many newspaper stories as he had. His pictures are still on the walls of The Well, Cousin Bee's, the poolroom and the barber shop.

CARL: Yeah, my old man was a bad dude in his day. He was scared of Uncle Buck and Daddy Cooper though. He used to say they were kin to John Henry. I sure am glad Mary took after her mother.

JESSIE: *(Smiling)* Yeah, me too! *(Pauses)* All things aside, I now understand and I'm glad we all found peace and love before they died. I think he died with a sincere fondness for us. It took a while but I think he realized how much we loved each other and had planned on getting married. I wonder how we're going to be when we have daughters?

CARL: Good question. I hope I don't be like them!

JESSIE: I don't know. Look how you do your 14-year-old niece on Eight Mile. You got all those brothers afraid of you.

CARL: Getting my bluff in before they get theirs in! That's all!

JESSIE: I believe that's exactly what Daddy Cooper and Uncle Buck did to us.

CARL: It was a long time before they changed. At first I think they thought their daughters were too good for us. Then they realized how much we all cared for one another. Plus Jessie, you and I always hustled for money - whether it was at the car wash or working for Big Hank. We didn't mind working.

JESSIE: *(Sadly)* I kinda feel bad they didn't get the opportunity to see their daughters walk down the aisle with the ones they loved in their true virgin whites.

CARL: So do I, but I think they left in peace knowing their daughters were in good hands.

JESSIE: To be sure they did. They told Sister Johnson not to tell us how proud they were of us. Yeah, we all found peace just in the nick of time before the tragedy struck.

CARL: *(Sadly)* You know, Jessie, I think about it a lot. What if Tracy and Mary were with their parents when the accident happened? Man, I don't know if I could've taken it.

JESSIE: Yeah. I think we would've died with them. All those years of us dreaming and planning our future together. *(He shakes)* Man, that would've been an ugly nightmare.

CARL: I know, man! I just can't help it. What happened then to our future wives and us was worse than 'Nam. Two families - best friends on their way back from vacation, wiped out in a flash by a drunk driver. To this day, our wives still have nightmares at times.

JESSIE: Man, it hurts thinking about how beautiful our wives are. I'm so glad we're all together. 'Nam sure made me appreciate what we have in this community of our world - our wives, family and friends. We're rich, my brother.

CARL: I believe we got the best of the best. Best wives, best friends and best community. I couldn't have friends as beautiful as you, Mary and Tracy. You're closer to me than my brother B.U. I love you, man!

JESSIE: Hey, I love you, too, man! We've been best friends ever since kindergarten. You're the brother I never had.

CARL: *(Changing the subject)* Hey, Jessie, I got a great idea. Once we start working steady and Mary has the baby why don't we renew our vows? Save up enough money and give the girls the kind of wedding they used to always talk about when we all were growing up. Sister Johnson and Uncle Buck helped us to have a nice wedding and all but circumstances cancelled the dream part for them. They talk about it sometimes.

JESSIE: That sounds really cool. They deserve more than what they had with us going into the service right after we were married. Was it one month later for you and for me two months later than that?

CARL: Think about it, Jessie, we've been married almost three years and this is the longest we've been together in all those years. It's seven months for me and three months for you. We've been in the service on each of our anniversaries. We sure haven't had the opportunity to enjoy each other very much, have we?

JESSIE: Naw. It's been a rough two and a half years for all of us but especially them - losing their parents and us going into the service. They probably had some lonely, troubling moments those years without us. That hurts both of us - not being here for them. First time in all our years growing up we were not there. Thanks to Sister Johnson and Uncle Buck they were looked after. *(Trying to inject humor)* They sure were mad at us for leaving them - telling us they wouldn't be here when we got out.

CARL: Let's do it! Let's give them the best wedding - their dream wedding with all the trimmings. We'll stay at the Bonaventure and wear tuxedos like we had always planned.

JESSIE: *(Excited)* Let's do it! Let's see, she'll still be pregnant this coming Valentines' Day, so let's make it for the next one. That will give us plenty of time to give them an unforgettable wedding. As soon as we start working we can start saving. I bet you and Tracy will be pregnant before long, too. Watch what I say!

CARL: You may be right. I truly hope you are. Me - a daddy! You - a daddy! Man, we'll be on top of the world!

JESSIE: *(Smiling)* Yeah! Our wives and our images!

CARL: That will be the two happiest days of our lives. Getting married to Mary and Tracy and having children with them.

JESSIE: This is so beautiful sitting here talking about good things - not letting this world for a moment bother us. We're just sharing brotherly love and love for our world and its people. These are the moments I dreamed about... us sitting here on a warm night with our wives and friends or just us together like we used to do; laughing, telling jokes and lies or just rapping and drinking Stroh's.

CARL: *(With a sly smile)* Hey, Jessie, did you know any other virgins beside Mary and Tracy as you were growing up?

JESSIE: *(Thinking)* Hmmm, let me see… I would say maybe the skinny French sisters and Mr. Peeler's daughter.

CARL: Those French sisters were so skinny they had to stay at home from school on windy days and Mr. Peeler's daughter, Kathleen, was so homely, her cousin, Jerome, took her to her prom. You know, looking back now I guess I can be glad nothing happened back then. *(Smiling)* Of course, I wouldn't have turned it down. *(They do a high-five slap in agreement)*

JESSIE: Yeah! Thanks to Daddy Cooper and Uncle Buck who turned it into a test of time and love without submission of influence.

CARL: You mean thanks to the fear they put in us because we had been some begging fools. Huh, man, that Uncle Buck, every time we came around, he looked at us as if he wanted to beat the living daylights out of us with those big old hands.

JESSIE: I bet Daddy Cooper is looking down on us smiling.

CARL: He still left Uncle Buck around to keep an evil eye on things. He sure is a lot different now. Man, I don't know what we would've done without Uncle Buck sometimes.

JESSIE: He has been like a daddy to the girls. He really helped us out taking care of our ladies while we were away.

CARL: You know, Jessie, our wives are blessed. You and I are some together brothers if I have to say so myself. We may not have it all right now but I see a bright future for us and our ladies.

JESSIE: Right on! Pretty soon we'll finish automobile school and be working for old man Whitser in his garage until he decides to retire and sell it to us.

CARL: I think he's just waiting on us to come in and get our feet wet. Then he's going to retire, sell it to us and move to Texas with my old man and Aunt Teresa.

JESSIE: He and your dad's sister got a thing going on, don't they? I mean he convinced us to go to mechanic's school.

CARL: Yeah, they've been grooving for a long time. She's been trying to get him to come and live with them. That's why I think he'll retire soon.

JESSIE: I guess that's why he won't sell to anyone but us.

CARL: *(Smiling)* Aunt Teresa put her mojo on him to come live with them. He's going. Bet he can retire comfortably.

JESSIE: Our own business! Our wives can quit Hudson's and take care of the books for us.

CARL: Sister Johnson said she would retire and take care of the babies for us.

JESSIE: That would be cool. We could pay her. She and Uncle Buck were life savers to the girls while we were in the service.

CARL: Yeah! Uncle Buck helped pay for the wedding and helped the girls to pay off their homes and go to school. But he doesn't need our money, so let's do all his mechanic work free for him.

From the opposite end of the street, Junior Boy Allen, incognito, wearing a pulled-down brimmed hat, sneaks into view. Jessie and Carl see him sneak into the building that Luella and Francine live in.

JESSIE: *(Quietly)* Wasn't that Junior Boy?

CARL: Sure looks like him! What is he doing sneaking around this time of night? He just went into the Army eight months ago.

They look at each other.

JESSIE: *(Changing the subject)* You know I really feel bad about Rabbit, man. Throughout the years he had our backs - looked after our ladies when we weren't around. He's a true friend!

CARL: I know you feel bad, Jessie. In reality everyone does.

JESSIE: I mean, he's our man. Always been there. I know how you feel but think about it. Everybody has had their hopes and faith in

Rabbit ever since junior high. We put a lot on him and most of the time he came through for us.

CARL: Jessie, you're right! We did put a lot on him. We grew up with him and played sports alongside him. Yeah, I guess you can say he was the only person in this community with the most - *(Pauses)* we felt - opportunity to be our hero and we sure needed one for a long time. I mean, my personal feelings for him are torn between love and hate at the same time.

JESSIE: I'm not making excuses for him. I understand and I'm not trying to justify what he did. I'm just saying we, this community, did put a lot on him. It's not easy living up to human expectations. One slip and it turns from sugar to lemon. Rabbit is tough, strong and very talented but not the brightest person in the world. In fact, he's pretty weak in some things. We helped him academically throughout junior and senior high school. In college, without people who cared like us and this community, folks took advantage of his popularity.

CARL: Jessie, understand, man, the brother is someone like many others that we know or have heard about in this community. We all have had our struggles. His is no greater than others in the inner cities. I hate what he became and the letdown for many around here who really needed heroes. I mean we need heroes because they may be able to make other heroes who may have lost hope and faith. Heroes save lives. Heroes give others hopes and dreams. Heroes put new paint on a city and a community and heroes bring the trophy of pride home. Think about Joe Louis, Martin Luther King Jr., Muhammad Ali, Berry Gordy Jr., Malcolm X, Jim Brown, Maya Angelou, Huey Newton, Angela Davis, Willie Mays and others. Rabbit, to us, had the potential of being one of those people.

JESSIE: I know, man. I was glad to block for him in football, to pass him the basketball, to be the third man that handed him the baton in the 220-yard relay. Rabbit won us the State Championship in basketball, football and track. He's a hero, man. I think in my mind we also owe him something – to be there for him. In times of trouble, we're a family. Turn your back on family and we have no one.

CARL: You're right, you're right, Jessie! I understand and I feel for you but my heart is just not as sympathetic as yours. Some things I just cannot accept. You tried to help him and he won't listen to you. *(Pauses)* He won't listen to no one.

JESSIE: The last I heard he was doing well. That's why he left to get away from the elements. Hey, let's all go to Chicago one weekend and visit him.

CARL: That sounds good. I really hope he's doing well.

JESSIE: I know you do. Everyone does.

CARL: *(Changing the subject)* Hey, Jess, Tra left me a note. Why don't we go in, drink more beer and listen to some jazz like we did back when. The girls are staying over at Sister Johnson's tonight.

JESSIE: *(Getting up)* Cool.

They disappear into Carl's house.

END OF SCENE THREE

ACT III

SCENE FOUR

A few weeks later / Tracy's big announcement - she is pregnant...

It is an overcast afternoon. Jessie and Mary are sitting on Sister Johnson's porch. Jessie is wearing a sweatshirt, sitting on the porch floor with his back resting comfortably against the porch's beam; his legs stretched across the entrance to the porch. Mary is sitting on the porch's swing and has on a long-sleeve sweater. Sister Johnson comes out bringing three cups by the handle in one hand and the other she carries a thermos with a handle on it. Sister Johnson is also wearing a lightweight sweater. Jessie rises and grabs his and Mary's cups and gives one to her. He takes the thermos and pours Sister Johnson, Mary and himself tea and then repositions himself. Sister Johnson sits next to Mary on the swing.

JESSIE: *(Sips the tea)* Thanks for the tea.

SISTER JOHNSON: You're welcome, son. That rain last night sure cooled down things pretty good, I say.

MARY: *(Sipping tea)* Your tea sure makes it nice though.

JESSIE: These are the days I remember so well. I cannot wait for when it gets cold so we can come over here and you *(Sister Johnson)* make that hot apple cider with your fireplace going and we sit at the dining room table talking or playing cards. We all back together again!

MARY: That all sounds good as long as it doesn't get as cold as it got this past winter. Shoot, none of us wanted to go out for anything unless it was for something important such as work and groceries.

JESSIE: You wrote and told me that. I bet Cousin Bee's was still busy.

SISTER JOHNSON: *(Sipping tea)* She wasn't as busy. Some days it was just too cold for anyone who didn't have to be out. Folks around here were sometimes her only customers. Bernie's was shut down for a week - couldn't get deliveries. I tell you it was cold! I don't ever need to see anything again as cold as this past winter - not even a refrigerator!

JESSIE: You all are exaggerating. Carl said it was not all that bad. I'm still looking forward to winter.

MARY: He's lying - just trying to show his macho behind to you. Ask him what he did when our heat went out! I've never seen a grown man complain as much as he did! You weren't here but I tell you this past winter's weather scared us.

JESSIE: Awww... I think it was because I wasn't here. Now that I'm back you remember how we looked forward to winter time? House parties, chili, card games, The Well's Friday night fish fry, basement movies and popcorn Saturdays.

SISTER JOHNSON: None of that was going on this past winter. Folks stayed in the warmth of their homes. The only time they went out was to check on the other folks to see if they were okay. Some days it was just too cold to go to work. Even my boss called and told me to stay home. That's how cold it was!

MARY: When you did see folks out you didn't recognize them because of all the clothes they had on. They looked like Arctic Eskimos.

JESSIE: I don't believe y'all. It couldn't have been that bad!

MARY: *(Exaggerating)* Ask Page. That man was delivering mail at nine o'clock at night - when he did deliver the mail. He would stay a few minutes longer at every house he delivered mail so he could warm up enough to deliver mail to the next house.

JESSIE: *(Laughing)* Y'all need to be on TV...

SISTER JOHNSON: *(Changing the subject)* Carl and Tracy still at the unemployment office?

MARY: Shoot! You should have seen all those people there. We waited nearly an hour and a half the last time we were there. Tracy wouldn't have had to go back if she had told them about Carl's work record - the two months he worked when he first got out of the service. He didn't think he was eligible for unemployment. As Mary continues speaking, Carl and Tracy come around the bend. Tracy is carrying a bag. Jessie sees them first as they approach...

JESSIE: *(To Carl and Tracy)* Don't tell me you hit the numbers and didn't tell us!

CARL: *(Smiling)* You know how I like to spend what I don't have.

MARY: *(To Carl)* At least you're honest. Must really be something you needed for Tra to make you bring it home - let's see what you got!

TRACY: *(Smiling... to Mary)* Don't be so nosy. *(Changes the subject)* Y'all, the unemployment office was so packed it was two hours before we saw someone. I almost lost my turn when I couldn't find Carl. He ran into D, Washington and Domino. Of course, they had to go outside just about that time when they called this fool's name. If it wasn't lucky that Cora Watkins was the one who called him, we'd still be there. She interviewed me until he got back. Seems like everyone we knew was in there. I'll be glad when this strike is finally over.

SISTER JOHNSON: I tell you, this is the worst strike I've seen.

JESSIE: *(To Carl)* When did Domino get out?

CARL: I don't know. He was out when I got out of the service.

MARY: *(Answering the question)* He got out about a year ago.

SISTER JOHNSON: That child has been in there more than he's out.

TRACY: He seems like he may want to stay out this time - opened a barber shop over on Dubois.

JESSIE: Maybe I'll go over there and get me a haircut. Last time I saw Domino we were in the eleventh grade.

TRACY: He's been out a few times since then but he does something stupid and winds up going back in.

MARY: I still want to know what's in that bag you're holding on to.

TRACY: *(She and Carl glance at each other)* Well, we were thinking about you all *(Mary and Jessie)* while we were out and brought back a gift. *(She reaches in the bag and pulls out a maternity dress).*

MARY: *(Grabs the dress and hugs her)* I'm going to be one fine pregnant sister, you hear me? *(She dances around while holding the dress in front of her)*

JESSIE: *(Responding)* She's got enough maternity clothes to last for two nine months.

TRACY: *(Snatching the dress back)* That was not your gift. It was my gift from my man.

Everyone is stunned for a moment except Carl and Tracy...

SISTER JOHNSON: *(Catching on)* That child is pregnant.

JESSIE: *(Looking at Carl)* Is this for real?

TRACY: *(Puts her arm around Carl smiling)* Why you all looking so shocked? You all thought he didn't have it in him, huh?

CARL: *(Boasting)* I had to give her what she wanted, man.

MARY: *(Jumps up from the swing and hugs Tracy)* Ohhh, thank you, Jesus! Girl, we're going to have children a few months apart.

JESSIE: *(Embraces Carl)* Congratulations, my brother!

SISTER JOHNSON: *(Rising from the swing)* Now I finally got me some grandchildren! *(Hugging Carl first and then Tracy)*

MARY: *(To Tracy)* You're cold! I told you and Sister Johnson before I told anyone - even Jessie!

TRACY: *(To Mary)* Girl, you don't know how hard it was for me to hold this in. I wanted to tell you the minute I thought I was pregnant but Carl wanted to be sure. *(Looking at Carl)* That's why we didn't want you all to go with us today. We had a doctor's appointment. You all should have noticed the way my man has been carrying on lately.

SISTER JOHNSON: I did notice a slightly different strut these last few days.

Everyone is smiling and happy.

TRACY: *(Joking)* That man has been walking around here like a great warrior.

CARL: *(Admiring Tracy)* Look at my Queen… carrying a little Prince *(Pauses)* or maybe Princess Carla.

Everyone is laughing at their antics.

TRACY: *(Teasingly reacting to Carl)* Y'all, if I had not gotten pregnant I don't know if my man could've lasted much longer. Last few weeks he was running on fumes. *(Hugging him)* He pushed it to the limit and look here.

CARL: *(Boasting)* Shows you all what a great warrior I am.

TRACY: *(Hugging and kissing Carl on the cheek)* Awww, sugar, you're the greatest! I've been whupping butts over you since we were in elementary school and will still do it.

Everyone briefly looks at Carl disappointedly.

SISTER JOHNSON: *(Trying to bring back the joy)* This is sweet potato cobbler time along with some greens, fried corn and cracklin' bread.

JESSIE: *(Catching on to Sister Johnson)* Shoot, I'm hungry now!

MARY: *(Happy again)* What does everyone like to put on their greens?

They all start singing... everyone likes to cha cha cha.

END OF SCENE FOUR

ACT III

SCENE FIVE

Weeks later - late in the afternoon: The poolroom is raided

It had been an overcast, damp and chilly fall day. The weather with gray skies was an indication that it would not get any warmer. The season was getting close to the time of storing away the porch furniture and putting up storm windows. This afternoon, pedestrian traffic is lighter than usual on Side Street because of the earlier rain showers. The vegetable cart sits across the street in front of Bernie's store, but it is covered over because of the rain and Mr. Crimple is not there. Three men, one black and two white, wearing matching soiled blue overalls with "Wayne's Construction" written on the back of them, pass the laundromat and enter Cousin Bee's Café.

Sister Johnson comes out of her front door onto the porch wearing her late husband's cardigan sweater and carrying a cup of steaming tea in her hand. She sits in a chair next to the railing so she can see the comings and goings of the street. She acknowledges the passersby, and notices two men wearing raincoats playing dominoes in front of Bernie's. The thought of winter being close at hand briefly encompasses her mind as she looks up and down the street and up at the gray sky. Acknowledging her porch-sitting days, domino games, fish and vegetable man, in a few more weeks at the most it will soon be over. Outside of having to go places and do things, for the next five or six months Detroit's winter inhabitants will be confined indoors. The big picture window in Sister Johnson's living room will be her only association and communication to the world of Side Street. Wrapping both hands around the cup of tea, a look of gleefulness shows upon her face as her thoughts change. She sings softly to herself.

SISTER JOHNSON: *(Singing)* He's got the whole world in his hands.

One reason for her joy is because Carl and Jessie hit the numbers the other evening for a nice sum of money. This morning they left, taking Tracy and Mary out shopping. Sipping her tea, she begins to reminisce. She truly considers all four of them as her adopted children because of Mary's and Tracy's parents. She promised their parents that if anything ever happened to them she would always look after the girls. Remembering this, her first duty after they were deceased was for her and Uncle Buck to talk Carl and Jessie into marrying the girls much sooner than planned before they left for the Army. The girls loved her as their adopted mother. They say she acts more like a sister than a mother to them and that is why they recognize her as Sister Johnson.

Sister Johnson smiles at Tracy's and Mary's portrayal of her sometimes. "A pretty hip old lady," is what they say about her. She truly enjoys their pampering of her, taking her to so-called sophisticated places and showing her off to their friends because of her fashionable appearance. The children think she is naturally attractive. They just don't know how much work it takes in order to keep it up. (A flashback) Remembering when her husband, Theodore, passed away, Mary's and Tracy's mother and father looked after her as if she was their own family. They were always there for her. Her mind brings her back to the present and she smiles.

Mrs. Washington comes out of her front door carrying food inside a covered picnic basket. She is not wearing a sweater or coat and feels the chill, as her pace accelerates to the rooming house next door. From the list of names on the wall she rings a bell. From the upstairs window a shade and window quietly rises, and Luella cautiously sticks her head out the window. She pulls her head back in after recognizing that it's Mrs. Washington at the door. A minute later, the door partially opens and Mrs. Washington gives the basket to Luella. The door closes and Mrs. Washington, going back to her house, stops as she hears Sister Johnson's voice.

SISTER JOHNSON: Kinda chilly, Mrs. Washington! Don't want you to catch a cold. You know how this here weather is.

MRS. WASHINGTON: *(She doesn't see Sister Johnson until she calls out to her)* Had I known it was this cool, I would've put on something warm like you have. I guess winter is getting pretty close.

SISTER JOHNSON: I think you're right. Guess the boys will be taking our porch stuff and storing it in our basements until next spring pretty soon.

MRS. WASHINGTON: *(Climbing her stairs)* Oh, that reminds me, *(Pauses)* at the end of next month I'm going home to New Orleans for three or four months. If any of you all need to get in the house, Ernest and Bee will have the keys. *(Opening her screen door)*

SISTER JOHNSON: You know I had planned on going to New Orleans around November but my sister and brother are driving up here for Christmas.

A couple come into view, speak to Sister Johnson and Mrs. Washington as they pass by and go into the poolroom.

MRS. WASHINGTON: Well, I'll be seeing you, Sister Johnson!

SISTER JOHNSON: *(Stopping Mrs. Washington briefly)* Awww, Mrs. Washington, I just wanted to say you've been through a lot these last few years and it's understandable what you're doing. *(Referring to her bringing food to Luella and Francine for Junior Boy)*

MRS. WASHINGTON: I'm glad folks understand, Sister Johnson. Thanks! *(She closes the door)*

Two men come onto Side Street wearing the exact same overalls, a bit dirtier than those worn by the three men who went into the Café earlier. They acknowledge Sister Johnson as they pass. She watches as they join in the domino game. Housecoat Pearl appears in front of her window in her housecoat with a glass of vodka in her hand. She raises the window briefly, peeps her head out, looks up and down the street. She sees Sister Johnson, the domino game and a slower-than-normal flow of traffic. Housecoat sees the young black couple pass beneath and go into the poolroom. All the activities on the street seem normal as she disappears back into the house and closes the window.

An older-looking, bearded white man wearing a lightweight coat comes onto Side Street and passes the laundromat. He walks towards the vegetable cart and begins uncovering it like he is setting up for business, but he is not Mr. Crimple.

Reverend Peters, wearing a light sports coat, exits the church. He starts to walk in the opposite direction, but he notices Sister Johnson sitting on her porch and changes his course and approaches her.

REVEREND PETERS: *(Approaching)* Good afternoon, Sister Johnson!

SISTER JOHNSON: Same to you, Reverend Peters! Looks like you're ready for winter.

REVEREND PETERS: It doesn't seem too far away. I'm not used to seeing you sitting here by yourself.

SISTER JOHNSON: If I sit here long enough by myself, Reverend *(Teasing)* someone interesting is bound to come and bide my time.

Reverend Peters feels awkward when talking to Sister Johnson because of his fondness for her, which she is fully aware of. (She enjoys her devilishness with the preacher as he is somewhat of a square man.)

REVEREND PETERS: *(Sits on her steps)* Is that a compliment, Sister Johnson? If it is, I thank you.

SISTER JOHNSON: Reverend, it is indeed!

REVEREND PETERS: I reckon pretty soon Carl and Jessie will be top-notch mechanics. Heard Mr. Whitser plans on eventually selling them his shop. Guess I have to split my business with them and Deacon Grady.

SISTER JOHNSON: *(Teasing)* I better not see you taking your car to Deacon Grady anymore when they own that shop. If I do, you aren't getting any more of my sweet potato pies and cobblers.

REVEREND PETERS: That would be unkind! I feel like I grew up on your sweet potato pies and cobblers. And you know I must be fair. After all, I'm a minister and Grady is one of our fine deacons in the church.

SISTER JOHNSON: *(Having fun)* Don't get me going on Deacon Grady. You just let him work on your car after my boys are mechanics and own their own shop. It's not only pies and cobblers that you'll not get but I'll tell the whole church how Deacon Grady don't like working on ladies' cars because he thinks ladies should be at home cooking, cleaning and having babies - just like his poor wife once did.

REVEREND PETERS: *(Smiling)* Would you really do that, Sister Johnson?

SISTER JOHNSON: *(Demonstrating)* I declare I would step out from that choir, walk up to the front of that church and I would preach it. Preach it like you preach about alcohol, hot pants and miniskirts.

REVEREND PETERS: Now Sister Johnson, you know when I speak of those things I'm speaking of poison and lustful temptation.

SISTER JOHNSON: I ain't saying nothing about the alcohol, but you know as well as I do a woman alone is temptation enough for man. We could have on Eskimo clothes and still you lust with temptation. *(Imitating)* Oooh, baby, you sho looking good in them Eskimo clothes!

REVEREND PETERS: *(Smiling)* Now that may be true in some instances, Sister Johnson, but my job is to try and cut the Devil's odds, that's all. Hot pants, short skirts and tight-fitting clothes are designed for *(Apprehensive)* ah… you know what I mean.

SISTER JOHNSON: *(Smiling)* You mean clothes designed for vital signs.

REVEREND PETERS: Exactly! Those are all Satan's allies.

SISTER JOHNSON: Well, now, if that be the case answer this for me, Reverend. I hear Ray Charles and Little Stevie Wonder are as horny as a bull looking at a flock of heifers and they can't even see.

REVEREND PETERS: Ahhh… well, Sister Johnson there are exceptions, I reckon, but *(Sister Johnson interrupts Reverend Peters)*…

SISTER JOHNSON: Well, now wait, Reverend Peters. You seem to be quite healthy looking, I must say. Are you eliminating yourself from man's runaway hormonal condition?

REVEREND PETERS: *(At a loss for words)* Sister Johnson, why do you… ah… when we talk somehow manage to get me hemmed in a corner? I declare, I believe you take a liking to the tongue-lashing of a preacher man.

SISTER JOHNSON: I can't lie to you, Reverend. It's a pleasure for me but not for any preacher man - just for you.

REVEREND PETERS: How do I get into these conversations anyway with you? How in the world did mechanics turn into hot pants and miniskirts?

SISTER JOHNSON: Ahhh, Reverend, you know you look forward to these kinds of conversations every now and then. They give you a little spruce - wake up them sleeping dogs!

REVEREND PETERS: *(Smiling)* Sister Johnson, have you ever heard of the old saying - I'll rephrase it – "let sleeping dogs lie"?

SISTER JOHNSON: Ahhh, Reverend, all things need to wake up sometimes, if but for a brief second, for a breath of fresh air or a fleeting memory.

REVEREND PETERS: You're a very persuasive woman, Sister Johnson.

SISTER JOHNSON: *(Smiling)* Is that a compliment, Reverend?

REVEREND PETERS: I suppose it could be dangerously construed as one.

SISTER JOHNSON: You don't think God is going to confuse our tongues so we can't talk to one another, do you, Reverend?

REVEREND PETERS: *(Smiling)* I don't think so. He knows you're a good person *(Pauses)* but then again, there's that sweet potato cobbler issue that may cause a little disturbance in his church.

SISTER JOHNSON: Ahhh, Reverend, a little persuasion from you may make me want to bake you a cobbler and a pie every now and then.

REVEREND PETERS: *(Explaining)* I'll remember that, but I'm not speaking of me. I'm speaking of what your pies and cobblers, tools of persuasion, have created amongst some of our male church members.

SISTER JOHNSON: *(Curious)* What have I done, Reverend?

REVEREND PETERS: Now you know as well as I, Sister Johnson, that the folks at church know how persuasive your sweet potato pies and cobblers have been in church affairs. Just like when the choir wanted new robes and the church members, led by you, wanted a new bus or when the musical director wanted a new organ, he called on you and your sweet potato pies and cobblers. *(Pauses)* Well, now it seems your sweet potato pie and cobbler method of persuasion is beginning to upset some of the deacons and male members of the congregation.

SISTER JOHNSON: Where do I fit into this, Reverend - outside of my sweet potato pie and cobbler?

REVEREND PETERS: Well, as the chairman of our female church body, your methods of persuasiveness seem to have rubbed off on some of the sisters. Some of the wives have taken a liking to it and are practicing your methods of persuasion at home - with a certain amount of success, I might add. *(Pauses)* The deacons aren't too happy.

SISTER JOHNSON: *(Proud)* I didn't know that had happened. Sounds like something I'd be proud of. About time some of those women stood up for what they believe and as far as those deacons are concerned, let me tell you what I think about them. I sure wouldn't like to be on their team when it comes time for God's wrath.

REVEREND PETERS: Yes, ma'am! Your sweet potato pie and cobbler have surely made a reputation for themselves in this community.

SISTER JOHNSON: *(Modest)* Guess folks love their sweets. *(Flirty)* Is it the sweets or is it me? Can you guess which one?

REVEREND PETERS: I declare, Sister Johnson; sometimes you ask questions that should be left unasked and unanswered.

Reverend Peters and Sister Johnson see Carl, Jessie, Mary and Tracy coming around the corner carrying shopping bags and they seem very happy until they see Reverend Peters. They had hoped they were not going to see him while they had the bags.

REVEREND PETERS: *(Smiling as he's getting ready to leave)* Sister Johnson, I'd better be going. It's a rather busy day for me. *(Speaking to Carl, Tracy, Jessie and Mary as they come closer to the porch)* Afternoon! You all make it feel like Christmas around here with all those bags.

JESSIE: *(Smiling)* How are you, sir? I guess sometimes Christmas may come a little early.

CARL: *(Smiling)* Thanksgiving, too!

REVEREND PETERS: I tell you it sure makes me feel good to see folks out shopping and bringing needful things home again. Maybe it'll rub off onto this community. It has been a while since folks around here have been enjoying the little pleasures of life. You all are always an inspiration to this community.

MARY: *(Being nosy)* Hi, Reverend Peters! What have you and Sister Johnson been talking about?

CARL, JESSIE and TRACY: Yeah!

MARY: Remember, you're a reverend. You aren't supposed to fib.

Sister Johnson and Reverend Peters look at each other and smile.

SISTER JOHNSON: Do you want to tell them or do you want me to?

REVEREND PETERS: Why don't you tell them, Sister Johnson?

MARY: Oh, no, Oh, no! Let the preacher man talk!

REVEREND PETERS: *(Assuming they have hit the numbers)* I tell you what. Let us have a fair trade agreement. I'll be glad to tell you what we talked about if you'll give me a good sermon to preach about on Sunday so I can show the congregation how they, too, can have an early Christmas and Thanksgiving like you all are having in these hard times.

Sister Johnson hides her elation over the Reverend's comment, since she never thinks of him as being a witty person. Carl, Jessie, Mary, and Tracy look at each other. They know what Reverend Peter's sermons are like and he, not believing in gambling, sure could make an embarrassing sermon for them on Sunday.

CARL: We can't do that at this particular time, Reverend.

MARY: Am I correct when I say I believe he has outsmarted us?

TRACY: I think you are correct.

REVEREND PETERS: *(Beginning to walk away)* I'll be on my way. I'll be talking to you again, Sister Johnson and *(Turning to Mary, Jessie, Carl and Tracy, says)* you all have a wonderful day.

TRACY: *(Speaking to Sister Johnson)* Did you tell him about us hitting the numbers?

SISTER JOHNSON: *(Smiling)* Of course not! I think the Reverend seeing you all with those bags and the way things are, he probably had a pretty good idea where the money could have come from. I like his smarts today.

Page comes around the corner without his mailbag, dressed loudly in civilian clothes. He goes into the laundromat for a brief second and comes out and goes into Cousin Bee's. He comes out and does the same thing at every business until he reaches Sister Johnson's porch, where Carl, Jessie, Mary, Tracy and Sister Johnson are sitting.

PAGE: Have you heard the news? The strike is over and the Teamsters have reached an agreement. Longest strike I've ever seen.

EVERYONE: *(Applauding)* Yeaaah!

PAGE: *(Continuing)* I heard that anybody who wants to work will have a job full or part-time; and all those workers who are being called back to work better be prepared to do a lot of overtime. Warehouses are overflowing. They say it'll take months before things get back to normal.

SISTER JOHNSON: Thank you, Jesus! The folks around here are just about at the end of their rope.

MARY: Doesn't the Lord work in mysterious ways? He isn't going to give you no more than you can bear.

CARL: Looks like we're going to have two Christmases and two Thanksgivings!

PAGE: *(Getting ready to leave)* I'm going to get a haircut. *(Speaking to Jessie and Carl)* Y'all hit for a nice piece of change the other day, huh? Has Big Hank been around yet?

JESSIE: Not yet! We're waiting. He said he would be coming around this time.

PAGE: He will if he said he would. *(Walking away)* See y'all later. *(Turns back to them briefly)* I forgot to tell you, folks. Got mail today about Junior Boy leaving tonight heading to Canada.

Page sticks his head into the beauty shop.

PAGE: The strike is over! Factories and other businesses are hiring anybody who wants to work.

Page goes into the barber shop.

TRACY: I sure hope the Devil doesn't come and mess things up. All the goodness of this day. You know how he hates to see folks having a good time. It's like he sticks his feet out and tries to trip you every time.

SISTER JOHNSON: Y'all are a mess! This here has been so wonderful. I woke up feeling kinda strange this morning. You know when something just ain't right, but this day has been nothing but sunshine in the sky and in our spirits. *(Pauses)* By the way, a few minutes ago I saw Big Hank and his boys go into the poolroom.

JESSIE: *(Speaking to Carl)* I guess we better get ready to go. You know he moves fast.

CARL: Yeah, just long enough to collect and pay his debts.

MARY: You all better be going if we want to get to the bank before it closes. It's nearly five o'clock now. We don't have that much time left.

TRACY: Sure enough! We aren't planning on putting that under no mattress or in no cookie jar.

CARL: Why don't you three be ready when we get back? We'll go to the bank then over to the Rooster Tail.

MARY: We're ready. We haven't got anything else to do but put our bags in the house.

SISTER JOHNSON: *(Rising from her chair)* Well, now, I need some touching up. I better see what I can do to improve upon age.

TRACY: Hush your mouth! You could go just like you are and look better than most folks - including us. We'll leave our stuff at your house 'til we get back, Sister Johnson.

The three of them go into Sister Johnson's house. Carl and Jessie look at each other.

CARL: *(Smiling)* No use waiting any longer.

JESSIE: I'm ready, my brother!

Jessie and Carl step off the porch and walk to the poolroom. The activity on the street begins to change as soon as Carl and Jessie enter the poolroom and close the door. Traffic suddenly slows down. A few minutes pass and all that remains visible on Side Street are four men playing dominoes, the man at the vegetable cart and Housecoat Pearl looking out her window. A man comes onto Side Street wearing beige pants and a matching shirt with a tool belt around his waist and stops at a telephone pole right at the beginning of Side Street. He takes a key from his pocket and opens the big black box mounted on the pole. Then he reaches in his tool belt, pulls out a tool, does something inside the box, puts the tool back into his belt and closes the black box. After making eye contact with the man at the vegetable cart, he turns and goes back in the direction from which he came. On the back of his shirt is written "Michigan Telephone Company." Two men get up from the domino table, walk in the opposite direction and disappear around the bend. The three men wearing overalls come out of Cousin Bee's, look over at the bearded man at the vegetable cart then disappear around the bend near the laundromat. The two remaining men playing dominoes get up and walk over to the vegetable cart.

Housecoat Pearl begins to look curiously at the happenings from her window. She notices the three men that left Cousin Bee's wearing overalls coming back onto the street wearing guns and green undercover police attire with bottom pant legs inside their boots. Seeing the three men come back, the one man at the vegetable cart takes off his mustache and beard and the other two men take off their jackets and coats revealing guns and police uniforms. Pearl, seeing that a raid is going down, desperately tries to contact the poolroom by telephone, becoming frustrated and helpless as she realizes her telephone line has been cut. She races to the window to yell to alert someone of what is happening, but realizes it is too late.

The three men at the vegetable cart merge to the right side of the poolroom door while the other three men go to the left. One of the policemen pulls out his gun and the others follow suit. He then raises his hand and they all swarm into the poolroom together and the sounds of a ruckus can be heard.

END OF SCENE FIVE

ACT III

SCENE SIX

Rabbit comes back home...

Big sign reads: MILTON'S BARBER SHOP

The barber shop has three chairs, a long pew, a card table with a domino game and a milk crate with a board on top of it being used for checkers. There are two teenagers, eating chips and drinking pop, sitting on the pew along with other customers reading magazines while waiting their turn.

Reverend Peters sits in the barber's chair listening to a conversation and watching the domino and checker game while Milton cuts his hair.

MILTON: *(From time to time glances out the window and looks up at the sky)* Almanac says we're going to have another cold winter.

MALE VOICE: *(Older gentleman)* I'm not going to pay attention to that almanac, not when I got Jesus who can change winter to summer and summer to winter *(Pauses and snaps his fingers)* just like that! Am I right, Reverend?

REVEREND PETERS: I surely can't say you're wrong.

CUSTOMER: I'm going to be more prepared this winter. Getting up at five o'clock in the morning and going out in that weather to warm the car up to go to work is murder. I saw a report on television of how they can put something in your car that you can start it right up from inside the house and warm it up. I'm going to have one put in my car next month.

MILTON: How much do those contraptions cost to install and do they work? *(He mutters out loud)* All these newfangled gadgets!

TEENAGER: They do. My cousin did that to his car.

MALE # 2: *(In the barber chair)* You all think this past winter was cold? Heck, in 1967 we had days when it was 8, 9, 10 and 11 degrees below zero! I remember one day it was 22 below zero. Now that was cold!

REVEREND PETERS: I seem to remember those days you're talking about. It was one of the coldest times I can remember.

OLD MAN: *(Playing checkers)* Y'all have not felt a winter until you've been in the winter of '58 and '59. I don't believe we had a day over 31 degrees the whole winter. We had days of 18 and 22 below zero and they said it was over 45 inches of snow. Some days we couldn't get out of the house and it took a few days before our streets were plowed. The markets ran out of food and schools were closed. I mean there were days when it was so cold you couldn't start your car.

TEENAGER #2: We were out of school for a week this winter. The boiler busted.

TEENAGER #1: We had fun in the cold.

MILTON: *(Turns and speaks to the teenagers)* When you get older, you'll change your mind. The cold does something to your bones. Make them ache.

MALE # 2: Mine's aching just talking about it.

Milton, finishing up with Reverend Peters, looks out the window.

MILTON: I wonder who is parking that fine new convertible Eldorado out front. They must have hit the numbers.

Reverend Peters gets up from the barber chair and looks out the window while Milton brushes the hair off his clothes, head and shoulders.

REVEREND PETERS: *(Still looking at the car)* That's sure a fine looking automobile! Wonder who it belongs to?

TEENAGER # 1: *(Seeing the Cadillac out the window)* That's a bad hog *(car)*!

CUSTOMER: *(Leaning to see the Cadillac from his seat)* During these times there's not too many ways you can afford a car like that - and most aren't legal.

MILTON: I wonder who that is. Who hit the numbers?

REVEREND PETERS: Reckon you'll find out soon. He pulled up in front of this shop for a reason. *(Standing, looking out the window)* Well, well, if it isn't Brother Nicholas Jones!

Everyone's eyes are on Rabbit, his appearance and his car. (There seems to be a unanimous expression from everyone.)

MILTON: *(Brushing the hair off Reverend Peters' collar and neck)* From the looks of it, that boy leaving Detroit seems to have done him good.

Everyone is in agreement.

TEENAGER: He looks like a celebrity.

CUSTOMER EARL: He looks like a new person since the last time I saw him. It's like night and day.

Reverend Peters is putting on his coat as Rabbit walks into the shop.

RABBIT: *(Trying to be humble as he walks in)* Afternoon, everybody!

The customers in the shop come over and give him a handshake and a hug.

CUSTOMER: Good to see you! What's happening, my brother?

OLDER CUSTOMER: *(Shakes Rabbit's hand)* How have you been? You're looking mighty good, son.

RABBIT: I feel good, too!

YOUNG CUSTOMER: Boy, that sure is a bad hog you got there!

RABBIT: Thanks, my brother!

Rabbit waits until Milton and Reverend Peters finish. Both are as eager to talk to him as Rabbit is to talk to them. Milton comes over as Reverend Peters looks in the mirror and tidies himself up.

MILTON: *(Hugging Rabbit)* It's good to see you, boy! We were talking about you just this morning. Seems like the folks around here been kind of concerned about you. *(Looking out the window at the car)* I say, from the looks of things you seem to be doing all right though. You ain't doing nothing illegal are you? Ain't seen many folks driving a new car - especially a Cadillac!

RABBIT: No, sir! I ain't doing nothing illegal.

CUSTOMER: *(Somewhat joking)* Well, you sure look mighty prosperous! You must have hit the numbers for a whole lot of money then. *(Everyone laughs)*

MILTON: Have you seen Jessie?

RABBIT: *(Looking very serious)* No, sir! This is the first place I came to since I got in town. *(Looking at Reverend Peters)* I called the church and they told me you were here getting a haircut.

REVEREND PETERS: *(Goes over to Rabbit and they briefly embrace)* Brother Nicholas, I must say it's good to see you looking so well. What can I do for you?

RABBIT: Well, sir, I have news that I want to share. Since you're the leader and the voice of our community, I thought it would be fitting if you would be with me when I share what I believe is good news. But first, I want to share it with Jessie and you before I share it with anyone else.

MILTON: Son, you sure have come to a bad place talking like that. This here is a barber shop.

RABBIT: I know and I beg you all to understand. Jessie is my main man who deserves firsthand information about me. No one gets to know before the reverend and Jessie.

MILTON: Well, now, let's do some compromising here. Tell you what, my boy, Reverend Peters and I, more than anyone, know how much Jessie and you have meant to each other through the years. We wouldn't want anything to spoil any good news about you that you have for Jessie. Since you and the Reverend are both here in the barber shop it just doesn't seem right for you all to walk out of here with good news. Are you going to Side Street when you leave here?

RABBIT: Yes, sir!

MILTON: I'll be willing to bet you before you get to the end of Side Street we'll know everything you said, plus what you didn't say. Folks cannot wait to get to a phone to call and tell us the news. Outside of the church, the barber shop is the soul of the community. This place here is the news capital of the ghetto. We'll tell you this; we promise that whatever you share with us no one will hear it from us until after you've told Jessie and Side Street.

As Milton turns to everyone in the shop they nod in agreement meaning that they promise not to talk.

REVEREND PETERS: *(Speaking to Rabbit)* I don't think they'll let us out this door right now. Do you?

RABBIT: *(Smiling)* No, sir! I don't think they will. *(He pauses)*

Reverend Peters sits back down in the empty barber chair and listens to Rabbit as he continues...

RABBIT: Okay, *(Pauses)* one thing I'm proud to tell you is that I'm completely free of all my bad vices, thanks to you all, the Nation of Islam and especially Jessie.

Everyone in the room shouts with cheer and applauds for Rabbit's victory.

RABBIT: *(Gestures with gratefulness as he continues)* Thank you very much! When I left here, my cousins took me to a facility for drug and alcohol addictions. It's a place where professional athletes, entertainers and others go. It really helped me a lot. They had a gym and football field and I played basketball and football with some professional athletes. I was in there for ninety days. I started working harder than I had ever worked in my life to get myself together and to get in the best physical and mental shape ever.

CUSTOMER: You look good, boy!

RABBIT: *(Acknowledging his compliment)* Thank you. I still have a long way to go yet but I'm slowly getting there.

MILTON: You sure know how to keep folks in suspense. You got us all on pins and needles.

RABBIT: *(Laughing)* Okay! I'm just as excited as you all… but please, I beg you not to let the cat out of the bag. *(Pauses)* My cousins got me a chance to try out for a semi-pro football team in Gary.

Everyone in the room stands in attention on pins and needles with anticipation of Rabbit's next words.

RABBIT: Well, after a month of practice and working out, they made me their starting running back! Our team played a team in Canada and I played really well. Scored two touchdowns! *(Applause)* Thanks! I didn't know until afterwards that Canadian football scouts were there at that game and they were pretty impressed with me and my performance. So much so, that they came to two other games to watch me play. Each game I played I got better and better.

CUSTOMER: *(Junior High School Football Coach)* Not trying to interrupt you, son, but I just want to say something. I can remember watching you in high school in football, basketball and track. You were a born natural! No one could be taught to do what you did. Why I'm saying this is because you've only been out of school a little over three years and by this time you should have been finished with college. I believe you still have what you had back then. You just have to re-establish yourself.

Everyone in the room mumbles in agreement.

RABBIT: *(Smiling)* Thank you, sir! I sure am trying. I don't know if I have what I used to have but I still got something. I sure stirred up quite a lot of interest in those last games I played.

Rabbit pauses and smiles, reaches in his inside suit coat pocket and pulls out an envelope. He reaches inside the envelope and pulls out a paper, unfolds it and holds it up in the air.

RABBIT: I may not be good enough to play yet for the NFL but I have here a signed three year contract *(Pauses)* to play professional Canadian football for the Grey Wolves!

There is more applause and cheers from everyone, including Reverend Peters.

REVEREND PETERS: Brother Nicholas, this will be a monumental day for our community and for the city of Detroit. Folks have been waiting for this moment and they're going to be real pleased.

A customer in the shop asks Rabbit if he will be starting.

ANOTHER CUSTOMER: *(Responds)* You know he is! Shoot, the way he moves no one can catch him.

RABBIT: They thought enough of me to give me a contract. I've been practicing with them for two weeks and so far they seem to like what they see. I can't say I'll be starting but I'm looking pretty good out there, if I have to say so myself. They do have some real good backs I'm competing with.

CUSTOMER: I bet you it won't be long before you'll be playing for the NFL. *(Everyone claps and cheers and some of them come up and shake Rabbit's hand with congratulations)*

ANOTHER CUSTOMER: Maybe you'll be playing for the Lions. Wouldn't that be something?

MILTON: We're proud of you anyway, my boy. I know when Jessie hears about this he'll be the happiest person in the world!

REVEREND PETERS: *(Rising from the chair)* Well, I guess we shouldn't be holding you up any longer. It seems like you've got a busy day ahead of you.

Everyone moves towards the door to bid Rabbit goodbye and wish him luck as he and Reverend Peters exit the barber shop. They keep their positions in front of the plate glass window as they watch Reverend Peters and Rabbit get into the car. The car drives off about the same time the telephone rings in the barber shop.

MILTON: *(Answering the phone)* Barber shop! *(He pauses, and then hangs up the phone and speaks loudly to everyone)* The poolroom on Side Street is being raided and you can't call in or out. *(There is a look of shock and disappointment on everybody's faces.)*

END OF SCENE SIX

ACT III

SCENE SEVEN

At the poolroom...

Carl and Jessie are angry that the poolroom got raided as they stand with three other people handcuffed with their backs against the poolroom wall. Big Hank and his men are also handcuffed on the opposite wall of the poolroom door. Two boxes of number slips and briefcases are brought out. Everything has been confiscated, including their winning ticket. This means they may not get paid.

Sister Johnson comes out of her house with Mary and Tracy. All three were unaware of the happenings until they looked up the street and saw the policemen. As they stepped off the porch they see Jessie and Carl standing against the poolroom wall.

SISTER JOHNSON: Oh, my Lord!

TRACY: Carl!

MARY: Jessie!

They all run towards the poolroom but are restrained from moving further down the street by a policeman in front of Mrs. Washington's house. Luella and Francine, hearing the noises, raise the window shade, let up their window and stick their heads out. They see the raid and notice Mary, Tracy, and Sister Johnson being restrained. They also see a similar situation taking place in front of Bee's Café with Bee, Ernest and Ernestine. Junior Boy pops his head out and is quickly pulled back in as they quietly shut the window and pull the window shade back down. They were unaware that their building had been under surveillance by the two men in overalls who were playing dominoes, left and returned.

While the attention is focused on the poolroom, the two men who had on raincoats and played dominoes earlier with the policemen have returned without their coats. They are wearing Army uniforms and on their sleeves are bands that indicate they are MPs. Both have pistols in their possession. They pull Army caps from their pockets and put them on their heads. While no one is paying attention to them, they casually walk to the entrance of the rooming house. One produces a key and unlocks the front door as they both enter.

A policeman comes up, pulls out a key and unlocks the handcuffs and releases Carl, Jessie and the three individuals with them. Carl and Jessie walk over to where Mary, Tracy and Sister Johnson are standing. Everyone has been freed to leave except for Big Hank and his men. Ernest, Carl, Bee, Tracy, Mary and Sister Johnson all gather in front of Mrs. Washington's house.

BIG HANK: *(Speaking to Ernest as he passes them)* Call my lawyer, Elbert Henry!

Ernest acknowledges Big Hank's request.

A few seconds of loud noises and screams coming from the rooming house attracts everyone's attention. Then it's quiet. Moments later the front door of the rooming house opens. Everyone sees the MPs as they come out with Junior Boy between them, arms locked in a vice grip. Everyone's attention is on the MPs and Junior Boy. As one of them pulls out a pair of handcuffs, everyone watches as Luella and Francine run out the door and jump on the MPs' backs, startling them into loosening their grip enough for Junior Boy to break free and run across the field.

LUELLA: *(Swinging on one of the MP's back)* Run Junior! Run!

FRANCINE: *(Urging Junior Boy by hollering loudly)* RUN JUNIOR BOY! RUN… RUN… RUN!

Everyone at Mrs. Washington's house joins in by hollering… RUN JUNIOR BOY, RUN JUNIOR BOY… RUN...RUN...RUN. The MPs get the girls off them and take off running after Junior Boy. Luella and Francine join Carl, Jessie, Mary, Sister Johnson, Ernest, Ernestine, Bee and Bernie as they all watch Big Hank's poolroom door being padlocked.

JESSIE: Sometimes this street seems very long when you're trying to get from one end to the other.

CARL: This is what makes a brother go crazy - and I'm close to the cliff right now, man!

TRACY: *(Her arms around Carl)* We'll be all right, sugar.

MARY: *(Speaking to Jessie)* All I care about is that you're here safe with me.

SISTER JOHNSON: Nothing's going to change what happened and no one is going to feel better doing something that will bite them in the butt.

JESSIE: You just get tired sometimes. The door of opportunity opens, we peep inside and then it shuts right in our faces. It challenges our morals and faith. It seems we're always walking on the verge.

Page, dressed in his postal uniform, appears from around the bend. He is briefly restrained by a policeman. The door next to Cousin Bee's Café opens and Housecoat Pearl stands there mad and intoxicated. She holds a baseball bat in her hand and mumbles loudly as she steps out of her doorway, getting everyone's attention.

HOUSECOAT PEARL: Nobody is giving anyone around here anything! Not even a dime for a cup of coffee. Folks around here trying to live the best they can - barely making it without much. No jobs and you trying to take what little dreams and hopes we have away from us.

Housecoat Pearl walks towards the poolroom with her bat over her shoulder, causing over-reaction by the white police officers and causing them to flex their authority.

PAGE: *(Trying to calm the officers)* I know her! Let me talk to her!

Page gets near her before she reaches anyone. She raises the bat over her shoulder as if she may swing at him. Page knows her reputation and stops in his tracks.

PAGE: Guess I'll mind my own business!

The male and female cops approach Housecoat Pearl. Jessie is one of the few people that Pearl will listen to and he, knowing that she will hit them, quickly intervenes by putting himself between the cops and Pearl.

JESSIE: *(Speaking to the officers)* I can handle her. *(Putting his arm around her and gently comforting her)* Miss Pearl, we're going to get in trouble with that bat you're holding. It's making some folks around here pretty nervous.

HOUSECOAT PEARL: I'm ready to go to jail or to hell today.

BIG HANK: *(Speaking to Pearl)* Pearl, this isn't your fault. Why don't you go on back in the house? It's going to be okay.

As Carl walks towards Jessie, he is aggressively stopped by one of the white police officers. The officer places his hand on Carl's shoulder and says, "This is as far as you go."

CARL: *(Backing up as he is encouraged to do by the policeman)* Man, get your hands off of me!

Big Hank, seeing the behavior of the police officer towards Carl's resistance, steps forward.

BIG HANK: Hey, take it easy! That boy ain't bothering anyone!

END OF SCENE SEVEN

ACT III

SCENE EIGHT

Rabbit is dead / Tracy miscarries and loses her baby...

From the opposite end of the street from around the bend, Rabbit and Reverend Peters appear unnoticed. They stop briefly, visibly stunned at the happenings. Rabbit, reacting as his natural instincts have always done in the past, seeing Carl in somewhat of a confrontation with the police officer, hurries to his defense. Reverend Peters follows behind him in an attempt to help calm things down.

REVEREND PETERS: *(Talks to Rabbit)* Hold on, son! Let me handle this. *(Loudly to everyone)* Calm down! Calm down, everyone!

Reverend Peters and Rabbit head towards the ruckus. The police officers are holding everyone back and one of the black officers recognizes Reverend Peters and slows down the aggression, knowing the reverend will be able to calm things down.

POLICEMAN: *(To his officers and the crowd)* Hey, let the Reverend here handle it!

THE WHITE POLICEMAN: *(To Carl, whom he's still in confrontation with uses his fingers and taps Carl on the shoulder forcibly)* You take it easy and settle down!

CARL: *(Pushes his hand away angrily)* Get your damn hands off me, man!

BIG HANK: *(To the policeman)* Hey! That boy ain't done nothing and not bothering anyone!

The situation is becoming volatile as the white officer sees Mary, Tracy, Ernest and the others congregating and reacting to what he is doing to Carl.

TRACY: *(Yelling at the policeman... Mary and Ernest holding her back)* Get your hands off my husband!

SISTER JOHNSON: *(Knowing Carl)* Oh, Lord!

The policeman, not hearing the command of his fellow policeman because of all the chaos and loud chatter, reaches for his gun when he sees Rabbit break away from Reverend Peters.

RABBIT: *(Approaching white policeman)* Whoa, wait a minute... cool it, man!

The officer's feels threatened as Rabbit approaches him and he lifts his gun to his waist just as Rabbit comes between the policeman and Carl. Seconds later a gunshot sound penetrates the air.

Tracy screams and breaks from Mary and Sister Johnson.

TRACY: *(Screams thinking it's Carl)* Carlllllllll!! *(She gets a few feet and collapses onto the ground)*

MARY: *(Running to Tracy)* Tracyyy!

Sister Johnson and Ernestine go over to Tracy. All three of them kneel and lift her up until she comes to. Sister Johnson and Mary hurry her into the house. The policeman holds his gun down by his side, stunned as the other officers and Reverend Peters calm the situation down.

REVEREND PETERS: *(Kneeling down by Rabbit's side)* Someone call an ambulance!! *(To Rabbit)* Be patient, son. An ambulance is on its way!

Bee rushes into the café. Carl gets down on his knees and lifts Rabbit's upper body on to his lap and cradles his head in his arms. Rabbit reacts looking up at him. Jessie is stunned and kneels down next to Rabbit.

BIG HANK: *(Mad)* This was not necessary! Somebody is paying for this! I promise you!

REVEREND PETERS: *(Noticing the hostility growing by the crowd)* I want everyone here to stay calm. We don't need any more pain than what we have!

BEE: *(Hurrying out of the café... yells)* The phones are off!

The female officer acknowledges Bee.

POLICEWOMAN: The ambulance is on its way!

RABBIT: *(Turns to Jessie and extends his arms, talking weakly...)* I didn't let you down, Jess! You hung in there with me, Jess! I didn't let you down. *(Rabbit grimacing... slowly reaches into his pocket and pulls out an envelope)* Read it Jess... read it. *(He feels the pain from the gunshot wound)* Oww, it hurts. Read it, Jess!

JESSIE: *(Opens the envelope and pulls out the letter... reads it tearfully with his voice breaking)* It is hereby declared that Nicholas Jones has agreed upon a three-year contract to play for the Canadian Grey Wolves Professional Football Team.

RABBIT: *(Trying to smile)* I didn't let you down, did I, Jess?

JESSIE: *(Keeps talking to Rabbit as the siren sound nears)* Hang in there, Rabbit! Help is coming. You're going to be okay, hang in there!

RABBIT: You're my main man, Jess. *(To Carl)* I love you, too, my brother!

CARL: *(Teary-eyed)* I love you, Rabbit! I do. Hold on, my brother, please hold on!

RABBIT: I'm sorry. *(He hollers)* MAMA!

Rabbit becomes silent as the ambulance pulls in near the street entrance and seconds later two men come around the bend with the stretcher.

Next Day- Late morning - inside Tracy's house ...

Mary and Sister Johnson come from another room into the living room of Tracy's house. Mary has a bag full of Tracy's maternity clothes. Sister Johnson is shaking her head sadly.

SISTER JOHNSON: Those poor children! They wanted a child so bad. I know this situation will mend, but right now I just feel for what they're going through.

MARY: I sure wish there was something we could do for them Sister Johnson. Why does this always happen to us, Sister Johnson? When something good happens, something worse happens and crushes the happiness. Is God testing us?

SISTER JOHNSON: It's not God. It's the revenge of the Devil, testing our faith, trying to change and convert us to hell! As bad and dark as it seems there is a bright light at the end of this tunnel. *(Pauses)* Did you get all the baby clothes and her maternity outfits out of the closet?

MARY: Yes, ma'am! Carl said they were all in the bedroom closet and drawers. Lord, the blood on this street from yesterday will never wash off.

SISTER JOHNSON: *(Putting her arm around Mary)* A tornado tore through this community yesterday! Now it's rebuilding time, child. Sometimes losses can produce great gains. You just have to keep trusting in the Lord. What time are they supposed to be home?

MARY: Carl said he would call me when the hospital releases her. *(Pauses)* Lord only knows what Carl and Jessie are going through right now! Rabbit dying and Tracy having a miscarriage has burdened our world. Not like we didn't already have enough. *(Teary-eyed)* My poor husband! That man has lost the dream he's been carrying around with him since childhood. *(Pauses - thinking)* Sister Johnson, Rabbit didn't disappoint us, did he?

SISTER JOHNSON: No, he didn't, my child! Honey, yesterday, Jessie's dream came true when he read that paper that was in Rabbit's pocket. That said everything! Reverend said that Rabbit couldn't wait to show Jessie his contract. He didn't want anyone to know before Jessie. We may not see him play, but everyone knows he made it.

MARY: I think we can say he's truly our hero.

SISTER JOHNSON: He truly is!

MARY: Sister Johnson, I wonder what good will come from this.

SISTER JOHNSON: I think we're just going to have to wait on this one. It's too cloudy right now for any of us to see beyond the present. This community went through a lot. *(Pauses– looking around at the house)* It looks like we've gotten everything. When Tracy comes home she won't have to do anything but rest.

MARY: Yeah! All I've got to do is cook. When Carl calls, I'll start. I'm going to make pork chops, mashed potatoes and gravy with string beans. She won't turn that down.

SISTER JOHNSON: I made two sweet potato cobblers this morning - one I took to Mrs. Jones. *(Both heading towards the door)* I guess we better be going. Is Jessie still with the Reverend?

MARY: He called before we came down here. He and Reverend Peters are at the mortuary with Mrs. Jones. Poor lady! Lost her only child! She's a total wreck. *(Opening the door)*

SISTER JOHNSON: I think you need a little rest, too, child. You have also been through a lot. You have truly held up well and been strong for everyone else.

MARY: I'm trying. Lord knows I'm trying.

They walked out the door. (Fade)

Tracy is home from the hospital...

With the weather being a little warmer than it has been these past few days, Mary and Sister Johnson want Tracy out of the house and on the porch so she can enjoy the fresh air and talk to the neighbors as they walk by. Friends and neighbors have been visiting with Tracy who is home from the hospital recovering from her miscarriage. Mary comes out of Tracy's house with a more comfortable chair with a cushion and places it next to the porch chair. Mary and Sister Johnson help Tracy, who is wearing a muumuu, out onto the porch and sit her down in the chair. Sister Johnson sits on the porch chair and Mary goes back into the house and gets another chair to sit on.

MARY: *(Before sitting down, asks...)* Does anyone want anything from in the house before I sit down?

SISTER JOHNSON: We're fine. Just want to give Tracy a little fresh air… it may do her some good.

TRACY: Thanks, y'all. I sure have a heap of good friends, but none as great as you two.

MARY: *(Giving Tracy a hug)* You are the bestest friend anyone could ever have. I'm so glad you're all right!

SISTER JOHNSON: You're going to be back on your feet before you know it.

TRACY: *(Sadly)* Lord, my poor man! We sure were looking forward to a child. *(Starting to cry)* What is God doing to us? He's taking the joy of our lives away from us. Even when good things are about to happen, *(Pauses)* something awful comes along to add to our miseries.

MARY: I don't know what we've done either for all this to happen to us. *(Begins to cry and looks up into the heavens and says...)* We're good folks, Lord! We don't deserve this. We're all that our men have and the only wealth they may ever have. We are happy folks, Lord! It seems whatever little we have, even that's being taken away.

TRACY: Amen! We're stripped of what little hope and pride we have which make things so hard. We do not know how much more our men can take.

SISTER JOHNSON: *(Trying to console them)* I think, what we are experiencing, the devil is trying to make us believe that this is

God's doing. Our worth is much more than what we have undergone these last few days. Don't let him connive us into thinking of a way that will destroy our worth and bring it down to his level.

TRACY: What do you call it when a man like Nicholas, who battled and whipped all the demons dwelling within him, comes home a proud and dignified man, *(Pauses)* wanting to show his people and community he didn't let them down. *(Pauses)* He made it just in time to be our hero when we all needed one to keep our spirits up and this is what happens. It seems that no matter how we try and do good it's not needed. Why couldn't it wait until he was an inspiration to us all? When it happens like this, it makes it so hard to believe.

SISTER JOHNSON: I know right now everything seems that way, but we just have to keep on believing and have faith in spite of how hard things seem right now.

MARY: Sister Johnson! These past few years sure have been unkind to Tracy and me. How much more of this can we take? It's awfully hard to keep on having faith when these things keep on happening...

SISTER JOHNSON: I know, child, but we've got to keep pushing on or we'll wind up drowning in misery and sorrow. We just can't let that happen to us. We can't! I can't give you answers to why these things happen. But we cannot stop believing, hoping. We still have children and young people to inspire.

TRACY: I just don't understand! I'll be glad when the time comes when I can say, I understand. It's just too hard right now. *(Pauses)* Maybe God didn't want my child to live at this time in a world with so much destruction...

SISTER JOHNSON: Carl and your love created an angel. The Lord now has that angel. *(Pauses)* Remember all the days of your lives, no matter whatever else you all have, you still have an angel looking down on you.

TRACY: Thanks, Sister Johnson. It will be hard for Carl to see it that way, but I'm going to keep on trying to give him his image. *(Paus-*

es) I'm feeling better now... thanks, y'all. *(They all hug)*

MARY: *(Changing subject)* Black folks are pretty uptight right now. We better hope that Reverend Peters, Brother Man X and the other black leaders can prevent violence in this city. Ain't nobody going to get hurt or their property destroyed by violence more than black folks in the black communities.

SISTER JOHNSON: Reverend Peters and the other leaders of this city have spoken to other influential leaders to come forward and speak to the people. I hear Berry Gordy will speak and some of his artists who are in town will do a nonviolent benefit. Black folks right now are pretty distraught about everything.

MARY: There's a curfew out now. Jessie says that Man X said Muhammad Ali will be in town today. Folks listen to him...

TRACY: They had the National Guard and the police force all in place before they announced Rabbit's demise. They're trying their best not to have another 1967 riot.

Ernestine comes out of the cafe with a basket of food. She comes up to where Tracy, Mary and Sister Johnson are sitting.

ERNESTINE: Hey, y'all, Mama told me to bring y'all some food. *(To Tracy)* How you feeling, girl? You know we all are really sorry.

TRACY: I know! Thank y'all. Now that basket is making me feel good already.

ERNESTINE: I brought plenty, more than enough for y'all.

MARY: We can let Carl and Jessie eat the pork chops and stuff. *(To Tracy)* Girl, let's get back in the house and eat... I just got hungry all of a sudden!

SISTER JOHNSON: *(Speaking to Ernestine)* Have you heard anything?

ERNESTINE: Everything is pretty peaceful. It's kind of too peaceful. I heard there were a few incidents, but the cops were on them before any disturbances happened. I think the fact that black cops were involved made a difference also. I think we're going to be alright this time!

TRACY: We sure got a lot of bigwigs coming to town about this.

ERNESTINE: *(Leaving)* Hey, y'all! With the weather changing, porch-sitting days are almost at an end. *(Pauses)* Well, y'all will just have to put on extra clothes to sit on your porches these next few days or weeks as some interesting people are coming by. I ain't supposed to tell, but one of them doesn't eat pork!

MARY: I better go put on some nice porch-sitting clothes.

TRACY: *(Getting up weakly with Sister Johnson helping her- Mary carries the food basket)* I reckon I better get out of this muumuu and look a little presentable if I am going to porch-sit.

SISTER JOHNSON: *(Helping her into the house)* Now y'all cooking!

MARY: *(Closing the door)* I'm hungry.

END OF SCENE EIGHT

ACT III

SCENE NINE

Nine days later...

Side Street is empty. The cool, gloomy, overcast weather of earlier that day is subsiding. All the businesses are closed. Some paper cups litter the street and sidewalk. A large banner was taken from the high school where Rabbit laid in state, and now hangs above Side Street and reads, "In Loving Memory: A Tribute to Nicholas 'Rabbit' Jones, our Hero." These are the remnants still lingering from the events of earlier today when Rabbit's funeral took place. The quietness and emptiness now on Side Street is somewhat magical; for only hours ago, the church, the street, the sidewalk and beyond were overflowing with people from end-to-end like sardines in a can. Now everyone is at the cemetery for Rabbit's burial.

One hour after Rabbit's funeral...

The day begins to brighten as the moments pass. A few minutes later we hear voices coming from both ends of the street. From one end around the bend comes Bernie, Ernest, Ernestine, Bee, Page, Mr. Crimple, Big Hank and his men, Christine and Jackie Lee. Around the bend from the other side comes Sister Johnson, Mrs. Washington, Carl, Jessie, Mary, Tracy, Luella, Francine, Beanpole, Fatman, Darnel, and Annie Mae. Everyone is well dressed. From their expressions, there is warmth, serenity and well-being. They all congregate from Sister Johnson's to Cousin Bee's, sitting and standing wherever comfortable.

MARY: *(Standing in front of Mrs. Washington's house)* I tell you all, this is a day we will likely never forget. One minute we're crying and the next minute we're smiling. You know, through all of what has happened this day, I'm feeling all right now, for I believe this may have been the only way for Rabbit to get the true recognition he deserved and he got it today.

EVERYONE: Amen! Amen!

BERNIE: In my lifetime I've never seen such a funeral. I thought Eunice's was, but never like this one.

PAGE: I've never seen so many dressed-up colored folks in my life!

ERNESTINE: Why don't you go to church sometimes? You'll see many more.

BEE: You know, I don't think there is a building in Detroit that could have held as many people that came to that boy's funeral.

HOUSECOAT PEARL: Tiger Stadium could have!

PAGE: What do you know about Tiger Stadium or even baseball?

BIG HANK: Now wait a minute. Pearl knows her Detroit Tigers. I bet you she can name every player.

Pearl sticks out her tongue at Page.

SISTER JOHNSON: I'm agreeing with Bernie. It was more folks than a Joe Louis fight at that boy's funeral. Didn't he have a sendoff?

TRACY: I tell you, didn't we look good? Black kings and queens, princes and princesses!

MARY: Now that's the truth! *(Turning around smiling)* Even Beanpole, Fatman and Darnel looked like stars today. *(Everyone smiles)*

BEE: *(To the three boys)* You boys really sang a nice song today.

LUELLA: They sure did and so did Carl and Jessie. They nearly turned that church into a river.

FRANCINE: I don't want to think about it or I'll start crying all over again. Sister Johnson, your choir… Lord have mercy! No disrespect to anyone, but you all got to have the baddest choir in the country.

TRACY: That is the second time we've witnessed a performance - although our men *(Jessie and Carl)* were blowing horns with their voices today too.

MARY: Everyone performed for that boy today, including Reverend Peters. I don't believe that man has rested this week. He's been helping with the arrangements, counseling us at the church, meeting with city hall folks. I hope he's at home getting some rest - poor man.

TRACY: Yeah, he can hurt our feelings sometimes in his Sunday sermons - I'm a witness - but we've got the best preacher in Detroit.

Everyone applauds. Carl and Jessie, without saying a word, go into Carl's house.

BIG HANK: *(Speaking to Mary and Tracy)* Those boys are all right!

TRACY: I think so. I think they're just griping.

MARY: These past nine days have taken a toll on all of us - especially Carl and Jessie. *(To Tracy)* Plus, you and Carl have had a double whammy. *(Everyone in agreement)*

TRACY: *(Trying to make a joke of it)* Guess I'll have to put my man in overdrive again. *(Subtle laughter)* We thank you all for your support.

SISTER JOHNSON: *(Praising Tracy)* That's my girl. *(To Tracy and Mary)* We all are proud of how you girls kept your husbands strong in times of trials and tribulations. Folks around here are real proud of you. *(There is applause)*

BIG HANK: *(Tracy and Mary)* Y'all got yourselves some together young brothers. *(Folks agreeing)* Took their winnings to help pay for Rabbit's funeral until the city leaders decided to honor him. *(Applause)*

MRS. WASHINGTON: Hank, you've been a generous man also by helping folks in times of need for this community.

BEE: Ain't that the truth! Some folks would have been lost without you. You've been a godsend!

MARY: You've helped Tra and me when Carl and Jessie were in the service - made sure we were not without...

TRACY: Shoot, doesn't matter if they were away or not. You were there for us!

Luella, Francine and others raise their hands acknowledging Tracy's comment.

BIG HANK: You all got to give yourself praise. This community took me in when I was just a country boy with fifty dollars in my pocket. You're my family. Only family I got here - *(Joking)* and Pearl who has been my eyes and ears for years is a mighty fine woman and friend. *(Pearl acts proudly)* I will also tell you all the businesses on this street have gone beyond their part in helping this community. Bernie alone has come to my rescue many times.

ERNEST: I agree. Bernie has helped all of us out one time or another. When we couldn't get supplies, he found a way for us.

Page starts his carrying-on of Bernie...

PAGE: *(Joking)* That's because he takes what money we pay him and puts it in his brother's dairy farm and sister's chicken ranch and then makes us pay him again for the milk, eggs and those old hens.

BERNIE: *(Trying to sling dirt)* What chicken farm? Dairy farm? Maybe your brother milks cows and sister plucks chicken feathers.

PAGE: *(Laughing)* The fresh ones they send to A&P. That's why I go to A&P for my milk, chicken and eggs.

BERNIE: I wish you would go to A&P for pop, too. *(Changing subject... serious)* I know this community. I see children grow up here. You're my family! *(Everyone applauds)*

SISTER JOHNSON: The outpouring of love for Rabbit today from this community, this city and state. So many people! What an honor!

ERNEST: Sister Johnson, I think you hit the nail on the head when you were talking. Nicholas has touched us in another way. Because of this event today, look at us showing our respect and love for people like Bernie and Hank who have done a lot for this community. *(Pauses)* Old Reverend Senior, Lord rest his soul, sure taught you *(Big Hank)* a lot about community spirit. He made sure these kids around here had good Christmases.

BIG HANK: When I was a young boy, I ran away from home in Alabama with fifty dollars in my pocket. That was enough for two weeks of room and board at the Beaubian Rooming House and Café. I didn't know a soul. I ran out of money and they gave me a job washing dishes in the kitchen and cleaning up the café for my room and board. At the time, the café was one of Reverend Nathan Peters Senior's numbers pick-up routes. He was not a preacher back then. Everyone called him Nathan. He would come by every day, let me wash his car for extra change and I reckon he took a liking to me. *(Pauses)* Before long he had me counting his money in the back of the café after it closed. Not long after that he would take me on his route with him to let people know me and soon after that he had me running for him.

ERNEST: You used to come by the plant during lunch to pick up the slips!

PAGE: Yeah! Old Senior gave up all his illegal vices after his wife died. Broke his heart! That man loved his wife. She made him promise that he'd take care of Junior. He gave up all that for his son and his promise to his wife. He started going to his father-in-law's little storefront church. It held no more than twenty-five parishioners.

BIG HANK: That's true! Mr. Nathan said his father-in-law didn't care too much for him because of his vices. So when his wife died, he sold me seventy-five percent of the business and made me sign an agreement that ten percent would go for Junior's living and education and fifteen percent to the community's youth and seniors. I'm keeping my word.

SISTER JOHNSON: Well, you've done more than your share and we're grateful.

BIG HANK: I thank you all, too. We're a family together.

PAGE: *(Changing the subject)* Yes-sa. Today showed how loved and unforgotten Nicholas was. This was the only way.

ERNEST: He had a send-off all right! Never seen and probably never will see again a turnout like this!

ERNESTINE: If anyone can say that this community doesn't have a star, all we have to do is to let them see the funeral of Rabbit and that will answer all questions.

EVERYONE: Amen!

SISTER JOHNSON: *(Climbing to her porch to sit down)* It was something. There were so many cars and buses. I didn't think they would ever stop coming.

BIG HANK: As long as I've been here I've never seen them close off a part of Woodward Avenue for a funeral procession. And I have never seen anyone lie in state at a school gym!

PAGE: He had folks from all walks of life. Folks from all over this city and from other towns came to pay their respects to him. Look at all the policemen that were there, even though one of their own killed Rabbit.

ERNEST: He's been declared the greatest high school athlete in this city's history. Now that's saying something! We have had some pretty fine athletes.

Carl and Jessie come out of Carl's front door. They have bottles of beer in their hands as they walk off the porch and into the middle of the street. They hold their bottles of beer towards the sky.

JESSIE and CARL: *(In unison)* We love you, Rabbit! You are our hero!

Everyone cheers and applauds as Jessie and Carl return to Carl's house.

Reverend Peters brings good news to the neighborhood and introduces Nicholas Jessie Malaki Jones...

From around the bend, Reverend Peters walks towards the mix of the gathering as he passes the laundromat.

REVEREND PETERS: Afternoon, everyone!

EVERYONE: *(Responds in unison)* Good afternoon!

MARY: We didn't think you were going to make it, Reverend. We know how busy you've been these last few days. Thought you may be home resting.

REVEREND PETERS: *(Walking slowly and greeting people along the way)* Now Sister Mary, you know the Lord's work is never done. The minute I step onto this street I seem to find a burst of energy.

TRACY: *(Softly speaking)* You mean a burst of Sister Johnson!

SISTER JOHNSON: *(Having heard what Tracy said)* You hush your mouth, child!

REVEREND PETERS: I know this has been a stressful day for everyone. When I approached the bend I thought I heard cheering and clapping.

SISTER JOHNSON: You did indeed hear that! Everyone was acknowledging their love for Rabbit.

REVEREND PETERS: Well, I tell you, I believe you all may want to accentuate that more because I have some wonderful news that I think will brighten this day and days to come.

MARY: Should I get Carl and Jessie?

REVEREND PETERS: Where are they? They're just as much a part of this as anyone around.

MARY: *(Goes up to Tracy's porch, opens the screen door)* You all come on out here. Reverend Peters has some news for us.

Mary comes back down the stairs and joins the others. Carl and Jessie come out of the house and join the crowd.

REVEREND PETERS: *(Standing in the middle of the street)* This has been a day of ups and downs, highs and lows, sadness and joys. Today many shared in a farewell that this city will remember for years to come. Our brother and friend Nicholas Jones, better known as "Rabbit," has had one of the finest home goings I believe I've ever witnessed.

EVERYONE: Amen!

REVEREND PETERS: *(Continues)* His home going brought together families, friends, associates, acquaintances; and people from all walks of life, cultures, social and ethnic backgrounds; of all colors, religions and races; *(Pauses)* a floral arrangement of people in this city and from other places to pay their respect to a young man they remembered who, throughout his elementary, junior and senior years of school, dazzled many with rare and unbelievable athleticism. He was remembered at his best - not at his worst. For many people he was the history of storytelling. In the years to come he'll always be the athlete that people will compare to greatness - like a Joe Louis, Muhammad Ali and such. A once-in-a-lifetime, truly remarkable individual! *(Applause)*

Many in his community wanted this young man to be their hero because they believed if anyone could be, he could. If you noticed, (which no one couldn't) the turnout today showed all of us the tremendous amount of pressure this young man had to cope with day in and day out trying to live up to expectations, *(Stops and looks at their faces)* but through all his perils he didn't let anyone down. Let us reflect on how much love this city has shown for this young man. His athleticism united this city through many perils and difficult situations past and present. He has not been forgotten. There is respect and love for a young man who made color obsolete as he entertained like no other before.

PAGE: Amen to that!

Voices from the crowd... Amen! He sure did!

REVEREND PETERS: *(Continues - recognizing Carl and Jessie)* Brother Carl and Brother Jessie, his history will be your history. Pictures of his deeds and accolades will also be yours. You two have been with him from the beginning - not a bad place to be. *(He reaches inside his suit coat pocket, pulls out a folded paper and begins to unfold it, still talking)* I have something here I think will be a ray of light to this day. *(Pauses, holding the open paper in his hand)* After the funeral, some of our communities' civic leaders and I were invited down to City Hall to meet with other community civic and council leaders. There were news people there too. *(Holding up the paper)* I, along with other leaders of this great city, was given this document and told what it contained. I wouldn't read it until I was here so we all could share in this moment together. *(Turns and addresses Carl and Jessie)...*

Brother Carl and Brother Jessie, you both have always played sports with Rabbit and were the ones who helped him to keep his grades up and have been his biggest supporters. What you two knew about him we never realized. We all were just a few of the many fans he excited. Watching him made us realize whether it is football, basketball, baseball, track and field - he was outstanding in all. *(Looking at the paper in his hand)* Let's see, *(Pauses, putting on his glasses)* before I read this let me say that I was told that since Brother Nicholas' untimely death, there has been a great deal of research on him. This is part of the findings. It says here no high school in the city of Detroit and State of Michigan has had such a distinctive record as East River High - having been to the state championship in every sport nine times in three years and won six of those nine times.

Through thorough research, no athlete in the city of Detroit or State of Michigan has broken more records, won more trophies in more sports than Nicholas "Rabbit" Jones.

He has been elected Most Valuable Player in football, basketball, baseball, track and field seventy seven times in four years of school.

Applause and acknowledged accolades...

REVEREND PETERS: I know how exciting this is to everyone but I could get through faster if *(Directing his comment)* you all wait until I'm finished. Is that all right, Sister Mary?

Mary nods in approval.

REVEREND PETERS: *(Continuing)* Therefore, as of today Nicholas, aka "Rabbit" Jones has been declared by Sports Research Institute and Magazine "the greatest all-around high school athlete this city and state has ever known." He will be on the front page of Sunday's Free Press next week and Sports Research in next month's edition.

MARY: *(Too excited)* Hallelujah! Hallelujah! I'm sorry, Reverend. You can't hold jubilation in. I'm bursting on the inside!

Everyone laughs.

PAGE: Why doesn't somebody give her a peanut butter sandwich?

MARY: Awww, hush up, man!

REVEREND PETERS: Sister Mary, I know it's hard for you. It seems God just put a little more enthusiasm in you than most. I have just a few more lines. *(Quiet)* We all know that Brother Nicholas started attracting fans in his junior high school days and when he started high school they had to move all their games over to Metro Stadium and Auditorium, and some championship games were played at Tiger Stadium – well, the beginning of next year, East River High School and Detroit Metro Stadium and Auditorium *(Pauses)* will be renamed **Nicholas Jones High School and The Nicholas "Rabbit" Jones Metro Stadium and Auditorium**!

A burst of applause, screaming, hugging and shouting, as Mary runs up and hugs Reverend Peters. Carl and Jessie, near tears, em-

brace. Tracy, Ernest, Sister Johnson and Bee are all embracing. Page hugs Ernestine. Reverend Peters, smiling, waits until the jubilation quiets down.

MARY: *(Staring at Reverend Peters still standing)* Ain't you through, Reverend? Don't tell us you've got more?

Everyone focuses their attention back on Reverend Peters.

REVEREND PETERS: *(Hesitant)* I was expecting Mrs. Jones, Nicholas' mother. She wanted to come and thank everyone for their contributions and help in her ordeal. She was exhausted when I left her and she said she would come, but don't hold it against her if she doesn't.

EVERYONE: We won't!

REVEREND PETERS: Let me say this in respect. *(He looks over at Carl and Tracy)* Brother Carl and Sister Tracy, these past few days with Nicholas' funeral may seem to have overshadowed your own personal loss but we all want you to know how much we share in your sorrow and pain. We know how much you two were looking forward to a child but just remember God is still ruler and we know His blessings are...

From around the bend comes Mrs. Jones dressed in a dark suit walking with Rabbit's three-year-old son. No one is aware of who he is as yet.

MRS. JONES: Afternoon, everyone! *(To Reverend Peters)* I had to stop off at the mortuary and pick up the certificate. That's why I'm late, Reverend.

REVEREND PETERS: *(Trying to finish his statement before he introduces her)* That's mighty fine, sister! I was just finishing talking to Brother Carl and Sister Tracy. *(Continuing)* As I said, God's blessings for you will soon come. *(To everyone)* Now, I think Sister Jones wants to say a few words to you all. *(Applause and cheers)*

Mrs. Jones comes to the middle of the street in front of the poolroom.

MRS. JONES: *(Somewhat nervous)* I'm not one for speeches.

TRACY: *(Sympathetic)* That's all right, Mrs. Jones. We understand.

MRS. JONES: *(Looking at Tracy, Carl, Jessie and Mary who are standing the closest to her)* Thank you, child! I have lost my only child, *(Pauses sadly)* but I've gained the love of a city because of my loss and for that I rejoice inside.

REVEREND PETERS and OTHERS: Amen! Amen! Amen!

MRS. JONES: *(Continuing)* You all have made my burden so much lighter for me. I don't know what I would have done if it wasn't for all of your help and support. *(Looking at Reverend Peters)* You, reverend, brought me out of a deep, deep hole. I had given up and lost all hope. I thought I had nothing to live for when Nicholas died. I knew my son had turned himself around and was coming home to you all, his friends - *(Looking at Jessie)* especially you, Jessie - to celebrate his glory and show everyone he didn't let you down. Then when he died it was snatched away from him - like someone *(Teary-eyed)* didn't want him to have that moment of glory.

There is sadness and tears coming from Mary and others. Reverend Peters puts his arms around her.

MRS. JONES: *(Continuing)* You see, I'm not a church person like many of you all. I believe in God but *(Pauses)*...

REVEREND PETERS: All right, sister. God loves you!

MARY: Amen! We love you, too.

EVERYONE: Amen!

MRS. JONES: Thank you all! I'm just lost right now. I hope that God sees fit to allow my son to be in heaven and at peace. He had his share of demons controlling him.

SISTER JOHNSON: *(Comes down and stands next to her, putting* *her arms around her)* God knows Rabbit's heart, Mrs. Jones. Rabbit was a good, respectful young man.

REVEREND PETERS: Mrs. Jones, no one in this city could have been in more glory than Rabbit was today and now he's glory bound. Your worries for him should be no more.

EVERYONE: Amen! Amen!

SISTER JOHNSON: I've never seen a love like the love they showed for your son today. Rejoice!

EVERYONE: *(Applause)* Rejoice!

SISTER JOHNSON: *(Know who Nicholas is)* Who's that fine gentleman of a young man you have with you? He's been as quiet and well-mannered as can be.

MRS. JONES: *(Leans down to the little boy)* Tell everyone your name.

LITTLE BOY: My name is Nicholas Jessie Malaki Jones.

Everyone is stunned except Sister Johnson, Ernest, Bee and Reverend Peters. Jessie comes up to him bends down and gives him a big hug. Then everyone else does the same.

MARY: I knew that boy reminded me of somebody.

Reverend Peters smiles and waits until all the surprise of Nicholas' son ceases. Sister Johnson, unnoticed, has eased Carl and Tracy, Mary and Jessie right to the front of Mrs. Jones and the boy.

REVEREND PETERS: *(Still smiling)* I have one more thing I want to share with everyone.

REVEREND PETERS: *(To Carl and Tracy)* Brother Carl and Sister Tracy, *(Pauses)* young Nicholas has something to say to you.

MRS. JONES: *(Bending down to the little boy)* Go on, Nicholas, ask them!

NICHOLAS JESSIE: *(Happily)* Will you adopt me?

Everyone again is stunned.

CARL and TRACY: *(Looking at each other with tears in both their eyes)* Yes! Yes! Yes!

Everyone applauds with joy and happiness. Carl and Tracy come and hug the little boy. Carl picks him up and looks at Mrs. Jones who is crying with joy.

REVEREND PETERS: *(Looking at the joy on Carl's and Tracy's faces)* We have made all the arrangements. All you have to do is sign some papers and Nicholas will be your child.

MRS. JONES: I'll still be his grandmother and you'll let me visit him and keep him from time to time, won't you?

CARL: *(Full of Joy)* Yes, ma'am! Yes, ma'am! Anytime you like!

MARY: *(Excited)* We're his godparents! After all, he's named after Jessie!

PAGE: I'm his uncle!

The joy continues!

Something good from something bad;
Faith gave you this day... with a smile on your face;
If you believe the moon can turn into the sun and midnight into
  noon;
If you believe faith is the cross that bears forgiveness;
If you believe no worries about tomorrow;
If today you lived by your faith;
Hallelujah! Hallelujah!

THE END

CPSIA information can be obtained
at www.ICGtesting.com
Printed in the USA
FSOW02n0816091116
27101FS